WICKED TIES

A D JUSTICE

WICKED TIES

STEELE SECURITY BOOK 2

Steele Security Series
Book 2

A.D. JUSTICE

PROLOGUE

"Colt! Coming to you, buddy! Get ready!"

Colt widened his feet and slightly bent his knees, getting into his stance as the batter took a swing. Just as his coach predicted, the ball flew in low toward him in his shortstop position and bounced off the ground once before he caught it and whisked it to first base.

"Out!"

"Great job, Colt!" Colt heard his father call from the stands but he didn't take his eyes off the field. The sun was in his eyes but his baseball cap helped some in shielding his face. The bright spring day was perfect weather for a game. The vividness of the tulips, pansies, and daffodils in bloom colored the landscape. The slight breeze kept the sun from being too hot, but the heat didn't matter to Colt. He played all summer in the sweltering heat and loved every second of it. But this, this was a perfect spring Saturday for baseball with his dad watching.

Colt punched his glove a couple of times and took his stance again as the next batter swung. He loved this—the smell of the dirt, the feel of swinging the bat, and the sting of catching a line-drive. He was only seven, but he knew he wanted to be a professional baseball player when he grew up. That would make his daddy so proud.

"Let's get 'em, son!" He knew his dad's voice anywhere. He could pick it out of the crowd of parents on both sides of the dugouts with his eyes closed. He loved the game, he loved the crowds, he loved everything about baseball —but none of it compared to how much he loved his father.

His father, John, worked a lot of hours and had to travel frequently, but he never failed to make time for Colt. Every day that he was home, John spent time doing something—anything—with Colt. He taught him everything he knew about baseball in their backyard. They had just started working on football, too, since Colt was close to being old enough to start playing on the local recreation league team. But Colt insisted that baseball would always be his first love.

John also made it a point to teach Colt from an early age how to treat a lady. Even at seven years old, Colt could see how much John and his mother, Beth, loved each other. They unfailingly showed one another complete respect and trust. They were affectionate with each other and with Colt—keeping their small town Alabama home as cozy as possible. Colt felt loved, safe, and secure with his parents.

After Colt's team won the game, John took the family out for the standard celebratory dinner of pizza and ice cream. Afterward, John and Beth strolled hand in hand toward their home on the oak-lined street of their small town. Colt was secure on John's broad shoulders and thoroughly enjoyed being able to touch the lowest branches of the trees as they walked and chatted.

Late that very night, Colt heard voices coming from the kitchen. Sneaking out of his bed, he crept down the hallway, crouching low against the wall to keep out of sight. Just as he reached the opening to the kitchen, he heard his parents speaking in hushed tones. He could tell they were concerned about something but he couldn't hear what they were saying. When they started moving toward him, Colt rushed back to his room and jumped in the bed. Several minutes later, John knelt at Colt's bed, ran his fingers through Colt's hair and whispered, "Just remember I love you. Always, son."

The next morning, he woke to his mother's quiet sobs. Walking softly to his parents' room, he saw his mother holding a piece of paper. He silently crept closer and closer to her until he could read the note over her shoulder.

She never knew he was there and he silently made his way back to his own room.

He was only seven, but he could read the one line the note contained. And he knew he was forever changed because of those eight little words.

"You and Colt are better off without me."

1

CHAPTER ONE

The reception for the newlyweds, Mr. and Mrs. Noah and Brianna Steele, was in full swing. They intentionally kept the wedding small, with only immediate family and close friends invited. Some of the close friends in attendance—like Shadow, Rebel and Bull—were all also employees of Steele Security, Noah's security firm located in downtown Miami. The unbreakable bond was sealed between the "brothers" when all the men served together in the Army as Rangers, and finally in a remote area in the Middle East in the clandestine Delta Force unit.

Noah and Brianna exchanged vows at sunset on the beach, with the bride radiantly glowing in her early pregnancy and the groom smiling from ear to ear, like he was the luckiest man in the world. Noah and Brianna's relationship had been through hell and back over the past several years. But with Brianna's return to Miami, they managed to pull the pieces back together and move forward as man and wife, stronger than ever.

Engrossed in their nuptials and having eyes only for each other, neither Noah nor Brianna noticed the figure lurking in the shadows. The one person who tracked their every move, while keeping out of sight of the guests, the wedding planner, the caterer, and other workers. The one uninvited guest, who had crashed their private party, but remained unannounced, unseen, and unheard. The one who patiently waited for the right opportunity to make a move toward the happy couple.

When the wedding party moved inside an outdoor event tent, the uninvited visitor patiently waited outside. There were plenty of ways to blend into the background—to be invisible and silent—when it was absolutely necessary. This was one of those times. It was absolutely necessary to keep quiet and stay hidden. The intruder's sole focus was to wait them out, knowing that they eventually would *have* to leave the sanctity of the tent and head for their waiting limousine.

The intruder patiently waited as the wedding guests danced, laughed, and thoroughly enjoyed themselves inside the fully air-conditioned tent. For everyone except the blushing bride, the champagne flowed freely.

Bull, Rebel, and Shadow all met Brianna in the Middle East when she was on assignment as an investigative reporter. They were actually her assignment, but in a short span of time, they developed a close relationship. They became her brothers, in the same manner that Noah was their brother, and they each took that unspoken oath seriously.

Bull's commitment to Brianna and Noah was unconditional and unwavering. As Brianna and Noah's brother, he felt a keen responsibility to keeping them safe, watching their backs, and being available whenever they needed him. He loved Brianna like the little sister he never had and she had more than proven her worth in his eyes.

Brianna shared dances with her new husband, Noah, and then with Shadow and Rebel, throughout the evening. But Bull waited until the end of the evening to request his dance. He viewed his relationship with Brianna as a special one. He didn't easily trust people and she had earned his trust—actually twice in one lifetime. *No one* had ever lost his trust and then won it back again. No one until Brianna, that is.

"Can I have this dance?" Bull's smile lit up his handsome face as he leaned down and offered his arm to Brianna. She had just taken a seat next to her husband to rest her weary, swelling feet when Bull approached.

When Brianna first met the team, it was Bull who was the hardest for her to get to know. She knew right away that he regarded loyalty and trust as the ultimate test of friendship. If anyone failed that test, they would never get another chance. For those who passed the test, they would never find a more loyal friend.

"I don't know if that's a good idea, man. Her feet are-," Noah started to respond, but Brianna cut him off.

"It's okay, Noah," she patted his arm and turned to Bull, smiling warmly. "I would love to dance with my brother. I thought he'd never ask." Brianna smiled as she stood and walked to the dance floor with Bull.

Noah smiled proudly as he watched one of his best friends walk off with his glowing bride on his arm. There was no jealousy in their relationship. Noah knew very well how Bull viewed allegiance, honor, and trust in their tight-knit group. He knew when he met Brianna in the desert that he would one day marry her. There was absolutely no reason to ever question her love and faithfulness to him. She'd already proven that to him with everything they had been through.

Bull was hurt when he thought Brianna had betrayed him. His trust in her was temporarily shattered. After she revealed the truth, and Bull understood all the events of the past, he realized he had been wrong about Brianna's intentions.

When Noah thought about it, he had to admit to himself that he was relieved that Bull was able to forgive Brianna for her breaching his trust—even if it was for a good cause. It would've been hell living between the two strong-willed, hard headed people he loved had Bull not relented.

Arm in arm, Bull escorted Brianna to the dance floor and gently twirled her around to face him as they began swaying to the slow music. Bull looked around the tent, taking in all the happy faces, the toasts and cheers accompanied by glasses clinking. The bride and groom's deep-rooted love was evident to anyone who even glanced at either of them. He knew his friends would have a perfect life together. Not that there would never be problems, but their trials had only made them stronger and better prepared to face whatever the future may bring.

Bull had accepted long ago that he would never have *this*—a wife, someone who holds his heart, someone with whom to share his thoughts or someone he could trust with every facet of his life. He was happy for his friends but it just could never be in his cards. That decision was made for him—inside him—long ago. He didn't share his feelings, dreams, fears—or his love—with anyone outside of his group. He sure as hell didn't give his heart away to anyone who could hurt him.

"You look gorgeous, Sunny," Bull said, referring to her with the nickname she'd earned when she first met them while on assignment. "It was a beautiful wedding and Noah is a lucky man. I can't wait to be an uncle and help Noah teach that baby boy a few hand-to-hand techniques."

Brianna burst out laughing and put her forehead on Bull's expansive chest. His high school football coach gave him that nickname because of his enormous and formidable stature. Following through on his duties was tantamount to his sense of honor—and one of his duties was to be an uncle to the baby growing inside of her. And his honor would not be impugned.

Brianna shook her head in only slight disbelief at his statement and asked, "What if it's a girl?"

With an equally serious face and tone of voice, Bull answered. "She can learn, too."

When Brianna laughed, Bull finally conceded and laughed along with her. "Seriously, Brianna, I am looking forward to being an uncle. You and Noah will be great parents."

"Thank you, Bull. That's so sweet of you. I mean that," Brianna responded before straining on her tiptoes to kiss his cheek.

"I want you to have fun on your honeymoon, but I want you to be careful, too, Bri. Don't leave Noah's side if you can help it. I don't want anything to happen to you. *Promise me*." His smile was gone and so was any glint of humor. He was instantly back on soldier duty and she was his charge.

Bull's sudden seriousness and frankness caught her by complete surprise. Bull was normally a man of few words, but when he did find it necessary to issue a command, he meant what he said. For him to specifically ask her to stay close to Noah and be careful meant he knew something she didn't know. She'd learned that much about him, and she also knew better than to quiz him about it. Years of working on a "need to know" basis made him keep information to himself much more than the average person.

Still, Brianna searched his eyes for any trace of worry or any other sliver of information she could use later to pry everything out of Noah. Bull felt her penetrating stare, knew what she was looking for, and steeled himself against it. The last thing he wanted was to add undue stress on her, especially while she was pregnant, but he learned to rely on his instincts many years ago. Those instincts had kept him alive in many hazardous conditions.

Realizing she would have better luck penetrating Fort Knox than penetrating Bull's thoughts and feelings, Brianna nodded in agreement. She responded, "I promise, Bull. I don't intend to leave Noah's side the whole two weeks unless I absolutely have to."

Satisfied with her word, Bull escorted her back to Noah, who waited patiently at the bride and groom table. As they approached, Bull watched Noah's eyes take in his new wife. He was amazed with how they instantly filled with love and admiration every time Noah looked at Brianna. They also demonstrated how possessive and protective he was of Brianna.

He became even more possessive and protective of her after he learned of her pregnancy. In honor of the love that flowed between Noah and Brianna, Bull made a silent oath to do whatever it took to keep Brianna safe. He meant what he said—he was looking forward to being an uncle and he would use any means necessary to protect his family.

Noah's eyes reluctantly left Brianna and met Bull's. Brianna saw the immediate shift in Noah's demeanor—the crinkling of the outer corners of his eyes, the hard set of his jaw, and the deep breath he inhaled that drew Noah up even taller than his normal Greek-god self. She knew he saw something in Bull's countenance that set him on guard. Noah and Bull had worked together for too long and had too many full conversations without ever saying a word for Noah to have missed it. She just wished *she* knew what it was.

Noah took Bri's hand and pulled her into him for a full body embrace. Since he towered over her, Brianna couldn't see the looks he and Bull exchanged or even guess at what the looks conveyed to the other. When she pulled back, Noah lowered his head and gently brushed his lips on hers, his hands on either side of her face, then deepened it to kiss her thoroughly and completely.

It really didn't matter how many times he'd kissed her in exactly that manner, every time made her weak in the knees and gave her heart palpitations. Mr. Noah Steele was one fine specimen of a man, and she was so thankful that their lives were reunited.

"It's time to go on our honeymoon, *Mrs. Steele*. Let me take you away from here now," Noah whispered seductively to Brianna. Brianna knew full well that his words held a triple meaning. It actually was time to leave, he wanted to get her alone, and he knew something was wrong and he wanted her as far away from it as possible. She decided to go with the meaning that she liked the most.

"Take me away, Mr. Steele. *Take. Me. Away*," she replied as she wrapped her arms around his neck, stretched on her tiptoes, and kissed him back. As his strong arms wrapped around her, she forgot about Bull's warning. She forgot about the guests who were most likely watching. She forgot about anything and everything else that the world wanted to throw at them.

It was time for her honeymoon with the man she loved.

2

CHAPTER TWO

The wedding reception ended with the tradition of the bride throwing the bouquet and the groom removing and shooting her garter into the crowd. The crowd whistled catcalls when Noah lifted Brianna's dress and slowly dragged the garter down her leg. She blushed bright red when he stopped midway and softly kissed her thigh. The smoldering look he gave her left no room for doubt of exactly what he had in mind.

Bull, Rebel, and Shadow each took their assigned locations to guard all sides. Each man automatically covered and protected Noah and Brianna's flank without giving it conscious thought. Bull's position put him in the optimal location to catch the lucky garter when Noah shot it into the crowd.

The surprised and disgusted look on Bull's face at catching the feminine adornment was priceless. He was such a big, macho man but he had no clue what he was expected to do with the girly garter Noah had just removed from Brianna's leg. He turned it over in his hands, smirking at the crowd of people who clapped him on the shoulder to congratulate him, though he had no idea why they thought it was such a big deal.

Brianna teased him, telling him it was the male equivalent of the bridal bouquet. It meant he would be the next male there to get married. He quickly tried to pawn it off on any other single, unsuspecting male but no one would have it. He vehemently argued with his brothers that he would never get married. He had big plans to be a career bachelor.

With the festivities and fun coming to an end, Brianna and Noah left the shelter and sanctity of the tent and took their exit as man and wife. Their friends and family tossed birdseed onto them as they left. They entered the waiting limousine with beaming smiles, obviously excited to leave for their two-week honeymoon at a secluded resort in Fiji.

The uninvited guest was still hiding in the shadows, trying unsuccessfully to catch a glimpse of the newlyweds as they walked from the massive tent to the waiting stretch limousine. A giant man strategically blocked every viewpoint of the bride and groom. None of the men moved until the happy couple was safely tucked away in the limousine and the car was then driving away.

Bull, Shadow, and Rebel exchanged glances and turned back toward the tent and beach area, each man taking a different route and moving with the confidence and prowess of a well-trained reconnaissance team. After a few minutes of nonchalantly mingling with the few remaining friends and family members, each man's eyes conveyed their path he would cover as they separated. A few members of Brianna's family were still gathering the last of the wedding gifts as the three men made their way around to the area behind the enormous tent.

Their time together in the military made them a lethal machine that could operate without any verbal communication. The way they could communicate and read the other's thoughts was more than a little intimidating to others. They stealthily moved into position, quickly identified the culprit's location, and descended. Focusing too much on where Noah and Brianna were, and not enough on the immediate surroundings, the intruder was suddenly cornered by the three intimidating giants. And there was no way out.

One of the giants spoke first, his voice low and instinctively threatening. "This is a private party. And since I don't know you, I know you weren't invited."

When the intruder didn't answer, Bull spoke more forcefully. "Tell me what you want with the bride and groom. *Now.*"

"I have business with Noah Steele," she finally answered, tentatively.

"Not today you don't," Bull responded in an end-of-discussion tone.

"You don't understand. I have to talk to him," she argued.

"No. *You* don't understand. He's married now, so whatever you think the two of you had once upon a time is long over. You have no business with him now."

Confusion etched her face for a moment as Bull's words sunk in. "Oh, no, it's not like that at all. I, um, I," she stammered under his watchful glare.

"Yes?" he prodded, his irritation and disbelief obvious in his voice.

"I'm in trouble and I need protection. Noah Steele—he owns Steele Security, right?" she hedged, pressing on with her questions about Noah.

Bull's threatening stance toward her didn't change. He instinctively knew there was more to this lady than she revealed. Her persistence in reaching Noah, at his wedding of all places, was blatant and now she was asking questions to which she obviously already knew the answers. He decided that he would get answers from her and then he would personally escort her from the premises.

Bull narrowed his eyes, tilted his head, and thoroughly examined her from head to toe. He knew from the first glance that she was accustomed to looking and behaving in a more refined manner than her current casual appearance displayed. She wasn't someone who had lived a life in the criminal element. In other words, she didn't appear to be very street smart, but Bull never trusted anyone at face value.

She had long, black hair that was thick and naturally wavy. The natural tan glow of her skin made her mint-green eyes stand out and be noticed. Her lean, muscular frame fit her five-foot-seven height with perfect proportions.

She wore khaki mini-shorts with a stylish, flowing tank top that showed off her tanned arms and shoulders. Her fingernails and toenails were expertly manicured and she wore the exact amount of jewelry that was considered appropriate but not overdoing it. She was truly a beautiful lady and he would definitely be interested under better circumstances. Interested for a night or maybe two, that is.

When her mint-green eyes fearfully looked up into his, Bull felt electricity arcing between them. The attraction was immediate but he didn't trust that feeling. He was never one to give in to sudden impulses, so he mentally shook those thoughts away and continued with what he knew best.

"I think you know Noah *Steele* owns *Steele* Security. But what I don't know is why you came to his *wedding* to ask for protection instead of calling his *office*. The office that has manned phones, twenty-four hours a day, seven days a week," Bull retorted, his Southern drawl more evident now than earlier. He'd learned to hide his accent fairly well, but it was still ingrained in him.

The extra few seconds that it took her to respond told Bull everything he needed to know. She didn't have an answer for not calling Noah's business line and she had no business being at his wedding. He reached down and took her hand, intending to lead her away. Her reaction was completely unexpected.

"*No, please don't!*" she pleaded as quietly as she could while she resisted his attempts to move her. "Please—I'm really scared." Her eyes were wide open and darting around the open area, looking for hidden dangers and safe passages. She recoiled into the shadows, trying to stay hidden from sight.

Bull stopped moving but kept her hand in his. He squeezed it lightly to catch her attention. He knew that look—the wounded look, deer-caught-in-the-headlights look, the near full-blown-panic-attack look.

"You really need our help?"

"Yes," came the whispered, strained reply. He knew she was

simultaneously fighting tears while internally determining whether she would fight or flee. He was leaning heavily to the flee option, if her demeanor was an accurate indication.

Taking a deep breath and letting it out with an acceptance of resignation, Bull softened his voice. "Alright. You'll have to come with me and answer a few questions. We'll figure out how to best help you."

Shadow and Rebel silently witnessed the entire exchange. Bull looked at each of them and the unspoken request was conveyed. They surrounded her and walked her to Bull's waiting Steele Security SUV. Once she was safely seated inside, Bull pulled away from the curb and stole a glance at her.

She drew her sandaled feet up in the seat, bent her knees, and rested her chin on them. Her arms were bent and also resting on her knees, almost completely covering her face as her eyes darted back and forth from the windshield to the side window. Bull realized this part of her story was true—she was very scared of something or someone.

"What's your name?" Bull asked, breaking the silence and making her jump unexpectedly.

"Chaise," she answered after several long seconds. Bull noted she didn't give a last name. "What's yours?"

"Bull," he answered, thinking to himself that two could play that game.

"I can see why," she mumbled under her breath.

Bull chuckled at her bravado, the sound reverberating through his chest, and said, "Let's start over. I'm one of Noah's best friends and a long-term employee of Steele Security, Colton Lanier."

Bull held out his hand to shake hers while keeping the other one on the wheel. She looked at him for a second before relenting and taking his hand in hers. "Chaise," she paused and Bull noted that her eyes darted to the *Quickie-Mart* sign as they passed before she added, "Martin."

"Well, Chaise *Martin*, it's nice to meet you," Bull replied, emphasizing her last name and letting her know that he didn't believe her, but he decided he shouldn't push the issue any farther. He knew true fear when he saw it and she wasn't so good of an actress that she could fool him on that aspect. Her terror was real and he would allow her some anonymity for now—until he felt he had given her enough time to trust him.

She nodded once in response and let go of his hand to wrap her arms around her legs again. She let out a long breath of exasperation and Bull had the feeling she was about to start crying on him. He didn't do *feelings* too well.

"Want to tell me what's going on, Chaise?" Bull asked in a much more relaxed tone than he felt inside. He didn't want to add to her stress and make her start crying, but he needed to know what he was dealing with in this case. He had to keep himself and the other men safe, but his main concern at the moment was Brianna and Noah's safety.

She started to speak a couple of times but stopped both times before she got the first word out. She studied Bull's profile, trying to determine what she should and shouldn't say. He could tell by her rapid eye movement and her increased breathing rate that she was very uncomfortable in his presence. He just didn't know why that was.

"Um, Colton, right?"

Bull nodded. It felt strange being called by his given name but she seemed more comfortable with it, so he would deal with the discomfort for the sake of a client.

"Colton, I'm scared, okay? Really, *really* scared," she spoke slowly and emphasized each word. "I don't know who I can trust."

"But you trust Noah?" Bull asked and noticed how her body immediately tensed even more at the mention of his name. Bull stopped at the red light and turned to look her directly in the eye. "Chaise, do you trust Noah?"

She nodded her response and bit her bottom lip in apprehension. "Yes, I do. But I know him." She turned her face away and peered out the side window for a few seconds before adding, "Or, I used to, anyway."

Bull clenched his jaws and gritted his teeth. He really didn't like the vibes he was getting from Chaise *Martin* regarding Noah and Brianna.

"Look, Chaise. It seems like something else is going on here. I told you—whatever you think you and Reaper had together, you don't. He got married today, and even if he wasn't married, he's completely in love with Brianna. I will protect them both from anyone or anything that comes against them."

"The light's green," she answered, purposely avoiding Bull's direct comments. Bull stomped on the gas in response.

"You need to start explaining some things to me, Chaise, or this is the end of the line. You can get out here and call a cab," Bull stated with finality.

Chaise obviously believed him because she jerked her head in his direction, her mouth parted in surprise, and her eyes opened wide in fear. "I told you—it's not like that. I knew Noah when we were in school. He's a little older than I am, but we were not romantically involved *at all*. I just didn't know anyone else to go to."

"About?" Bull asked, but before Chaise was able to answer, Bull continued in a stern, commanding voice. "Hang on, Chaise. And keep your head down."

Bull jerked the wheel to the right and made a sudden last-second turn. The car immediately behind him did the same and he knew without a doubt that they had a tail. He calmly picked up his cell phone and called Rebel. Chaise had no time to process his command or to even determine if she should be afraid.

"Black full-size truck, Florida tags, black-out tinted windows. Yeah. Let me know. Thanks, man."

Bull's clipped phone conversation gave Chaise no indication of his intentions or why he was talking about a black truck with tinted windows. His demeanor change was almost imperceptible. The only real difference was now his eyes darted between his rearview mirror and the road ahead instead of trained on her.

"Colton, what's going on?"

"We're being followed. Rebel is going to shake our tail for us so we don't call unnecessary attention to ourselves," Bull answered in a tone that belied the severity of the situation. It was as if she had asked for the time and he was merely supplying her with the information.

"Shake our tail?" she asked, dumbfounded.

Bull laughed. "You know, I never really thought about how that sounded until you said it like that. Rebel's going to make the bad guys lose us in four, three, two, one."

Suddenly, another Steele Security SUV darted out from a side street immediately in front of the large, black truck that had been tailing them. The driver of the truck barely had time to slam on the brakes to keep from hitting Rebel. With nowhere else to go, thanks to oncoming traffic and Rebel's SUV blocking the rest of the road, the black truck had to come to a complete stop.

Bull drove on and watched as Rebel and Shadow exited the SUV and approached the truck with their pistols drawn. Confident the two men were capable of handling whoever was following so closely that their tail was immediately made, Bull took Chaise to one of the rarely used mainland buildings of Steele Security.

3

CHAPTER THREE

ecurely inside one of the safest buildings in the state, Bull escorted Chaise to a "discussion room" for a little talk. The staff didn't like to call them "interrogation rooms" because that term immediately created a negative image. These discussion rooms were plush, with comfortable, overstuffed leather chairs and couches, easy lighting, and a warm, inviting appeal. When they weren't sure of their guests' integrity, they found this atmosphere was much more likely to promote information sharing than the harsh rooms they used during their military days.

Chaise took a seat in the comfortable leather chair and Bull poured her a drink before taking the seat opposite her. He noticed a slight tremble in her hands as she took the tumbler from him. He again noted that she wasn't acting, her body language matched the tremor in her voice, but he still didn't trust her. Her words and actions had shown that she was too invested in Noah and not enough in Brianna. That didn't bode well with him. There was no way she was a current friend of Noah's but didn't know about Brianna.

"Back to our conversation earlier. You say you trust Noah, right?" Bull asked nonchalantly while keeping his all-seeing eyes fixed on Chaise's reaction.

She didn't make eye contact when she said, "Right."

"Then you can trust me. I've known Reaper for a long time. We've had each other's backs more times than I can count or even talk about."

"Why do you call him *'Reaper'*?" Chaise asked, her voice full of curiosity.

"Same reason he calls me 'Bull,'" he answered with a single shoulder shrug.

"Were you and he in the military together or something?"

"Yes."

Chaise waited for Bull to expand on his tour of duty with Noah. The non-committal answers of his were wearing on her already frayed nerves. She knew he needed to feel like he could trust her, but she needed some confirmation that she could also trust him. After all, she was the one who had people coming after her to prevent her from sharing vitally important and damning information.

She looked at him expectantly and twirled her hand in the universal sign to keep talking. Bull considered her request for a moment before carefully continuing.

"Yes, we were in the Army together. He was my Captain and he's been my friend for a great many years now. I've worked for him since the day I left the military and he opened Steele Security," Bull explained.

"How many years has that been?" Bull could see Chaise trying to do the math in her head, counting back the years.

"Six or so," he answered, knowing full well exactly how long it had been to the exact day, but he would only give answers in approximates.

Her head nodded in understanding, but her eyes said she was deep in thought, worlds away from the room they were in. She was thinking about the last *'six or so'* years that Noah has been out of the service.

"How long since you last saw Reaper—um, I mean Noah?" Bull asked.

Chaise looked back down at her glass for a second then turned her face away from Bull. Her hand came up and quickly whisked away a tear before she turned back to him to answer. "Um, I'm not sure, much longer than that, obviously." Her voice was shaky and she actually sounded hurt by just the thought of their length of time apart.

Bull's eyes narrowed to mere slits in suspicion. "You know his *wife* is pregnant, right?"

Chaise quickly looked Bull in the eye and her mouth was agape. "I-I thought she may be," she stammered, "but I couldn't really see them very well from where I was standing. I did notice he kept putting his hand on her stomach. There's usually only one reason a man would do that," she finished with a humorless laugh.

"My soon to be nephew," Bull said proudly, "or niece. Either way, I'll be *Uncle Bull* soon." All the color drained from Chaise's face at his statement and her eyes welled up with tears that she quickly tried to stamp down.

She didn't know what to say when Bull confirmed that Brianna was pregnant with Noah's baby. A million different feelings flooded her instantly and she knew his keen eyes didn't miss a thing. She tried to mask the hurt and regret that filled her eyes as quickly as possible at the thought of Noah's baby.

Bull continued, "And the *only* person who will protect that baby better than *me*, is Noah himself. And that's only because I don't live with them." He looked at her pointedly to make sure she caught his meaning.

Chaise swallowed hard, swallowing the tears and trying but failing to hide the pain that was evident on her face. "I'm sure you will make an excellent uncle, Colton."

Bull couldn't help but smile at this. "That I will, Chaise. That I will."

An hour, two drinks, and a couple of cartons of Chinese food later, Bull realized he had enjoyed his amiable meal and conversation with Chaise. He actively fought against his almost instant attraction to her. He kept trying to remind himself that she was a client at best and a threat at worst. But there was something about her, something that drew him in and made him want to get to know her better—as a person, not as a part of his job.

These warring emotions were so far removed from Bull that he wasn't sure how to handle them. His training told him to proceed with caution. The man in him urged him to pursue the attraction and enjoy it while it lasted. The logical part of him told him to play the middle of the road as long as possible so that he could find out her true intentions and assess the threat she posed to Noah and Brianna.

Bull was intentionally friendly and relaxed with Chaise as he continued to gauge her body language. When he was content in his ability to make Chaise feel at ease in his presence and trust him, he decided it was time for her to start sharing her story. He needed to know the whole story—why she was hiding, what scared her so much, why she needed Noah's help, and why they were followed.

It was time for her to give him a few answers.

Chaise had watched Bull all evening—from the moment she saw him standing by Noah at the wedding, when he approached her outside the tent, in the SUV on the way to the building, and inside the comfortable, cozy room. She didn't want to feel the intense attraction toward him.

But, dear lord, the man was *fine*. The natural blond highlights in his light brown hair were no doubt from the strong Miami sun, as was his tanned skin. His stark blue eyes innately penetrated and captivated anyone who dared to hold his gaze. He was intense, and though he had been friendly over dinner, he was also powerful and intimidating.

He was a little taller than Noah, which had to put him at about six-foot-five and he had the biggest arm muscles she'd ever seen. They just kept rippling and flowing down from his neck to his wrists. His expansive chest stretched his shirt tight across the middle, showcased his impressive build, and made her involuntarily salivate and gawk like an inexperienced school girl.

Bull had made it plain to her, in more ways than one, that he didn't trust her and he wanted her to leave. He questioned her motives, he questioned her integrity, and he questioned the reason why she specifically sought Noah out. But these things only made him more attractive—his loyalty, his protectiveness, and his unyielding resolve. He clearly loved Noah, Noah's new wife, and their unborn baby. Men of his caliber were nearly impossible to find. He reminded her of Noah in so many ways.

If she told him everything, would he believe her? Or would he turn her away, push her out the door, and leave her to figure it out alone?

No, that definitely isn't an option, she thought. *There is too much at stake to risk that.* She decided she would tell him what she could— what she had to tell him to ensure he gave his help. But she would give no more than the bare minimum until she absolutely had no other choice. If, or actually *when*, that time came, she would pay the piper then. In the meantime, she didn't really see any other choice.

Chaise could feel Bull's eyes burn into her as he studied her every movement. It was quite unsettling to be scrutinized so thoroughly, like she was a specimen under a microscope. She shifted slightly in her seat and immediately knew that Bull detected her uneasiness. His eyes narrowed slightly as his head ever so slightly cocked to the side as he studied her.

"Where is the restroom?" Chaise asked, hoping to convince him that her distress was from the need to use the facilities rather than from being so near to him. Or from having secrets she wasn't ready to disclose.

Bull stared her down for a couple of seconds too long for it to be a coincidence. He really didn't trust her in the least, but there was also something else in the way he looked at her. There was a hint of masked desire. It was so faint; Chaise wasn't positive that was what she had actually seen or if it was just the reflection of her desire in his eyes.

"This way," he finally said as he stood. He led her out of the discussion room and down a dimly lit hallway. "Right here," he motioned to the door on the left as he leaned against the wall on the opposite side. He apparently intended to wait for her to finish and escort her back to the main room.

Chaise smiled warmly at him as she entered the windowless bathroom and closed the door behind her. She looked around for a minute but the room only held the bare essentials. No doubt it was the "guest" bathroom. She took her time, washed her hands, and splashed water on her face. She dragged the towel down her face to dry it and stopped when she caught the reflection of her eyes in the mirror.

"You can do this," she whispered to herself, "you *have* to. No matter how hard this is."

A knock on the door startled her. "Everything alright in there?" Bull called from the other side.

She opened the door and put on her best smile again. "Fine. Just fine."

Leaning against the doorjamb when Chaise opened the door, Bull pushed up to his full, intimidating height as he crossed his bulging biceps over his equally bulging chest. Chaise's eyes couldn't help but wander to the impressive mounds, and for just a second, she forgot to be nervous around him.

Her slow perusal of his imposing upper body made her momentarily forget where she was. That is, until her eyes found his eyes, the ones that were hard-as-nails and were currently piercing her without saying a word.

"Look–" he started when the sound of the main door opening caught his attention. Before she could even react, Bull had pulled his gun from God knows where and was silently stalking toward the sound. Male voices came from the direction of the door and Bull suddenly stopped, holstered his weapon, and stepped into the open doorway from where the voices emanated.

"That's a damn good way to get shot, man," Bull said and then chuckled. He turned and saw Chaise was still rooted to the spot where he left her. He motioned for her to come to him, and somehow her feet got the message before her brain fully understood.

Chaise's heart was pounding and she felt dizzy as she moved toward the waiting Herculean giant. When she first heard the voices, she was certain they had found her, had come for her, and she was completely frozen with fear. Chaise couldn't remember a time when she had been so scared before.

It must have shown in everything about her because Bull's countenance changed from being stern to showing concern. "Are you all right?"

Chaise managed to nod but still couldn't make a sound to answer him. She didn't trust her voice just yet. As she reached Bull, the other two men came into view and she immediately recognized them from Noah's wedding. Finally breathing again, she held out her hand and introduced herself to them.

"I'm Chaise," she said, intentionally not stating her last name.

"Yes, this is Chaise *Martin*," Bull added, intentionally emphasizing her last name yet again. She cut her eyes to him and couldn't help but shoot him an apologetic look in return. He knew she was lying but he didn't know why yet. Maybe he would understand when she was finally able to tell him everything. She hoped so, anyway. He didn't seem to be the type of man she could cross and get away with it.

"This is Rebel and Shadow," Bull continued as he pointed at the other two men. "They both work for Noah, too. And, yes, we all served in the Army together, so you can trust them, too."

She smiled and shook their hands as Bull formally introduced them. She noted that although Shadow was bigger built than Bull, which in itself was really saying something, he had a friendlier natural carriage about him. Rebel wasn't quite as large as Bull but his eyes weren't as hard and suspicious as Bull's, either. He caught the emphasis Bull placed on her last name and gave her a look of understanding as he shook her hand. Even though Noah wasn't there, she was sure she was in good hands.

"What's the word, then?" Bull asked Rebel and Shadow. Chaise looked between the three of them and instantly felt invisible.

"Low-level hired hand. Amateur. He was supposed to follow her and see where she went. Didn't know shit about tailing someone," Shadow answered with a laugh.

Rebel picked up the story, "Thing is, he was hired by the *leader* of the Latino gang, *Tres Seises*. They're not someone a nice, pretty lady would normally mess with."

The three men turned and stared Chaise down. The weight of their stares was palpable on her skin and made her involuntarily take a step backward. Their size alone was intimidating, but being under all three of their hard, probing stares was enough to make her squirm.

"Well, Chaise?" Bull spoke and turned to face her fully. Her eyes searched his for any hint of empathy but found none.

She felt the tears stinging the back of her eyes as she fought to keep her emotions under control. She had been on one hell of an emotional roller coaster and she was so ready to get off the damn ride.

"I think it's time for us to have that talk. Right now," Bull finished as he advanced on her. Wrapping his enormous, thick fingers completely around her bicep, he easily steered her back toward their "discussion room." Rebel and Shadow fell in step behind them and she suddenly felt something she'd never experienced before— complete claustrophobia.

With her eyes downcast to her feet, Chaise focused on putting one foot in front of the other. One step at a time, she allowed Bull to guide her as she tried her best to block out the unwanted feelings. Entering the room, he marched her to the chair she had vacated earlier and let go of her arm. She instantly missed the warmth of his touch on her and the security being linked to someone else provided, even if only for a moment. Even if he hadn't intended for his grip to be considered a lifeline, that's exactly how it had felt to her.

As Shadow started to close the door, Chaise startled. "No, please, leave it open!" Bull eyed her suspiciously again. "I'm just feeling a little claustrophobic. Can you just leave the door open?"

Wordless glances exchanged, Shadow replied in an easy manner. "Sure thing, sweetheart."

Bull watched Chaise's heaving chest carefully as her breaths slowed slightly, showing that she was at least telling the truth about her incident. Her respiration rate had been close to hyperventilation, but he wasn't convinced it was related to a sudden bout of claustrophobia. From his viewpoint, it only came on when he said it was time to talk.

Chaise took her seat and waited patiently as the men moved chairs around to make it easier for them to hold a conversation. She looked to each of them nervously and didn't even try to hide her feelings. They all knew she was scared and she had no reason to try to convince them otherwise. She wanted them to know she was scared out of her mind so they would help her.

4

CHAPTER FOUR

"Why would the *Tres Sieses* be interested in you?" Bull asked with obvious scrutiny. He didn't waste any time, she had to give him that. "That particular gang isn't known for having people *followed*. They're known for making people *disappear*."

Her hand immediately went to her mouth as tears sprung to her eyes and spilled over onto her cheeks before she could stop them. Quickly wiping them away, she pursed her lips and looked down, trying to quickly collect her wits so she could intelligently explain what was happening. She knew from experience that hardened, ex-military men don't appreciate emotionally unstable, babbling women.

Swallowing her tears and anxiety, her eyes found Bull's and she asked with as much confidence as she could muster. "Do you mind if I just start at the beginning and explain? Then if you still have questions, you can ask them?"

Bull leaned back in his chair, crinkling his eyes as he slowly took in her posture. "By all means. Go right ahead then," he replied, but she detected at least a little disbelief in his voice.

"My nineteen-year-old intern is missing! Suddenly and mysteriously. It's not like her and I know someone took her. I've been looking for her and I've apparently gotten too close to someone who doesn't like it," Chaise blurted out hysterically before she could stop herself.

"Okay. What is your intern's name?" Bull calmly asked.

"Aura Perez."

Bull cut his eyes to his friend and nodded. Shadow quickly moved to click a few keys on the laptop while they continued talking.

"She's nineteen, right?" Bull asked and Chaise nodded to confirm. "That's pretty young—she's probably just off having fun with friends, not taking her job seriously. Maybe being an intern wasn't her thing," Bull suggested, shrugging his shoulders like it wasn't as big of a deal as Chaise was making it out to be.

"No, she's not like that. This is completely unlike her and she's been missing for several days now. I know they got her—somehow, somewhere. I have to find her before they do something terrible to her," Chaise retorted, desperate to make them understand.

"Have you had some kind of run in with this gang that would draw attention to you and Aura?" Shadow asked.

Chaise began wringing her hands and looking around the room at each of the men. "How long did you say Noah would be gone?"

Bull quickly answered. "I didn't say."

Rebel gave Bull an odd look and answered Chaise's question. "Two-week honeymoon on a tropical island. There's no way we can reach him without going there ourselves. And I'm not ruining *Reaper's* honeymoon."

Chaise nodded in understanding. "Well, I can't wait that long, anyway. It's already been way *too* long." She took a deep, calming breath in and let it out before continuing. "I work as a field human resources consultant. Companies without full time human resources professionals will hire me as a consultant to make sure their employee files are in order, ensure the policies and procedures are being followed, and that payroll policies are maintained. That sort of thing," Chaise explained.

"Anyway, Aura is a college student and she was assigned to me as my intern. I found some discrepancies between the employee paperwork and the payroll paperwork, so we started investigating them together. When we saw there were just too many *coincidences,* I told Aura to stop looking into the documentation. Something was terribly wrong and we were being pulled into the middle of it. I wanted to find out more on my own and leave her out of it. I'm afraid it was too late, though," she finished.

"What information did you find?" Rebel asked, as Bull shifted his position to lean in closer.

Before she could answer, an explosion from outside rocked the building, sending all three men scrambling for cover. Bull grabbed Chaise from the comfortable chair on his way to the floor, secured her in one spot, and then crawled to the windows to look out.

"There's a car on fire in the parking lot," Bull called to Shadow and Rebel. "It's the one Chaise and I rode in on the way over here."

"Time to move, people," Shadow commanded. "They know where we are and they want her. We need to get her to an unknown location. I'll have one of our other men meet the police here, but we need to split *now*."

"Let's split up, divide their attention," Bull responded. "I'm taking her south. Rebel, head west. Shadow, head north. We'll rendezvous tomorrow at thirteen-hundred hours."

The sound of gunfire erupted outside, but Chaise appeared to be the only one concerned with it. Bull relieved some of her fear when he simply stated, "Bulletproof glass." He led Chaise down the hall, through a doorway, and down the stairs into the underground garage.

Once inside his truck, Bull slowly pulled forward to exit from a side entrance. When he was satisfied that the exit was clear, he pulled onto the street, weaved in and out of traffic, and circled several city blocks to ditch any possible tail, before heading toward the south-bound interstate ramp.

Chaise watched Bull as he navigated his full-size truck expertly through the downtown Miami streets. His eyes constantly searched and assessed possible threats. He was definitely in his element and Chaise thought she caught brief glimpses of what he must have been like when he was in the military. With Noah.

"Did you do this kind of thing in the military?" Chaise asked, unable to hold her curiosity any longer.

Bull glanced at her over his shoulder before responding. "Not exactly the same thing. We learned to do most everything and anything. And we were good at it."

Chaise knew he wasn't being conceited. His tone was humble and the thoughtful look on his face conveyed his nostalgia without saying a word.

"You miss it, don't you?" she asked, trying to pry information out of the man who seemed intent on only giving single syllable answers.

"I do sometimes—I miss parts of it, anyway," he answered. "The best thing about the military is here with me, though—my brothers and Brianna."

Chaise smiled at his reference of his *'brothers and Brianna.'* "You love her, don't you?" The words poured out before she could stop them.

Bull's face took on a serious look as he answered. "She's *earned* her place as my sister. Just like the others *earned* their place as my brothers. I love her like a sister—nothing more."

"I didn't mean to offend you. I wasn't implying you'd betray Noah like that. You just always include her when you do talk about them, so it's pretty obvious that she holds a special place in your heart," Chaise explained humbly. Bull was protecting her and the last thing she wanted to do was offend him or appear unappreciative of his actions.

Bull shifted uncomfortably in his seat and took a moment before he responded. "Trust and honor are very important to me. Sunny— uh, that's Brianna's nickname—well, it's a long story, but I misjudged her and turned my back on her once. I won't ever do that again."

"Well, she's lucky to have someone like you in her corner. And while I'm at it, I'm lucky to have you in mine, too. Saying *'thank you'* seems grossly negligent, but I really don't know how else to say it. Thank you, Colton, sincerely, for helping me, saving me," Chaise fought back the emotions that were threatening to take over her voice.

Bull gave a single nod as his response. He wasn't accustomed to taking compliments. He was used to taking orders and seeing that his duty was performed to the best of his abilities. His commanding officers didn't say the words *'thank you'* for a job well done and they sure didn't show emotions when they told him he did a good job. He thought maybe he should lighten up on her since she looked like she was about to lose her composure.

Chaise wasn't normally such a crier, but the sudden dump of adrenaline was starting to wane and her emotions were on a crazy roller coaster. Everything that she had experienced up until that point was weighing on her as the severity of her situation started to sink in.

Chaise's coping mechanisms were being greatly tested. Aura was missing, a notorious gang was having her tailed, someone blew up the car she and Bull had been in, and then someone started shooting at the building. She was no military expert, but it was all a little too much to be considered a coincidence.

She chuckled under her breath at the absurdity of that thought. *A coincidence?*

"What's so funny over there?" Bull asked with an amused smirk.

"Well, Bull, it's pretty simple. It's either laugh or cry. And since I absolutely hate crying, I figured I had better start laughing really damn soon," she replied with a hint of witty sarcasm in her tone.

Bull let out a full belly laugh at her statement. Chaise was suddenly captivated at how his smile transformed his whole face. There was a light in his eyes that was normally masked, his white teeth shone against the stark contrast of his tan skin and his dark chin stubble, and the deep, masculine rumble of his laugh was hypnotizing. Having only seen his serious side, she was curious just how many people had been blessed with his rich, deep laugh that reverberated through her very core.

She felt herself smile a genuine smile for the first time in weeks—since the whole sordid mess started and she found herself in such a precarious predicament. Bull looked at her for a second or two longer, with this full-on smile still in place, before turning his eyes back to the road.

"Well, Chaise, I have to admit I'm glad to hear that. If I was a betting man, I would've put money on the tears," he replied with a smidgen of teasing and playfulness in his voice.

Chaise hoped she was beginning to see the real Colton Lanier, the one she knew he kept hidden from most everyone. The real part of himself that he kept reserved for only those whom he trusted. That thought left her with a sorrow she couldn't quite shake.

She had only met him a few hours before, but in that short time, he had helped her more than most people had in her entire adult life. But the part that was weighing most heavily on her was that she knew she wasn't being fair or completely honest with him.

"I guess it's a good thing you're not a betting man, then. Unless, of course, you'd actually made that bet with *me*," she playfully jabbed back at him.

His amused chuckle rippled through Chaise and his eyes lingered on hers again before turning back to the road. She noticed, with more than a little satisfaction, that his smile lingered just a bit longer that time. She hated to be the one to remove that smile from his gorgeous face, but with the interruptions they'd already encountered, she felt a dire need to finish as much of the story as she could.

"So, Colton, where are we going?" Chaise asked while turning sideways in her seat. She put her back against the door, the seatbelt strap under her arm, and pulled her knee up in the seat to get more comfortable.

Bull glanced over to answer her and was hit with a sudden and severe craving for all that was Chaise. The way she was sitting was unintentionally provocative and every cell in his body automatically gravitated toward her. Her question purred from her lips, inadvertently sounding alluring and sexy. Bull shifted in his seat and cleared his throat, taking a moment to gather his faculties before responding.

He had only met the woman and the attraction he felt toward her bordered on insane—for him. While he enjoyed the sight of a beautiful woman, and had enjoyed his share of one or two nights with them, he couldn't remember ever feeling such an intense pull to anyone else. Bull fought to keep his mind on the job and not on her as a person.

"We have a couple of choices—a safe house in Key Largo or we can go to my place for now. The house in Key Largo is rarely used so I doubt there are many supplies left for us. But it could be a good place for us to regroup," Bull stated confidently.

"We're, what, about an hour from Key Largo?" Chaise asked.

"Yeah, around there. Is there somewhere else you need to be?" Bull asked, somewhat playfully, still trying to keep the tension light.

"Well, I need to check my schedule," Chaise retorted with a laugh. Then she suddenly remembered. "Oh—um, can we go by my apartment first? I really need to get some clothes and other things together."

Bull checked the rearview and side mirrors and then changed lanes as he checked for any signs that they were being followed. When he was certain they were in the clear, he asked for her address and made his way to her South Beach condominium. Bull circled the block before he turned into the condo, where the armed guard on duty stopped him.

The guard cautiously approached the truck as Bull rolled his window down.

"Hi, Paul, it's me, Chaise. I don't have my gate opener with me. Do you mind letting us in?" she asked sweetly.

"No problem, Miss –"the guard started but Chaise promptly cut him off.

"Thank you so much, Paul! We really appreciate your help!" she quickly responded. Paul smiled and keyed in the electronic override code to let them through.

"Have a good night," Paul called as Bull slowly pulled through the gate. Bull waved in response.

Chaise was infinitely relieved that she was able to stop him before he said her last name. That would cause a whole new set of problems she wasn't ready to deal with, including confirming to Bull that she lied to him. He already knew, she had no doubt of that, but she wanted to be the one to explain it. Having someone else reveal it before the right time could be disastrous.

Bull gave her a knowing look as he rolled up his window and inched forward. She smiled apologetically, yet again, and the urge to explain everything was overwhelming.

"Colton," she stated hesitantly, drawing out his name. She was obviously unsure of how she could explain without explaining, and without making the situation even worse than it already was.

"Chaise, I understand. Martin isn't your last name. You're scared, and until you trust me, you want to stay anonymous. Just know that needs to change soon," he stated sincerely.

Chaise's thoughts immediately went to his statement implying that she didn't trust him. *That couldn't be farther from the truth*, she thought. She knew for a fact that if Noah could trust him, she could, too. The problem existed in him learning of *her* true identity. Would that destroy the delicate tendrils of trust that he was just beginning to form with her? Would he even give her a chance to explain?

Mentally chastising herself, she pushed those thoughts away to deal with at a later time. Bull looked at her, clearly expecting a response, and she realized she'd been lost in her own thoughts.

"I really appreciate that, Bull. You just don't know how much," she responded truthfully, maintaining eye contact with him as she reached to touch his arm. She wanted to tell him that she did trust him. With everything in her, she wanted to reassure him that he was good, honest and trustworthy. Unfortunately, she couldn't convey that to him without opening herself up for the questions she wasn't yet able to answer.

She directed him where to park in the parking garage underneath the oceanfront, high-rise condominium building. Bull looked around and gathered Chaise in close to his side to protect her. The unfamiliar arc of electricity shot through him immediately upon the physical contact. The look on her face told him she felt it, too. But she moved in closer to him, willingly wrapping her arm around his waist as he tucked her under his thick, muscled arm. Chaise couldn't imagine a safer place in the world to be.

5

CHAPTER FIVE

Bull stood at the massive picture window on the twenty-second floor of the luxury high-rise condominium. Chaise's *apartment* was really an eight thousand square foot, two-story luxury condo with an unbelievable view of the Atlantic Ocean from every room. A very talented interior decorator had apparently been utilized to create a natural flow from one room to the next in the open-air design. Feelings that had been stamped out and forgotten suddenly surfaced within Bull. Thoughts of ineptness and questioning if he was good enough to be there appeared from nowhere.

Bull sternly reminded himself that she was in danger and she needed the help that only he could provide. He was there for a reason and that reason was his job and *only* his job. His internal discussion proved successful as he pushed away the insecurities of his youth.

Bull slowly walked around the condo, taking in the few personal pictures that were scattered around the massive first floor, noting that Chaise wasn't in any of them. Just as he was nearing the kitchen, where a stack of mail laid piled on the counter, Chaise bounded around the corner from the back stairs and plowed into him.

She let out a shriek when she met the wall of muscle and bounced off of him. Bull grabbed her forearms, pulling her slightly toward him and steadied her footing. She let out a scared chuckle as she playfully swatted at his chest and said, "You scared the shit out of me!"

Bull laughed easily as he responded, "This place is big enough to get lost in. I'm lucky I found you at all. I must be in the wrong business."

Chaise looked around the luxury condo as she replied on a sigh. "It is great, isn't it? I'm obviously in the wrong business, too."

Bull looked at her quizzically, obviously confused by her statement.

Chase quickly amended her statement. "Oh, this place isn't *mine*. I could never afford this on my salary. It belongs to the company I'm consulting for—they use it for executives, important visitors, people like that. Since my contract with them is only for a short time, they are letting me stay here for free."

The red-alert hairs on the back of Bull's neck were now at full attention, standing on end, and making him tingle in a not so pleasant way. In his experience, if something seemed too good to be true, it usually meant that it wasn't true.

"The same company where you found discrepancies and where your intern worked when you believe she suddenly disappeared? They have access to the condo where you're living?" Bull asked slowly as his hand moved to unsnap his side holster.

All color drained from Chaise's face as she gasped and took an involuntary step back. "You don't think they'd come after me here, *do you*?"

"You haven't told me what you found, but from what I've gathered, you think there's something highly illegal going on at that company. If that's the case, I wouldn't make the mistake of underestimating them," Bull answered truthfully. "Don't forget they've already tried to come after you while you were with me."

Chaise nodded slowly, her eyes wide open, and her pupils fully dilated from fear. "I need to tell you everything, Colton. In case something happens to me, you need to know what I've found. So you can find Aura."

"Let's get out of here. You can tell me in the truck. You got everything you need?" Bull asked, pointing to the small suitcase she still held in her hand. She nodded her affirmation and he took the suitcase from her hand. Bull led the way out of the condo, stealthily moving and checking around corners to ensure a safe route for Chaise.

Bull couldn't shake the feeling of being watched. His gut instincts told him that something was awry in the condo and it wasn't safe for Chaise to stay there any longer. He pulled her in close to his back as they neared the elevator, using him body as a human shield. Once inside, he maneuvered Chaise to the front corner of the elevator. She was caged in the corner by his body. His hands were planted on the walls on either side of her face.

"We need to finish that talk real soon, Chaise." His smooth, deep voice lowered an octave as he nearly whispered his command. His face was close to hers—so close, in fact, that if she lifted herself up just enough, their lips would touch. His warm breath caressed her cheek as he leaned in closer, dropping one hand near her waist. She waited for the warmth of his touch to ignite her already pulsing body.

Instead, he reached to push the button for the lobby. Waves of disappointment rolled through her as he straightened his back and stepped away from her.

What the hell am I thinking? Chaise mentally chastised herself for such inappropriate thoughts in the most inappropriate times and places. She glanced at her watch, noted the lateness of the hour, and decided she must have been even more exhausted than she thought. She also decided she had waited way too long in between relationships.

Stress and anxiety can do funny things to the mind. That had to be reason why she was picturing Colton without his shirt on, the feel of his sinewy muscles and tan skin against hers, the silkiness of his sexy, mussed hair between her fingers. The dinging of the elevator reaching the first floor brought her out of her daydreams, or night dreams, as it was officially way too late to be considered daytime. She quickly masked the smile that was plastered on her face the instant before Bull turned to her.

"Are you ready for this?" Bull asked.

Chaise stammered for a minute, wondering if she had actually spoken the thoughts aloud before she realized he was asking if she was ready to leave the safety of the elevator. "Yes, I'm ready," she managed to respond.

"Stay close to me, Chaise."

"Okay." *No arguments from me,* she thought.

Once safely inside Bull's truck, Chaise breathed a little easier. She leaned her head on the window and closed her eyes. Her thoughts drifted to her intern, Aura, and she wondered where she could be. *Is she safe? What have they done with her?*

Bull's voice pulled her from her thoughts again. "It's late. If it's all right with you, we'll stay at my place tonight and regroup with Rebel and Shadow tomorrow to come up with a plan."

"That sounds great, Colton." Chaise's relief resounded in her tone.

Before she could start to tell him about the discrepancies and coincidences she uncovered, she fell asleep in his truck. Cocooned in the warm, leather seats, hidden from dangers by an expert ex-military man, and the rhythmic rocking and swaying of the truck gliding down the interstate lulled her into a deep sleep. She hadn't slept well since she accepted her current assignment, but her insomnia had become even worse since Aura went missing.

She opened her eyes briefly when she felt a flying sensation. She saw Bull standing outside her door, sliding his huge arms underneath her, and scooping her up from the plush seat. Chaise wrapped her arms around his neck, clung tightly to him, and laid her head on his shoulder. Within a few seconds, she was back asleep, being carried into his house as if she weighed no more than a baby.

Bull maneuvered Chaise and her bags expertly through the front door and into the spare bedroom. It had been a long day and night for both of them, but he suspected the events of the day had taken a harder toll on her than she had let on. He still had so many questions and, truthfully, was looking forward to getting a lot of answers. He was disappointed on one hand. But on the other hand, he found it strange that he was enjoying carrying her to bed, pulling back the covers, and tucking her in safely.

His training and his mental conditioning didn't allow him to rest on his laurels. There was more than some local gang going after Chaise. They didn't blow up cars and fire multiple gunshots at a building that was well outside of their known territory. No, his gut told him that it had to a bigger operation that was only using the gang as a front. Whatever the organization was, it must have a significant presence to use a well-established gang like the *Tres Sieses*. There would be no sleep for Bull that night.

Chaise startled awake, unsure if the loud noise came from her nightmares or from somewhere in the house. As her eyes somewhat focused on her surroundings, she was momentarily disoriented and unsure of where she was. She vaguely remembered Colton picking her up from his truck, so she assumed she was at his house, as planned. She eased out of bed, quietly opened the door, and crept down the hallway toward the front of the house.

There was better light in the living room, shining in the windows from the security light positioned outside, so she was able to make out the furniture in the room. The large man-cave room held an impressive array of audio-visual equipment for the large flat-screen TV, an oversized, overstuffed sectional sofa wide enough for Bull to comfortably rest on, and a matching recliner. Bull had the chair fully reclined and his eyes were closed.

Quickly glancing at the clock on the wall, she reasoned he was most likely asleep at 3:45 am. Chaise jumped when Bull's voice challenged her before his eyes even opened.

"What are you doing out of bed?"

"Bad dream," Chaise answered softly as she moved around to face him. "Mind if I lie down in here with you?"

"Is the bed not comfortable?" Bull asked with genuine concern.

"It's great. It's just that ... well." Her voice trailed as she started biting her fingernails.

"Just that what?" Bull prompted.

"Don't laugh. It's just that I feel safer in here with you than back there. You wouldn't know if they came through the window to get to me," she replied shyly.

Bull held back a laugh since he could tell she was seriously scared of that scenario playing out. She seemed so young to him—or maybe *sheltered* was a better word. She didn't really seem like she had experienced a lot on her own.

He surmised, from his training in reading people, that she had a controlling father who didn't want to let his little girl find her own way in the wide, wild world. She wouldn't know that he had a state of the art alarm system and no one could get on his property, much less in one of his windows, without being riddled with bullet holes first.

Bull stood and led her over to the couch where he gestured for her to lie down. When she complied, he pulled a blanket out and covered her with it. As he leaned over to cover her, their faces were once again very close.

Unable to resist the urge, Chaise rose up and kissed his cheek. When he didn't move away from her, she moved her mouth to his soft, plump lips. She softly kissed him, a chaste kiss at first, then with more fervor as her tongue lightly grazed his lips. Bull's mouth opened, giving her entrance and returning the kiss.

Bull's hands went to her face and his fingers threaded through her hair. He tilted her head to the side to deepen the kiss. His response to Chaise's kiss was unexpected, but it felt so right. Bull's logical mind kicked in and told him to slow the freight train down before it crashed.

Gently ending the kiss, Bull brushed his knuckles across her cheek and said, "Get some sleep, Chaise."

"What about you?"

"What about me?" Bull furrowed his brow and titled his head slightly.

"You need sleep, too," she replied slowly, as if he were slow and didn't understand plain English.

Bull smiled as he remembered the missions, both in the service and in the employment of Steele Security, that had kept him awake for more than thirty-six hours at a time. But she was worried about him staying up half that time. "I'll make it," he replied genially.

Chaise mumbled something about stubborn, bull-headed men and snuggled under the blanket. Bull reclaimed his comfortable recliner and watched Chaise as she drifted back to sleep. He listened to her rhythmic breathing pattern, watched the softening of her face and relaxation of her entire body, and knew the exact moment she had succumbed to sleep. A fleeting thought flashed in his mind about wanting what Noah and Brianna had but he quickly pushed it away.

Mentally reprimanding himself for the momentary lapse in discipline, Bull steeled his thoughts and relaxed in his chair. He closed his eyes and listened to the sounds around the house. He knew every creak and moan and would know immediately if anything was out of the ordinary.

Bull was more relaxed while "on duty" inside his house because Steele Security monitored his alarm system from their central location. If his system suddenly quit, as in someone cut the line or they turned his electricity off, Steele Security would call his phone and they would immediately dispatch units if he didn't answer.

6

CHAPTER SIX

The smell of bacon frying and coffee percolating woke Bull from the best sleep he'd had in memory. Momentarily alarmed by the unfamiliar sounds and smells, it took him a moment to remember that Chaise was in the house with him. He silently rose from his chair, noted that she was missing from the couch, and he silently crept into the kitchen. He watched her from the doorway for several minutes without her ever knowing he was there.

The thought that she was being too reckless with her safety by being unaware of her surroundings crossed his mind and he had every intention of chastising her for it. Then he realized that she'd somehow walked past him, made herself at home in his kitchen, and had their breakfast almost fully cooked before he even realized anything. He decided that the chastising should really be more of a discussion about general safety precautions.

Besides, he really enjoyed watching her cook, in his kitchen, wearing her tight spaghetti strap tank top and cotton pajama shorts. She was making herself at home, but at the same time, she was also making sure to take care of him. No one had taken care of him, other than his brothers having his back, since he'd left home.

"Something smells good," Bull finally stated, making his presence known. The sudden intrusion made her jump and she let out a startled shriek. Bull's smile grew wider, reaching his eyes and making them dance with mischief.

"Colton Lanier!" she playfully yelled while laughing. "You will stop scaring me!"

Chaise tried to sound stern but she just couldn't do it when Bull was smiling at her like that. She stood transfixed, rooted to the floor as she watched him move toward her with his confident gait. His massive muscles flexing and contracting, his keen eyes assessing but also holding an unusual glint of humor, and one side of his mouth curled up in a sexy half-grin. *The man just woke up and he still looks sexy as hell,* she thought.

"Where's the fun in that?" he asked as he stalked toward the plate of crispy bacon.

"Oh, no you don't, Mr. Lanier!"

Bull's grim look conveyed that he'd been appropriately chastised so Chaise turned back to the stove to finish cooking. Bull snatched a piece of bacon when she wasn't looking and promptly chomped on it. The crackling noise made Chaise's head spin back toward him and he immediately stopped chewing. She narrowed her eyes suspiciously at him but he feigned an innocent look. She turned her head back and then quickly snapped it back to him just as he started chewing again.

She chased him out of the kitchen with a towel wound up, ready to snap him with it. They both laughed good-naturedly, genuinely enjoying the playful banter and easy-going morning lightheartedness. Chaise dared to hope that the new repartee signaled a positive shift in their relationship.

"You're going to make me overcook the eggs!" she playfully admonished him. Bull's smile lit up his face again as he popped the rest of the bacon in his mouth and aggressively chewed it in front of her.

"Here, let me help," he said, setting the plates and forks on the table.

Chaise looked at the plates and back to Bull. "That's it? That's helping?" she asked with a straight face.

For a few seconds, Bull looked unsure of how to answer that trick question. Unable to hold back her smile, Chaise quickly turned around to hide her face from Bull's all-knowing gaze. Soon, she was unable to hold in her laughter and her shoulders started bouncing up and down as she covered her mouth with one hand.

She was suddenly hoisted in the air by two strong arms that surrounded her and heard Bull's teasing voice. "Are you making fun of me, Chaise *Martin*?"

She squealed with amusement and screamed. "*The eggs!*"

Bull lowered her body back down, skimming his front with her back. The electricity arcing off of their bodies should have short-circuited everything within a fifty-mile radius, like an miniature EMP blast. When Chaise looked over her shoulder at Bull, the sultry, sweltering look he held would have melted steel.

Bull's hands rested on her waist, still holding her tightly to him, and he knew if he merely bent his head, their lips would touch and the damn eggs could burn to ashes. He felt his head incline slowly toward her, his eyes flitting back and forth between her plump lips and her accepting eyes. The memory of last night's kiss was on both of their minds, fueling the fire raging between them.

The shrill sound of his cell phone jolted him back to reality and he quickly let go of her, putting distance between them physically and mentally, before walking off to pick up his phone. Looking quickly at the screen, he noted it was Rebel before he answered. "Yeah, man."

Chaise listened to Bull's clipped end of the conversation but was unable to ascertain anything of use from it. Putting the food on the table, she filled their glasses with juice and filled her plate. She considered waiting for Bull to join her before she started eating but petulantly decided against it. As Bull finished his phone call, Chaise was finishing her breakfast. After rinsing the breakfast dishes and putting them in the dishwasher, she wordlessly left the room to shower and dress.

Knowing what the day held—her interrogation by the Steele Security team—she was not in a hurry to finish her morning ritual. The endless questions, the uncomfortable probing, the dubious glances, and the new issue of claustrophobia made the day downright dreadful. Now, with the mixed signals and wishy-washy temperament of Bull added, the day instantly became infinitely worse.

An hour later, when she left her room, she heard multiple male voices coming from the kitchen. Slowly and quietly skirting down the hall, she tried to covertly listen to their conversation before they became aware of her presence. The chatter suddenly stopped and she knew the team had detected her presence. It was their job, after all, but she'd hoped to at least get an idea of what she would be walking into.

Rounding the corner into the kitchen, she noted Rebel and Shadow sitting at the table with Bull. Bull was fully facing her and their eyes locked. His intense desire was still there, simmering like lava just beneath the earth's surface, only masked by his cool exterior. She liked that he reacted that way to her, but sensed any movement in their current status would have to be initiated by her. Bull's sense of professionalism and duty was deep and strong—he wouldn't likely make the first move on a client.

She'd purposely dressed in a short, light green dress that made her mint green eyes sparkle. It wasn't overly provocative but it wasn't boring, either. The V-neck halter tied around her neck, leaving it open to her mid-back. The loose fitting silhouette, along with the gracefully flowing hemline, made her lean legs go on forever. She paired it with long, elegant necklaces and light brown Grecian sandals to show off her dainty, painted toes.

Bull had been leaning on his forearms on the table, but the sight of Chaise in that dress had him sitting up at full attention. Her beauty was mesmerizing and had his thoughts racing about being alone with her again. The attraction was undeniable, like a moth to the flame, just as hot and just as likely to be burned. *If this is being burned*, Bull thought, *I can definitely handle the heat.*

He watched the slight blush creep up Chaise's slender neck to her cheeks, turning them a light shade of pink. She no doubt knew the look of a man who appreciated her beauty. Knowing she was just as affected as he was, and not hiding it, made her even more attractive to Bull.

"We were just talking about you. Perfect timing, Chaise," Bull's smooth voice welcomed her.

Smiling, she responded. "Good morning, Rebel, Shadow. And just what were you guys saying about me?"

Shadow started first. "Good morning, Chaise. I conducted a search for anything on Aura Perez but I found nothing of use. There's no missing persons report on file for her. Do you know why that would be?"

Chaise stopped in mid-step, shocked and unblinking before answering, "N–no. There's no report? You're sure? Her mom said she filed it. She was worried *sick*."

Chaise took a seat at the table, confusion and unrest imprinted in her features. She looked at each man and found only his assessing stares in return. "I don't understand. What happened to her missing person report? No one's been looking for her all this time?"

Shadow's deceptively calm voice set her nerves on edge. "There wasn't a report filed, Chaise. I checked for electronic reports and paper reports. I've talked to all my contacts at the sheriff's department."

"No, that's not right! Someone told you wrong," Chase adamantly refused to believe her ears.

Shadow looked at Bull and Bull took over the conversation. "Chaise, I think it's time you start from the beginning and tell us everything."

Chaise nodded but Bull noted the apprehension and tension settle in her face. "Okay, from the beginning. I'm an HR consultant, working under contract at Viboro Distributing. Aura was my intern. She was attending the University of Miami and was assigned to help me with all the cross-referencing data."

Rebel interjected. "Who assigned her to you?"

Chaise stumbled at his question. "Um, I'm not sure what you mean. She was waiting for me at Viboro and she said she was my intern."

"So, you didn't negotiate to have an intern? The managers at Viboro didn't introduce the two of you?" Rebel pressed.

Chaise gave it some thought before answering. "No, she was waiting outside the office I was assigned to when I got there."

"Okay, go on," Bull encouraged.

"Part of my job is to make sure all the paperwork matches—cross matching dates in the personnel files and payroll files—to make sure they've maintained accurate records. I started finding discrepancies in the hire and termination dates between the personnel files and the payroll files. Two different areas maintain them but they're supposed to communicate with each other.

"At first, I didn't think anything about the discrepancies—there were only a couple in the first dataset. I find that in every large corporation. The paperwork gets lost, someone keys in a wrong date, and usually it's no big deal to correct it. But then I kept finding them and started making a comprehensive list of names, addresses, and birth dates."

Bull repositioned himself, eager to learn more and dig further into the developing mystery. "Do you still have the list?"

Chaise regarded him for a moment before answering. "Yes, I have it."

"That's great. We can easily check that list against our databases," Shadow answered.

"Shouldn't I finish telling you everything before you just jump in and take over everything?" Chaise probed irritably.

Rebel couldn't contain his amusement. "I like her," he said to Bull and Shadow. "By all means, please continue, Chaise. We're all ears."

"I noticed every name on the list was a Latino girl, between eighteen and twenty-two years old, and it all was just too suspicious for me to ignore. At first I thought it was a blatant issue of racial profiling. But when I searched for a couple of them online, I found the fliers saying they were missing persons. One after the other, Aura and

I kept finding missing girls—all from Viboro Distributing, all Latino, and all very young.

"I told Aura to stop investigating it and leave it to me. I had the feeling we'd already raised too many suspicions with our questions. The next day, she didn't show up or call, so I went to her house. Her mother was absolutely distraught. She said Aura hadn't come home or called," Chaise finished.

"Did you call the police?" Rebel asked.

"No," Chaise answered tentatively. "I asked the head of security a few questions, but that didn't work out so well. Several strange things happened after that. That's why I ended up at Noah's wedding—I didn't know what else to do."

"Do you remember where Aura's mother lives?" Rebel asked.

"Yes."

"Good. Let's go talk to her mom today," Bull answered.

"All right," Chaise answered. "Can you take me to pick up my company car? I left it at the wedding reception yesterday."

"Sure," Bull answered. But Chaise didn't miss the suspicion in his eyes.

He still doesn't truly believe me, she thought solemnly.

Chaise rode with Bull, giving him directions to Aura's house, while Rebel and Shadow took a separate vehicle. When they arrived at the small house in the Hialeah Gardens area of Miami, Bull watched Chaise take a deep breath before exiting the car. They walked together to the front door while Rebel and Shadow kept watch around the perimeter of the house.

Bull knocked on the door, and when it opened, he was surprised to see an elderly Chinese man on the other side. He looked at Chaise, questioning her with his eyes, but she shook her head in confusion and had no answer for him. Bull turned back to the gentleman and gave him a warm smile.

"Hello, we are looking for Mrs. Perez. Is she home?" Bull asked.

"There's no one here by that name. I live here alone," the man answered.

"Maybe she left a forwarding address?" Bull continued his line of questioning.

"No, I think you must have the wrong address. I've lived here the last ten years," the man stated firmly, looking back and forth between Bull and Chaise.

"That can't be right—I am sure it was *this* house. I remember these red bricks on the driveway!" Chaise argued, confused and irritated about why the Chinese man insisted Mrs. Perez didn't live there.

"There are many houses in Hialeah Gardens with this kind of driveway, Miss. There's no Mrs. Perez here. Goodbye," he smarted as he stepped back in the house and closed the door in her face.

CHAPTER SEVEN

Chaise was quiet on the drive to pick up her company car from the beach area. Bull didn't have to say anything. She could tell exactly what he was thinking from the disbelieving look on his face. He made no attempt to spare her feelings with the look that he gave her. He thought she was making everything up. Glancing out the window, she saw that Rebel and Shadow were still following them.

"Why are they following us? We're just going to pick up my car, right?"

"Yes," Bull answered briskly without any further explanation.

"So, why are they following us?" Chaise pressed.

"Safety precautions," Bull answered.

Chaise knew better than to believe that excuse. Bull was keeping tabs on her because he didn't believe her and the Chinese man didn't help her case at all. "Well, I guess I should be completely safe then, right?"

"That's right," Bull snapped.

"Look, I don't know what's going on, but that's the house I went to and that's the house where I talked to Aura's mom. I'm not making this up!" Chaise could no longer hold in her frustration.

"If you say so," Bull responded with less sarcasm than before.

Chaise angrily huffed in response and was infinitely glad that they were arriving at her car. Placing her hand on the door, she readied herself to jump out and get away from the infuriating man beside her. It was just her luck that he burst that little bubble of hope before he came to a stop beside her car.

"Follow me back to my house. Shadow and Rebel will be directly behind you. You need to be on extreme alert for anything suspicious between here and my house. We will all be watching you," Bull informed her resolutely.

Chaise knew his message held the information she needed to be kept safe. But she couldn't shake the feeling that the same message was intended to *keep* her, period. They were following her and watching out for her, but they were also watching her and doubting her. Meeting Bull's eyes, Chaise felt the familiar butterflies in her stomach—the ones she got when she felt his stare penetrating deep into her thoughts.

Can he read my mind?

"Okay, I will follow you back to your place," she agreed, placating him and avoiding any arguments. Chaise lived by the motto to choose her battles and this wasn't one she wanted to fight with Bull. She would eventually have to talk to him about going back to work the following day. She knew how that would go over, though—about as well as trying to reason with an actual bull.

Back at Bull's house after an uneventful ride, Chaise popped the trunk of her company car and started removing all the contents. Bull, Shadow, and Rebel watched with curious and dubious gazes. When she started tugging on the spare tire, Bull wordlessly stepped in and removed it for her.

"Thank you," Chaise said in all sincerity. Bull simply nodded and placed the tire on the ground.

"What are you doing?" he finally asked.

Reaching under the jack, she retrieved a small, black cartridge and handed it to Bull. Upon inspection, he realized it was a tiny flash drive.

"That's the file that I was researching when I found all the discrepancies. I highlighted the missing girls I found online but there are plenty more to be researched," she explained.

Bull handed the flash drive to Shadow who was already on his cell phone calling his confidential contacts to start the investigation. When Bull turned back to Chaise, she could still see the apparent distrust in his eyes. Releasing a sigh of resignation, she started putting the contents of the trunk back together as Shadow and Rebel walked inside, leaving Bull and Chaise alone.

Unable to stand it any longer, she turned to Bull and firmly address him. "I am not lying. I'm not making this up and I'm not crazy. I don't know what's going on but I *need* you to believe me. Even if it is for no other reason than to help me find Aura. *Please.*"

"All right," Bull responded, sensing her sincerity. "But I still have questions you haven't answered yet. Simple questions—like your last name."

"Colton, that's not as simple as you think," she quietly explained, looking down at her hands. Meeting his sharp gaze again, she continued. "What else can I do?"

"I don't know, Chaise. I guess we'll have to take it one step at a time."

As Chaise and Bull entered his house, Rebel told them that there was too much information in the flash drive for them to digest all at once. He and Shadow would take it back to Steele Security headquarters to get Brad and the other technology guys to help them pull the information together and devise a game plan.

"I strongly suggest you two lay low until we get back with you. It may take a day or two for us to get everything in order," Rebel said. Turning to Chaise, he directed, "And you need to stay off the radar completely until we get this sorted out. This is nothing to mess around with."

Chaise nodded in agreement. "I will call and take the week off next week. I'll make up something, but I don't think I can stay away from work past that."

THE NEXT SEVERAL days seemed to drag by for Chaise. She called the general manager of Viboro and told him she had the flu and would be out a few days. She added a couple of fake coughs and made her voice sound gravelly and rough. He apparently bought her act as he told her to feel better soon.

"Well, that's done," she sighed as she hung up the phone. "That just bought me a few days off without appearing too suspicious."

Bull nodded. "Good. That gives us more time to talk. Doesn't it?"

Chaise cut her eyes to meet Bull's when he emphasized 'talk.' His vast chest expanded and contracted with his quick breaths, his nostrils slightly flared each time, and the temperature in his heated expression rolled off of him in waves. She knew without asking that *talking* was the last thing on his mind.

"Yes," she nodded while maintaining eye contact. "We have plenty of time to talk every day."

Bull blew out a forceful breath and squeezed his hands into tight fists. Chaise raised her eyebrows and flashed her best smirk at him. *So bull-headed*, she thought. *Well, two can play that game.*

Chaise enjoyed the time she had alone with Bull, getting to know him as well as he would allow it. She watched his routine and knew that he'd brought much of his military training home with him. The discipline, the organization, and the pride in keeping everything in perfect order were part of his DNA.

The unresolved sexual tension between Bull and Chaise continued to build over those several days they spent together inside the house. They had exchanged several heated glances and lingering touches during their internment. When their bodies brushed as they passed in the hallway, the heat between them was almost enough to start a fire.

"Excuse me," Bull murmured as they approached each other in the narrow hallway.

As he stepped into her personal space, Chaise turned to face him. His chest brushed across hers, and she softly gasped at the physical contact. Her eyes met his, the longing and desire obvious in them both, and she lifted her face toward his. Bull bent his head, his lips inexplicably drawn to hers. When their lips met, her hand slid around the back of his neck while his hand slid to small of her back.

When she moaned with need, Bull pushed her into the wall and pushed his body into hers. His hand drifted down to rest at the back of her thigh. Just as he was about to lift her off the floor, his common sense kicked in and he slowly release her leg. After he slowed their urgent, demanding kiss, he pulled away from her to allow his erratic pulse to slow back to normal.

"What's wrong, Colton?" she whispered, confusion marking her words.

"We can't do this, Chaise," Bull answered.

"You don't want me," she asked and stated at once.

"I want you so fucking bad I can barely see straight," Bull replied through gritted teeth. "Now isn't the right time, though."

Chaise looked at the floor as she replied. "Then I guess you can just let me know when the time is right." She stepped further away from him to give him room to pass her, but kept her chin dropped to her chest. Silently, she turned and walked away from him.

Bull was almost to his breaking point when Shadow called days later and said they were on their way over with the data. His thoughts were betraying his sense of duty and his commitment to his job. His professional demeanor was waning, and he was running out of excuses to keep avoiding his attraction to Chaise. She had made it painfully clear to him that she was interested. He only had to accept her invitation.

Chaise knew the distance that Bull had kept between them was intentional. She had tried to break down his walls and he had resisted her. She knew part of the reason he rejected her was because he didn't trust her. The other part of the equation was his professionalism, both on the job and in his life. When her open attempt miserably failed, she resigned herself to accept it could not be.

When Shadow and Rebel arrived at Bull's, they immediately opened the computer with the files the tech expert had dissected and had every document open and ready to discuss when Bull and Chaise joined them in the den. Shadow was busy clicking away on the secure laptop and chatting on his phone with his former CIA friends while Rebel was on the phone with Brad, the technology expert at Steele Security.

Their animated discussions centered on the information Chaise had provided. They were able to verify most of what she had already told them and linked many open cases to the girls' names on Chaise's spreadsheets. Bull raised his eyebrows at the two men and they both nodded affirmatively back at him.

"What was that all about?" Chaise asked.

"What was what all about?" Bull responded.

"Come on—I saw that. What's going on?"

"They just confirmed your story—or part of it anyway," Bull explained.

"Does that earn me any trust?" Chaise asked and Bull didn't miss the hopefulness in her tone.

"Some," he responded ambiguously. This earned him a full-watt smile from Chaise and he again felt the unfamiliar pull in his chest. He had to admit that their confirmation of her story removed some of his apprehension about her.

Relaxing his stance, Bull placed his hands on his waist and took a moment to simply observe her as she moved around his house. She moved with a fluid grace that was mesmerizing. Her long, lean body completely captivated Bull and pulled his thoughts from where he should be focused.

She walked between Shadow and Rebel, listening to their conversations and pointing out information over their shoulders as they talked about the names and the information on the lists.

"Ask them about Aura Perez," Chaise whispered to Shadow urgently.

"Yeah, can you run a check on an Aura Perez, nineteen-year-old female, University of Miami student? Thanks, man," Shadow said into his cell phone. Chaise waited on pins and needles, wringing her hands, and pacing back and forth in the three feet of space directly in front of Shadow.

When Shadow shook his head 'no' at Chaise, her pacing abruptly halted as she buried her face in her hands. Bull intently watched her every move, memorizing her body posture, her respirations, and her skin color. When she dropped her hands, he saw true fear and pain in her eyes. Chaise was sincerely worried about Aura Perez—it was no act. Seeing this, she earned another minute amount of his trust.

He waited for Shadow to finish his call before asking for an update. "What's the word, man?"

"Chaise is right—a lot of these names are tied to missing persons cases. Here's the interesting part, though. Several of these girls *used* to be listed online—pictures, fliers, everything—but now, almost all them have been taken off the Internet. I had to get a friend to hack into some servers and pull their restore files from a few weeks back to retrieve the information," Shadow explained gravely.

"What about Aura? What did they say about her? Did they find her missing persons report?" Chaise asked excitedly.

"There's no record of an Aura Perez—not at the college, not at Viboro, and not anywhere online. There's no missing persons report —not even one that's been deleted like the other girls. Either she never existed or she gave you a fake name," Shadow answered.

Bull watched Chaise's reaction to the information Shadow had obtained about Aura. She sat down hard on the sofa, confusion engraved on her face, looking around but seemingly not seeing anything in particular, then the tears started flowing uncontrollably. Before he realized it, Bull was at her side, wrapping his arm around her shoulders, and pulling her into him to console her.

"I don't *understand* what's happening," Chaise cried into Bull's chest. "She was my intern. Her mom was so distraught. Nothing makes sense!"

Bull tightened his hold on her, lightly rubbing her back as he lowered his voice to speak softly to her. "We've just started, Chaise. Don't give up hope yet."

When she wrapped her arm around his waist and hugged him tight, Bull was astonished at how *right* it felt to hold her in his arms. She fit perfectly against him, her soft but muscular body pressed to his as if she were cast from a mold that was meant only for him. The soft, sweet scent of her perfume enveloped him with her every movement.

Her soft cries into his chest propelled his protective instincts to new heights. She was his keep now and he would see things through to the end. Strange thoughts permeated his mind—thoughts of wanting her to still be around at the end of the case, to stay with him and make whatever attraction lingering between them become a living, breathing being. Whether its breath held fire or ice was yet to be determined.

Chaise's body became rigid when she realized she was wrapped around Bull and she was holding onto him so tightly. Fearing she had far overstepped her bounds, she tentatively pulled away from the safety of his comfortable embrace to look into his eyes. Both afraid and anxious to see what message they conveyed to her, she held her breath until their eyes finally met. In them, she saw desire and compassion—not the cold, unfeeling detachment she was certain she'd find. Her heart melted at the sight, and without conscious thought, her hand slowly drifted to his jaw line.

"Thank you, Colton," she whispered. "So much."

Without speaking the actual words, they both knew her appreciation was not only for how he consoled her or his oath of not giving up. They both knew the unspoken gratitude was also for the trust he was giving her—the chance that Bull rarely gave those he didn't know and never gave to those who hadn't fully earned it. He was taking an unheard of chance with Chaise and her outrageous story.

Their faces were so close. Their warm, sweet breath coated each other's faces and their lips were almost close enough to touch. Had they been alone, Chaise knew she would make the first move again, certain that Colton would not be the one to do it while he was on the job. She was thankful for the support that Shadow and Rebel were providing by researching the information she obtained. But she wished with all her might that they would suddenly disappear from the room.

Shadow and Rebel at least had the good manners of keeping their backs turned to Bull and Chaise while they reluctantly unfolded from their intimate embrace. Once they were again upright on the couch, Shadow and Rebel gathered their possessions, telling Bull and Chaise they would soon be in touch again, and Bull walked them out. Chaise took a moment to use the restroom and try to get her emotions under control.

As she entered the den, Bull was returning from outside. Their eyes collided and she was instinctively drawn to him. She couldn't have stopped her feet if she tried. It wasn't as if she had even wanted to stop. She floated across the room and directly into Bull's massive, welcoming arms. Their lips met with urgency—there was no slow, simmering kiss between them this time. It started blazing hot and continued until the fireball of desire consumed both of them.

Before she knew they had moved, Bull had backed her up against the wall and was passionately consuming her mouth. His tongue caressed hers with such finesse it felt smoother than the finest silk. Her fingers relished the feel of his hair as she feverishly massaged his head with her touch. She felt his strong hands move farther down her waist, across her hips, until he lifted her so that she could wrap her legs around his waist.

Supporting her with one leg, he used both hands to cup her face, tilting it to deepen his kiss and take more of her, which she willingly gave to him. Chaise tightened her legs around him, pulling up with her arms so that her chest was pressed hard against him. The heat of his hands penetrated the thin material of her dress, searing her skin with his brand and making her wish for more at the same time.

Tearing his mouth from hers, Bull pulled his face back to look her in the eye. "Are you sure about this?"

"I've never been so sure of anything in my life, Colton," she replied decisively while maintaining his gaze. Pulling his mouth back to hers, she reclaimed it as he shifted his arms underneath her and carried her toward his bedroom.

Chaise's fingers floated down his back, appreciating the ripples and striations of his muscles, until she reached the hem of his shirt. Lifting it slowly with one hand and trailing on his hot skin with the other, she languidly removed his shirt, breaking their kiss only to fully pull it over his head and cast it away on the floor.

The short length of her dress had her thighs rubbing against the rough texture of his jeans and heightening her anticipation of what was yet to come. When they reached his king-size sleigh bed, Bull stopped and stood her up at the edge of it. The yearning in his eyes and voice sent shivers down her spine when he delivered his alpha-male demand.

"My turn, Chaise—or more accurately, *your* turn," his deeply masculine whisper promised. He lifted her arms above her head. "Keep them up." He issued his command and she obeyed. His skimmed his hands along the outline of her dress, building the anticipation and pulling her deeper under his inimitable spell.

Unable to speak, she simply nodded in agreement, until she felt the warmth of his hands on her skin. She instinctively dropped her hand to his head, gripping his hair between her fingers, and her knees threatened to buckle as she whimpered unexpectedly. Bull took her hands in his, then gently pushed her arms back up. "You can hold on to the footboard for now. But when I'm done, I want your arms back up in the air."

"Okay." She was unsure of where the ability to speak suddenly appeared from or why she was instantly so willing to give in and do exactly as she was told.

His hands followed his tongue, moving up her legs, under her dress, until he found the innermost silky edge of her panties, directly covering her now soaked core. He skimmed his fingers slowly around the edge of her panties until he finally moved around to the sides. Slipping his index finger in each side, he languidly pulled them down her legs, skimming the surface and providing sweet torture, until they were finally in a puddle at her feet. When she stepped out of them, Bull picked them up and tossed them across the room.

"You won't be needing those for a while," his deep voice rumbled.

8

CHAPTER EIGHT

J ust the sound of his rich, bedroom voice was enough to melt her on the spot. Chaise released a soft moaned, ready for anything he wanted to give her. Dropping her head back, she gripped the bed frame tighter in anticipation of the things he planned to do to her. Her breathing was shallow, causing her chest to heave in and out in desire as if she'd ran a marathon.

"Chaise," Bull's voice commanded, it did not ask.

"Yes." *To whatever you want. The answer is yes!*

"Get ready to scream." Bull's fingers gripped her hips, pulling her tightly to him and to what she knew would be pure bliss.

The chimes of his cell phone stilled his actions, causing Chaise to groan in exasperation. *He was so close!* Their eyes were still locked, the desire burning in his like an open white-hot flame suddenly dimmed, and he sat back away from her to fish it out of his front pocket. She was still panting feverishly, still rooted to her place, her hands still gripping the footboard tightly as Bull supplied abrupt answers into the phone.

Ending his conversation, Bull stood and spoke. "The perimeter sensors have been tripped. Someone's here."

His voice held no indication of any sexual frustration or tension after what had just occurred between them was so suddenly interrupted. His demeanor was back to the normal, on-duty Bull while Chaise's head continued to spin out of control. *How can he go from red-hot to ice-cold in a matter of seconds?* Chaise thought to herself, with no small amount of annoyance and distress.

"Get ready to go. We need to leave," Bull stated matter-of-factly as he walked into the closet. He came back out with two more Glock .45 pistols and had put additional clips in his back pockets.

That sight seemed to suddenly snap Chaise into action as she dashed to his side, her eyes wide with fear and her breaths shallow, but for a completely different reason now. She followed closely behind him as he used his immense body as a human shield. His gun drawn and at the ready, he quietly moved through the house, checking the windows from the safety of the sides until he caught movement along the southern edge of his property.

"A security team is en route, but I need to get you out of here now," he turned his head to look at her. "When we get in my truck, keep your head down. Lie all the way down and don't get up until I tell you."

Chaise nodded, fear taking over and apparently rendering her voice incapable of responding at the moment. She knew someone was after her, but to hunt her down at Bull's house demonstrated an unyielding determination to get to her. *If I'm not safe here with him, I'm not safe anywhere*, she thought solemnly.

Chaise followed Bull down the hall, through the kitchen, and into his truck that was parked in the garage. Quietly opening and closing the doors, Chaise slipped in and hid in the floorboard of the backseat. The garage door was eerily quiet as it raised and Bull gunned the engine, making a quick exit from the garage until he reached the road. In his rearview mirror, Bull watched as the Steele Security teams arrived en masse to secure his home and property.

Bull had every confidence the men from Steele Security would thoroughly scrub the entire area until they either found the culprits or they deemed it clear. In the meantime, he made the decision of a safe place to take her—a place she could learn new skills to help protect herself and help him feel better. He would take her to the shooting range owned by Steele Security and teach her how to handle and shoot a pistol.

"Chaise, you can get up now," Bull had almost forgotten she was still lying in the floor in the back of his truck.

Chaise slowly rose and looked around before sitting up fully.

"I feel like I'm being chauffeured sitting back here alone," Chaise teased.

Bull smiled at her in the rearview mirror and her stomach did somersaults. He was more than gorgeous when he smiled. He didn't smile much, but when he did, it was more than worth the wait. She couldn't help but return the smile as she asked, "Where are we going now?"

"I'm taking you somewhere safe while they clear the house. We're going to the shooting range and you're going to learn to handle a pistol," Bull stated with a glint of humor and anticipation in his eyes.

"Oh yeah, because the shooting range is the best place for me," she replied sarcastically.

"Yes, it is. You think someone will try to get to you at a Steele Security shooting range, where everyone is armed to the teeth and an expert mark? No, sweetheart, that's the safest place for you to be right now," he explained.

"If you say so," she replied while looking out the window. Chaise was seriously dreading the situation. Her secret was killing her, and it just kept piling up. Should she pretend to not know how to use guns so that Bull could teach her? Or should she just go ahead and tell him that she was fairly well versed in handling guns and didn't really need instruction? Opting to reduce the backlash she was sure to get later, she decided to share some information with him.

"I'm actually pretty handy with a pistol already," she said nonchalantly.

"Really? Who taught you?" Bull was skeptical and watched her carefully in the rearview mirror.

"My dad and my brothers," she said softly. "When we were

growing up, my dad always said all his kids needed to be familiar with guns so that we had a healthy respect for them. He used to take us out in the back yard once a week to practice."

"Where are your dad and brothers now?" Bull asked, clearly not happy that they weren't helping to protect her.

She leaned up between the front seats to be closer to Bull but to also try to reestablish some connection between them. She couldn't tell him everything, but she wanted to convey in some way that she was telling him everything she possibly could.

"My dad and I don't have the best relationship. We haven't for many years now. I left home and have tried to make it on my own. He is more than controlling, Colton. He is overbearing and impossible to please. I talk to my siblings occasionally, but they all have their own separate lives. My mom is caught in the middle, so when I spend time with her, I try to leave everything else out."

Keeping her dress in place as best she could, Chaise worked her way between the seats and claimed the front seat beside Bull. "I know you're probably wondering why I haven't run back home to my family in all this. I just ... I can't do that, Colton. If you don't want to be stuck with me, I understand—you didn't ask for this mess. I just want you to *know* ... I want you to believe me when I say I mean no harm to Noah or his wife. And if my being here, with this gang and whoever else after me, puts *them* in danger, I will leave *right now* with no hard feelings."

Pulling up to a red light, Bull took a moment to read her body language, to study what she wasn't saying, and to decide what he should do next. *Do I cut her loose and protect Reaper and Brianna? Do I keep her close to keep an eye on her and protect them all?* She kept her eyes trained on him, never breaking eye contact, never flinching, and never showing that she was telling him anything but the truth.

"I don't want you go to anywhere," he finally replied. And that was the honest truth. He didn't want her to leave. He didn't know if he had it in him to pursue anything serious with her, but he couldn't deny the attraction. *For once*, he thought, *maybe I should give someone a chance.* "I believe that you don't mean them any harm. As far as danger, Reaper's job automatically puts him in danger and he's used to it—he's good at what he does. Brianna is pretty tough, too."

"She sounds great. I hope I get to meet her one day," Chaise replied absently, looking out the window. "And I hope we find Aura soon. I'm really worried about her, Colton."

After a couple of minutes, she realized he hadn't responded. Looking at him, she saw the muscle in his jaw jumping and recognized the hard set of his teeth. Aura was still a sore spot between them. Bull didn't completely believe her and she knew she wasn't lying. Before she could say anything about it, Bull pulled into the drive of a gated compound, keyed in the code, and soon they pulled into the parking area.

Bull reached across Chaise and removed a Ruger LCR .357 from his glove compartment. After grabbing a box of rounds, he and Chaise made their way through the secure building to the shooting range area. Bull wordlessly handed Chaise a pair of earplugs and the Ruger pistol. He set the rounds down on the shelf beside them and proceeded to put up a target and sent it out on the target line.

He stepped back, crossed his arms, and gestured toward the target. "Impress me."

It was definitely a challenge—and not just about her ability to shoot a pistol. She knew he was challenging everything she'd said to him. He was making her prove what she'd told him, and most likely using this test to gauge if she had told the truth about Aura. Unwilling to back down, or to risk the small advances they had already made, Chaise met his challenge head on.

She picked up the box of rounds and removed five bullets. Expertly popping the chamber open, she loaded all five bullets in and snapped the cylinder shut. She carefully put the gun down on the shelf, put her earplugs in and grabbed a pair of safety glasses. Once set, she took her shooting stance. She held the gun in her right hand, extended her arm and brought her left palm up underneath her right hand, wrapping her fingers firmly around her right hand to help steady her arm.

Letting out a calming breath, she aimed, and then slowly

squeezed the trigger five times in a row. Without looking at Bull, she put the gun back on the shelf, removed her earplugs and safety glasses, and pushed the button to retrieve the target. Chaise removed it from the line and smugly handed it to Bull.

"Is a one-and-a-half inch grouping at twenty-five yards enough to impress you?" Chaise asked with a hint of sarcasm and a hefty amount of pride. She knew it was good but she waited for his confirmation. But for good measure, she also hid the intense stinging in her damn hand from firing so many of the .357 rounds in such close succession.

Bull smiled, dropped his arms, and nodded. "Impressive, indeed. Remind me not to piss you off," he replied jokingly.

After Bull finished his practice shots, Chaise helped him pick up all their belongings and they walked back toward his truck. One of the other Steele Security men stopped Bull. Bull turned to Chaise, "Can you hold onto these for me for a few minutes?"

"Sure will," she said happily, taking the few .357 rounds that were left, along with the pistol, and dropping them in her purse. Bull walked off with the other man, leaving Chaise to walk around inside the building alone for a few minutes. She saw a large picture hanging in the main hallway and approached it. Instantly recognizing it as a company all-employee picture, she searched each face looking for the men she'd recently met.

She smiled when she found Bull in the midst of the all the primarily male employees. He was younger in the picture, but he had certainly only improved with age. She kept looking through the faces until she found Shadow and then Rebel. When she found the next face, her entire body froze. She would recognize him anywhere, even if she hadn't seen him in years. He had aged, of course, since she last saw him, but there was no doubt of who it was. He was still just as handsome as she remembered. It was Noah.

Finding her breath, she turned to move away from the picture and saw Bull watching her at the end of the hallway. Not missing a step, she smiled at him as she announced, "I found you in the company picture."

Bull nodded. "Who else did you find in it?"

"All of you," she answered honestly.

"Even Reaper?" He asked, cocking his head to the side and narrowing his eyes at her as if he dared her to lie to him.

"Yes, even Noah," she answered but refused to look away from him.

"Have the gun?" Bull asked, swiftly changing topics.

"Yep," Chaise answered as she patted her purse.

Bull cocked one eyebrow up at her. "You know that's illegal, right?"

"I have a concealed carry permit. I'm legal," Chaise replied with a smile at Bull's surprised look.

Back in Bull's truck, he made a decision. "I think I need to take you away for a while until the heat dies down."

Chaise knew his comment was only related to him doing his job, but the way he said it sent shivers down her spine. The thought of going away with Bull was more than enticing. But her determination to find Aura overshadowed her desire to run away from everything with the very sexy man seated next to her.

"As much as I'd love that, Bull, I can't. I have to go to work tomorrow." She kept her voice calm, projecting a confident outer image, but inside she was dying. She had been dreading that very conversation all day.

"Chaise, in case you haven't noticed, your employer is apparently into some very bad shit. The *Tres Sieses* are after you and work is the last place you need to be. Even though the breach at my house today was a false alarm, we still have to be careful."

Bull's last statement was the termination of that conversation in his mind. He was damn good at his job, but he couldn't protect her at Viboro—the very place from where she thought young girls disappeared. He was on the job for a reason, and he intended to make sure she stayed safe.

"Colton, I'm going. I have to find Aura. I know you don't believe me, but she was there. I talked to her mom, and I'm going to find her! I have to go back to work and try to back trace her from there,"

Chaise argued.

"No."

Chaise's head whipped around to Bull, her glare burned through him and the steam that emanated from her raised the temperature in the truck ten degrees in two seconds flat.

"No?" she asked incredulously. "Are you fucking kidding me? You think you can just say 'no' and that's it?"

"Yep."

"That doesn't work on me, Colton. I left my overbearing father behind years ago. I'm the customer in this scenario and I say I'm going back to work!" Chaise shifted in her seat to turn her body toward Bull as she spoke. When she did, her already short dress hiked up her thighs even higher and Bull was reminded that, in their rush to leave his house, Chaise had left her panties behind.

He suddenly forgot what they were arguing about, and he had a hard time focusing on the road. She was still sitting facing him, the flowing material of her dress moved with her every breath, shifting up and down her smooth skin. Every few seconds, it would ride up high enough just to torture and tease him with the threat of a very public display before it moved lower again.

She was still admonishing him with everything she had, but for the life of him, he had no idea what she had said. He was simultaneously dying inside and trying to focus on not killing them both by running off the road or driving into oncoming traffic. He felt like he could breathe again when his driveway came into sight.

"Damn! Finally!" He yelled before he realized that Chaise was still raking him over the coals, and he'd just interrupted her rant.

"Finally *what?*" Chaise asked irately.

Bull didn't answer her question. He simply turned into his driveway, parked his truck in the garage, and quickly jumped out. Chaise sat in the truck, stunned at his behavior, and contemplated the various scenarios that could occur should she just get her belongings and leave right away. The defiant part of her wanted to take the chance to handle everything alone.

Maybe it had been a mistake showing up at Noah's wedding and getting his company involved.

8

CHAPTER NINE

Chaise unbuckled her seatbelt and, with a heavy heart, resigned herself to the fact that she couldn't do it alone. Just as she started to reach for her purse, two strong arms pushed underneath her and easily lifted her out of the truck.

"What the hell-," she yelled, startled and confused momentarily.

Bull's deep-chested growl was his only reply as he swiftly moved from the truck to the door. Expertly maneuvering through the opening with her in his arms, he kicked the door shut behind him and continued straight to his bedroom. Inside, he put her down in the center of the bed and immediately covered her body with his own —clothes and all.

"Were you doing that on purpose just to make me crazy?" Bull's husky voice confronted her, and desire infused in his every word as his lips hovered just above the skin on her throat.

"Doing what?" She asked him as he turned her face to the side, giving himself full access to her neck.

Their mouths collided and Bull released a guttural moan of satisfaction that Chaise felt, warming every part of her body from the inside out. Bull's tongue lightly licked her lips, pushing its way through. He took his time, savored her and enjoyed the feeling of her slick, wet velvet tongue against his. Their erotic dance set Chaise on fire. She tried to take control, tried to increase the tempo, but Bull continued to keep his own pace, thwarting her attempts.

Ending their kiss, Bull raised his head to look at Chaise. Her plump, red lips were slightly swollen from their passionate kiss. Her skin was reddened and warm, her eyes were glazed over and full of heated desire. The quick rise and fall of her chest revealed her ragged breaths and her need for him to finish the sensual assault he'd started. And he had every intention of completely owning her before he was finished with her.

Bull took his time, ignoring the rising temperature between them and the intense pleading in Chaise's eyes. The time they'd spent getting to know each other had led to this moment. If he'd been honest with himself, he would've admitted he felt more than intrigue and distrust when he first saw her. She made him feel alive and gave him a renewed purpose to protect and serve. The job was important to him and would always receive his very best. But she'd become more than a protection detail, more than just another client, and more than

Using his knee to part her legs, he held his weight with one arm while the other hand slowly moved down her side. His touch left a trail of fire in its wake, branding her with his unique mark. When his fingers reached the outside of her leg, his skin on her skin, she thought she would come completely undone. His fingers traced circles on her skin until he reached the innermost sensitive part of her thigh.

"You're killing me, Colton!"

The carnal plea in her voice urged the primal side of him to take her right then, with no thought, rhyme, or reason. *Just. Take. Her.* The protective side of him, the side that she had awakened in him, prevented him from doing just that. That voice told him to take her slowly, to build her up to heights so high she would be ruined for any other man. It urged him to make it so that she could only think of him and what he alone could do to her senses.

His deep voice lowered to a whisper against the skin on her

neck. "That's how I felt in the truck. With this fucking short dress," he said as his fingers moved slowly up her thigh, "riding up on your legs."

"Colton, *please!*"

"Then it flared up, teasing me but never giving me what I wanted." He continued his languid movements as if she wasn't begging.. "Reminding me that your *fucking panties* were here on my floor. And I couldn't do a damn thing about it," he growled.

Chaise pulled on his short hair, tilting his eyes up to meet hers. Her eyes were like fire and her breathing was choppy and fast. "*Now*, Colton!"

His sexy smirk didn't help matters. He was dead set on claiming her at his own pace.

"Chaise, baby, you've only *read* about the things I will do to you. By the time I'm finished with you tonight, no other man will ever be able to even come close to pleasuring you. Just relax and I'll prove it to you—one touch at a time."

The promises of pleasure from the sexy man on top of her weighed heavy on her mind and her body, like a physical being, watching and waiting to fulfill every word he'd spoken. Chaise took a deep breath, trying to calm herself before the anticipation caused an anxiety attack. He pushed her hands above her head and held them with one hand. Their mouths met again as his other hand searched for something just out of her view.

The silky satin sensation on Chaise's wrist didn't register in her brain at first because all the nerves firing in every other part of her body. By the time she realized what he was doing, both of her wrists had been tied to the headboard. There was very little slack in the cloth. Regardless of how she moved, she couldn't reach Bull to touch him with her hands. She was both confused and excited at the possibilities. Regardless of the circumstances, everything she saw in him told her to trust him.

"Relax, Chaise. I won't hurt you. Far from it—you'll be begging me for more," he guaranteed.

Her answering sigh was all he needed as her signal of surrender.

"That's my girl." He praised her with a deep kiss, searing her to the core and driving her mad to feel his skin under her fingertips.

Her hands struggled against her restraints but her manacles both prevented it and served to heighten her senses. She was pleasurably surprised at how her body responded to being tied, how her mind gave over to complete submission for him to do as he willed and knew that she would enjoy every second of it.

When his hand left her body, she immediately missed the warmth and bliss it created. Opening her eyes, she saw a black velvet object in his hand and looked at him quizzically. He smiled assuredly and lightly stroked her cheek with it.

"Trust me, Chaise," he asked and commanded at once. Reassured by his eyes, she nodded, and he slipped the mask over her eyes. "You've never been blindfolded before?"

"No." She exhaled heavily.

"All you have to do is relax. I will do the rest ... until you fall apart in my arms and become completely mine."

"Oh, god," Chaise gasped.

"You can call me Bull ... or Colton." Chaise could feel his smirk without even being able to see his face.

"I'm going to call someone else if you don't get busy," Chaise deadpanned.

"Over *his* dead body," Bull retorted.

Before Chaise could say another word, she felt his warm, wet tongue lightly dragging down her neck and leaving chills and fire in its path.

Their bodies and minds melded into one, each relishing the feel and sensations of the other. Despite the pleasure he was determined to give her, somewhere in the back of her mind, Chaise sensed something was off. Something vital was missing, and until that something kept him separated from her. Finding out why he'd built walls and erected barriers around his heart and his body was off limits would be harder than getting out the restraints.

"Untie my hands. I want to feel you, Colton," she pleaded.

"Oh, you will feel me, Chaise," he assured her.

"I mean with my hands."

"You will love this. Trust me."

Bull remained still for a moment, committing her every line and curve to memory.

"Colton?" her small voice penetrated the silence.

"I'm here," he whispered in her ear, sending goose bumps down her arm. He stood and shed his clothes quickly.

The mask over her eyes was slowly removed and she blinked, slowly opening them to see him suspended over her.

"I want to see your eyes. I want to know the exact moment that you surrender to me ... the very second you realize that you belong to me," his bedroom voice whispered.

Chaise's breath seized in her chest at his words. Hope bloomed in her chest at the thought of truly being his, and he belonging to her. His eyes never left hers and she felt him reach deep inside her—physically and emotionally. And she knew what he meant. She knew immediately that he had touched her as no man had before. Even if she thought she'd been in love before, it was childish and immature compared to the barrage of emotions that flooded her at that moment. How could she explain it to anyone else when she didn't even understand? It couldn't be love—she had too much to learn about him with not enough time lapsed to give them true history.

But there was a connection to him that she couldn't break and there had been from the start. Even though he didn't trust her. Even though she hadn't told him everything—he knew that—but he still protected her, he still kept his word, and he still honored his commitment. Now, he wanted her in his bed, he wanted in her head, and he wanted to own her. Even as independent and self-confident as she'd been for the last several years after getting out from under her father's thumb, she wasn't the least bit offended by his declaration.

She didn't believe it was a total domination statement. It was simply to let her know that he was staking his claim on her. That he wouldn't share her with anyone else. He meant that the intimacy was between them only and not meant for anyone else. The feeling of belonging to someone in that sense, of surrendering all to him to love and care for her, wasn't so scary. It was comforting and fulfilling. She just hoped she was right, because he owned her, he possessed her, and she willingly surrendered her all to him.

Chaise was still riding the high of their union, unable to fully come down because he continued to rain down his pleasurable torture techniques on her. She knew she was done for when he leaned down and murmured in her ear.

"I'm not finished with you yet, Chaise. This is only round one." His eyes stayed glued to hers, never releasing her gaze as his hand deftly released her hands from their binds.

Repositioning her to lie in his arms, she curled up beside him with their arms and legs entwined. Content, thoroughly sated, and completed drained of all energy, she quickly fell into a deep sleep against Bull's warm body.

Bull stayed awake, listening to her breathing while he tried to keep his thoughts from racing. He had never allowed a woman he was involved with to spend the night at his place, and he'd certainly never gone to sleep with one in his arms. But something about their union felt different. Even though he knew she was still holding something back, he could only hope he wasn't wrong about her.

The next morning, Bull woke to an empty bed and felt the instant alarm run through him like an electric current. Chaise had slept with him the night before and he hadn't felt her leave the bed. Something about her was definitely throwing him off his game. Slipping on his lounging pants, he silently moved down the hall and found her in the kitchen again. She was sipping on a cup of coffee, reading the paper, and was fully dressed. For work.

"How did you get the paper? It was outside and the alarm was set," Bull smarted.

"Well, good morning to you, too, Colton. Yes, I did sleep well. Actually, I slept like a rock. You know, you are *so warm* it was like having my own electric blanket! Would you like some coffee?" Chaise spoke like there was no reason for concern and like he hadn't just completely chastised her without so much as a good morning first.

They stood staring at each other for a moment until Chaise

couldn't keep her eyes from roaming over his broad shoulders, firm chest, and chiseled six-pack. Her eyes trailed down the muscled V that disappeared into the waistband of his pajama pants. Her coffee cup was frozen at her lips as her eyes devoured the luscious form standing before her.

Bull's lips quirked up in one corner as he shifted his weight to one leg, placed his hand on his hip, and leveled his eyes at her. When her eyes met his, she blushed, the bright pink color filling her cheeks and neck. She smiled behind her coffee cup and quickly lowered her eyes as she took a sip.

"Oh, look at the time. I need to get going or I'll be late for work in the Miami traffic." Chaise tried to hide her ogling and announce her departure with one statement.

Out of the corner of her eye, she saw Bull's stance immediately change. Opening his legs farther apart, he crossed his muscular arms over his expansive chest and glared at her menacingly. Chaise pretended to not notice the difference in his demeanor.

"First of all, how did you disable my alarm?" Bull growled.

"I didn't—Shadow did. He brought something by for you," Chaise answered with an incline of her chin toward a large envelope on the coffee table.

"Okay. And I already said you're not going to work today. It's too dangerous," Bull commanded. "And don't forget your *missing* intern."

The suspicion in his tone felt like a literal slap to Chaise's face. She physically recoiled from the sting of his words and inflection of his voice. There it was and it may as well have been written in stone —he still didn't believe her. Not completely anyway. After everything Shadow and Rebel had recently found that corroborated her story, and after their night together, he still doubted her intentions.

Tears stung the back of her eyes and she swallowed hard to hold them back. She resolved that she would not give him the satisfaction of knowing that he hurt her as much as he did. Chaise calmly walked to the sink, poured out her coffee, put her cup in the dishwasher, and grabbed her purse off the counter. She walked directly up to Bull, who was now completely blocking the doorway and her exit route.

"Chaise, I can't let you go." Bull's tone had softened, as he was obviously aware of his mistake but he wasn't taking full ownership of it. His stance, however, was still threatening and unyielding.

"You can't stop me," Chaise retorted, emphasizing each word. "I'm not arguing with you, Colton. I am going to work and acting normal. Kindly step aside—you can't hold me against my will."

Bull drew in a deep breath, straightened his back, and pulled himself up to an intimidating height. Letting out an exasperated huff, he stepped aside to give Chaise just enough room to squeeze between him and the doorjamb. She seized the opportunity before he changed his mind and moved into the tight opening. Suddenly, both of his muscular arms came up on either side of her, boxed her in, and prevented her from moving any more than required to breathe.

"Chaise, I can't let you put yourself in danger," he said, his voice low but with a touch of tenderness to it. Her chest tightened in response, wanting to feel the intimacy he implied but the sharp sting of his prior words was still fresh.

"You can't stop me from doing anything I want to do, Colton. It's as simple as that. I'm leaving now," she stated firmly, meeting his eyes with her defiant glare.

While he was temporarily stunned, and before he could respond, she quickly ducked under his massive arm, slid her body against his, and walked quickly to the front door. She noticed that he made no attempt to stop her that time. She assumed he had done his duty—he had tried to stop her and she refused. It was by her very own decision, but part of her had foolishly hoped he would chase after her. The other part of her knew that was ridiculous since it was what she wanted to do in the first place and she had made that clear.

And this is why relationships never work. We're all damn crazy, she thought to herself as she got in her car. When she looked up, she saw Bull watching her from his front porch. His arms were crossed over his chest and his legs were spread wide in his fighting stance. But the look in his eyes stopped her. His eyes were fixed on her every move as if he was daring her to carry out her plan against his will. She couldn't explain—or escape—the feeling that she was betraying him somehow by simply doing what she'd planned to do all along. *Work.*

Remembering that she was still mad at him, she quickly put her sunglasses on, cranked her car, and pulled out of his driveway. Chaise couldn't help but wonder if she'd be welcomed back at his house at the end of her workday. She decided to cross that bridge when she came to it. She already had enough to keep her busy and stressed for the day. She'd decide what to do about Colton Lanier later.

Pulling into the parking space, she took a few deep, calming breaths before gathering her purse and walking into the building. She knew she'd been followed before going to Noah's wedding and she was sure it was because of what she'd found on the job. But she didn't want to show her hand just yet. She wanted to make them think she hadn't realized what she'd found so that she could keep digging. She wanted them to still feel smug and secure in their activities so they wouldn't change them. If they did, that would mean she'd essentially lost Aura forever. She felt responsible and wanted to find the young girl before it was too late.

She strolled into the building like she belonged there, exactly like every other morning. She smiled and said hello to the security guard at the front desk. He smiled and responded as he normally did. She breathed a sigh of relief, moved past him, and walked on to her office.

Putting her things down, she looked around her office to see if anything had been disturbed, but everything was exactly as she'd left it. If anyone had been snooping, they were experts because not one paper was out of order in her neat, organized world.

10

CHAPTER TEN

Deciding to face the music, Chaise drove straight back to Bull's house after work rather than going to the condo that had always given her the creeps anyway. When she first got in her car, she wasn't sure which way she should go. She hadn't heard from Bull all day and she hadn't called him, either. It stung a little that he acted so concerned about her going to work but then he never even called to see if she was safe.

As she pulled into his driveway, she had a moment of panic. She pictured him turning her away for not following his orders to not go back to work in the first place. She parked and placed her forehead on the steering wheel, conflicted and generally unsure of her next move. Her logical mind said she needed to be there with Bull, but she wasn't sure she could handle the reception she'd receive.

Her car door opened, and Bull's big hand gingerly wrapped around hers. She looked up at him, his cobalt blue eyes boring into hers, as he gently tugged on her to help her out of the car. He pulled her hand to his mouth and kissed each of her knuckles with his soft, plump lips. Chaise's heart both broke and melted at the sweet gesture. He was trying to be nice but there was still a huge chasm between them that she wasn't confident they would ever be able to bridge.

"I'm glad you came back here. I was beginning to wonder if you would," Bull finally spoke.

"I debated it—several times," Chaise answered truthfully.

Bull nodded in understanding. "I'm sorry for what I said, or rather, *how* I said it. I do believe that she is missing."

Bull reached in the car, turned the ignition off, and gathered Chaise's belongings. He carried them in the house with one hand and led her with his hand on the small of her back with the other hand. His words kept reverberating through her mind—both from that morning and from a few moments before. Once inside the house, Chaise decided to address the big, pink polka-dotted elephant that stood between them.

"You believe that she is missing because of the information Shadow and Rebel found. Not because of anything I've said. There's obviously a big problem between us, Colton.

"It was ridiculous of me to think last night would've changed anything—or that it meant anything to you. I *know* that, but I still wanted it to, honestly. I don't think my staying here is a good idea anymore. I won't go back to the condo, but I think I should go somewhere else," she stated sadly.

Bull admired how Chaise stood tall even though she was afraid. She faced her fears and didn't back down, although vulnerability showed in her mint-green eyes. Her long, black hair cascaded over her shoulders and her tan skin glowed with sun-kissed radiance. She was stunning at normal times, but when she was on a mission, she was absolutely spectacular.

And she was talking about leaving.

"I don't want you to leave," Bull stated plainly.

"You don't owe me anything, Colton. You've done what you said you'd do—you kept your word. This is my way of taking responsibility for my actions. I allowed ... this ... to happen between us and it was just way too soon. I don't regret it, but we don't really even know each other. I just don't want us to end up enemies," she said, exasperated. She was running out of steam.

All the events of the past few weeks were beginning to catch up with her and take a toll on her emotions. Discovering the missing girls, Aura's disappearance, seeking Noah after all this time, the complicated and untrusting relationship with Colton, and now going back to work where she felt eyes always watching her. It just all felt like too much and everything was closing in on her at once. The feeling of claustrophobia was returning with a vengeance, and she wasn't even in a small space.

She was about to have a full-blown panic attack. That's what was behind that feeling of everything closing in on her. The realization of that suddenly hit her. It was the same feeling she had when she was in the Steele Security building, and everything was so overwhelming. It was coming on again—just thinking about all the things she'd been through and all the things she still had to face. Alone. Again.

"Chaise? Chaise!"

She could hear his voice, but it sounded muffled and distant. Her legs felt like wet spaghetti noodles—completely unable to hold her weight or move of their own accord. She felt strong arms wrap around her and gently place her on the couch. Then the strong arms wrapped around her, pulling her into a big, thick chest and shielding her from the outside world. A low, murmuring voice chanted soothing messages in her ear and plump, kissable lips placed chaste kisses on her hair, forehead, and temple.

"Just breathe. Focus on just breathing right now. You're safe here with me. I won't let anything happen to you. Breathe, baby. That's it." The reassuring voice repeated the words over and over until they sunk in and took root in Chaise's subconscious, eventually bleeding over into her conscious mind.

And then the dam broke. Everything she'd held back, bottled up, and pushed down just broke free, and the tears started freely flowing. Bull felt the wetness, knew what was to come next. He pulled her securely into his lap and cradled her in his arms like a baby. Chaise welcomed it—she relished in the contact, the reassurance, and the support she felt flowing from him. She felt safe and secure in his presence and even though she would normally be embarrassed to have anyone see her cry, when her first sob broke through, she was relieved.

She felt relief that she could be herself and let the weakness show without being berated or chastised for it. She was relieved that even through her weak moments, Colton would keep his word and keep her safe. The anxiety she felt was in knowing that the troubles were not over and there were still things she needed to share with Colton. Although, maybe just not at that exact moment since she was a blubbering mess and couldn't seem to catch her breath between sobs. His hands rubbed her back and he still muttered comforting words instead of telling her to suck it up and carry on.

The sobs subsided and she was completely wiped out. She had no fight left in her, no energy to pretend she was all right and that she didn't need help. All she could do was close her eyes, inhale the masculine musk of the man holding her close, and sink farther into his protective embrace. Within minutes, her breathing returned to normal, and she fell asleep in his arms.

Bull looked down at her and marveled at how protective he'd become of her in such a short time. This type of thing never happened to him—he never allowed it. But he couldn't lie to himself and say he wasn't becoming attached to her. When he told her he didn't want her to leave, he meant it. When he said he would protect her, he meant with his life. Comforting her and calming her was new to him and he knew he'd fuck up again and cause her pain. Somehow, he had to make her understand why that was and figure out how he could make it up to her when he did.

Rubbing his nose and lips along her skin, he softly called her name until she stirred again.

"How long was I asleep?" Chaise asked, a little confused and her cheeks slightly pink with embarrassment.

"Not long. I actually hated to wake you, but I need to feed you," Bull answered, keeping his voice low and calm.

Chaise made no effort to move from her spot in his arms. She looked up at him for several long seconds without speaking before she raised her hand and let her fingers stroke along his jaw. The afternoon stubble pricked her fingers, and she liked the sounds it made as her nails scraped across it.

"I can't do this alone, Colton," she finally whispered her confession. Admitting to needing someone's help was tough for Chaise. She'd been on her own for so long and had always been the resilient one.

"I know, Chaise. You don't have to," the sincerity of his tone warmed her heart. "You don't have to leave. I want you to stay here. We can take it slower; get to know each other better."

"I'd like that," Chaise replied with a smile that Bull returned. She knew full well there was no going back for her. Taking it slow or not, there was something about that man that had captured her and refused to let her go.

After cooking supper and cleaning the dishes, Bull and Chaise settled back on the couch together. The atmosphere had lightened considerably since her emotional breakdown. She was just glad they were able to spend time together—talking, laughing, and sharing.

"How was work today?" Bull asked with an unmistakable smirk.

"It was okay. I swear I felt eyes on me all day, though. Made my skin crawl to think that they were watching me," Chaise animatedly replied while gauging his reaction.

"They weren't the only ones," Bull responded.

"What do you mean?" Chaise asked while sitting up then leaning toward him in a challenging posture.

Bull smiled his full on, mega-watt smile before answering. "Brad, our techie genius, hacked into their security system and we were able to keep tabs on you all day. Why else do you think I let you leave this morning?"

Chaise was stunned beyond speech. Her bottom jaw dropped open, her eyes widened, and she sat motionless for a moment.

"*Let* me? You *let* me leave?" she asked incredulously.

Bull chuckled. "Okay, now, don't take that the wrong way. I just meant that otherwise I would've had to go with you. We would've had to do things very differently if Brad hadn't been able to get into their surveillance system."

"Damn, no wonder I felt like I was being watched all day!" Chaise swatted at his arm playfully. She laughed harder when he pretended to be hurt.

"Did you notice anything out of the ordinary?"

"No, nothing. And I looked around my office. There was nothing disturbed. Nothing out of place from where I'd left it Friday. I didn't really push my luck too much today and get into anything I'm not supposed to be in. Now that I know you're watching, I will try harder tomorrow."

Chaise noticed the change in Bull's face at that statement. He didn't like it one bit and he was biting his tongue to keep from saying anything.

"Go ahead and say it before you bite your tongue in two," Chaise deadpanned.

Bull smirked. "It's just that if they caught you, we may not be able to get to you in time to stop them from taking you somewhere. If you're dead set on doing this, we'll have to outfit you with some of our *Inspector Gadget* toys first."

"No Bond toys?" Chaise asked teasingly.

"No, you haven't graduated to *spy* yet. Baby steps," Bull joked.

SHADOW, Rebel, and Brad came by Bull's house to bring their gadgets and show Chaise how everything worked.

"We will be able to see and hear you, but you can't hear us. The problem with that is, we won't be able to warn you if we see something happening before you do," Brad explained.

Bull recognized Chaise's worried expression as her eyes searched for reassurance from him. "Don't worry," Bull soothed her. "If it gets too dangerous, I *will* storm the building. I'll clear a path to you by any means necessary."

"You'll be close?" she asked.

"I'm never far away from you," Bull promised.

The other guys exchanged shocked glances but none of them were stupid enough to question Bull in front of her. Chaise's look of gratitude told them everything they needed to know. Whatever feelings Bull harbored for her were definitely reciprocated.

"Okay. I can do this then," Chaise replied as she stood. "Is anyone else thirsty?"

Bull, Rebel, Shadow, and Brad gave their drink requests and Chaise left the room. Rebel and Shadow took the opportunity to pounce on Bull.

"Want to tell us what the hell is going on here, man?" Shadow asked, giving Bull a pointed look, and inclining his head toward the kitchen where Chaise was.

"Uh—we are getting her ready to go in wired. Have you not been paying attention?" Bull snapped.

Rebel laughed, "You know what he's asking, man. Don't play fucking dumb with us. We know you better than that shit."

Brad was so enthralled with how the conversation was unfolding, he didn't notice at first that Bull was staring him down. Brad quickly lowered his eyes back to the electronics in front of him. Bull looked at his long-time friends and huffed out a disgusted sigh.

"Fine. Yes. Chaise. Me. Happy now?"

Rebel and Shadow both had huge, shit eating grins on their face at their friend's admission. Brad was even smiling but he didn't look up from his work to invoke the wrath of Bull for intruding on his private life. Rebel and Shadow slapped him on the back and clapped him on the shoulder. Bull, uneasy with the sudden intrusion of his privacy, told them to knock it off and walked off with them laughing heartily behind him.

Several minutes later, he reappeared with Chaise, and both had their hands full of drinks for everyone. Brad took a drink of his and turned the conversation back to business.

"All right, Chaise. You're all set—just remember what we've gone over tonight. Don't get the device wet. Try to keep your hands away from it. The rustling noises make it hard to hear. And you'll need to decide your code word that tells us you're in trouble. If we hear that word, we *will* rush in, so don't use it lightly," Brad explained.

Inhaling deeply, Chaise looked at each of the four men and saw a myriad of silent reactions on their faces. Rebel cocked his head to the side, crinkled his eyes, and studied her with a somewhat concerned look. Shadow stood tall, hands on his hips, and a troubled look on his face. Brad was confident in his equipment and its ability to help keep her safe. Bull was a different matter altogether. A mixture of feelings moved across his face—concern, awe, and agitation—almost simultaneously.

"I'll be fine. I have the best security team in the nation on my six. Nothing will go wrong." She tried to sound confident, but it fell flat, even to her own ears.

Brad stood and placed his hand on her shoulder. "It will be fine. We will take good care of you, Chaise."

After the men had left and they were alone again, Bull turned from the door and walked directly up to Chaise.

"You don't have to do this. We can work with the local authorities. We have enough to arouse suspicion and Shadow has some significant contacts. There are other ways—better ways—to do this," Bull reasoned.

"You're right, Colton. I don't have the expertise to pull this off alone. But I'm already inside and I am in a position to snoop into anything because it's my job. It would take too much time to get someone else in there now. We may never find Aura or the other girls if I quit now."

Bull didn't respond. He knew she was right but that didn't mean he had to like it.

"I don't think I can do this without you, Colton. Don't abandon me now," Chaise asked him. Her eyes beseeched him and she held her breath waiting for his reply.

"Not a chance in hell, Chaise," came Bull's promise.

Chaise tentatively lifted her hand and stretched it out to capture Bull's hand. Once she had it, she squeezed it and gave him a small smile of appreciation.

"Well, it's late and I have a big day ahead of me tomorrow, so I guess I should get some sleep," Chaise announced but she couldn't hide the anxiety in her voice. Not only did she plan to dive headfirst into shark infested waters, so to speak, she had much more pressing problems before her.

Where should I sleep tonight?

Bull's knowing smile did nothing for her discomfort. He knew what she was thinking and there was no point in even trying to lie her way out of it. They agreed to take it slower and to get to know each other better first. But in his arms, she just felt so safe, secure, and protected that she never wanted to leave them.

"Come on. I'll take you to the guest room," Bull answered with no hint of hesitation or the disappointment that she felt to her very soul. Chaise simply nodded and followed him down the hall.

At some point during the day, Bull had moved her belongings to one of the guest bedrooms. He reminded her where the towels and other toiletries were stored and made sure she didn't need anything else before he left her alone.

After getting ready for bed, Chaise lay in the big, comfortable bed and stared at the ceiling for what felt like forever. There was absolutely nothing wrong with the bed or the bedroom. It was perfect and comfortable. It was the fact that he was so close but so far away that was driving her crazy and keeping her awake. When she was still wide-awake just after midnight, she made a decision that Bull would just have to accept.

She tiptoed through the house with only her tank top and panties on until she reached Bull's bedside. He was lying on one side, on his back, and appeared to be sleeping perfectly well without her. She knew better than to assume he was asleep after the last time she made that mistake. Not waiting, or asking for an invitation, she carefully pulled the covers back and slipped into bed beside him.

She snuggled up as close to him as she could get and instantly felt better. The tiny bubble of anxiety that had started building in her chest instantly dissipated. Just as she was thinking that it might not be a good idea to rely on him to rid her of the anxiety, he spoke and disrupted her thoughts

"Did you lose your bed?" he asked as he wrapped his arm around and pulled her closer to him. His teasing and humor tone laced his words, telling her that he didn't mind sharing his bed with her.

"Actually, I was momentarily kicked out of *my* bed, but I found my way back on my own," she said in mock defense.

"Took you long enough. I was beginning to think you'd really stay in there," Bull laughingly replied.

Chaise replied with an elbow to the ribs. "You knew I didn't want to sleep in there, didn't you." It was intentionally more of a statement than a question.

"I knew," Bull replied earnestly, placing a kiss on her cheek. "And I'm glad. I wanted you in here, too."

11

CHAPTER ELEVEN

Chaise went to work every day that week, gathered additional information as the Steele Security team instructed, and went back to Bull's house every night. Every day she felt a little more anxious, felt more eyes watching her every move, and knew that time was not on her side. Aura had been missing too long at that point and Brad had found nothing on the other missing girls.

Bull had driven Chaise to work every day and picked her up. She had argued against it at first, feeling like her freedoms were slowly being taken from her. Bull explained that he didn't trust anyone to not tamper with her car while it was in the Viboro Distributing parking lot. If it were to break down and leave her stranded, she would be too vulnerable.

That day, she was infinitely glad that she had given in and heeded Bull's advice. The anxious feeling was at its peak and she knew she wasn't just overreacting. One of the warehouse workers had been in the office all day. He had watched every move she made, listened to her every conversation that occurred outside of her office and leered at her without trying to disguise it. She'd had an uneasy feeling all day and practically ran out the front door to Bull's waiting SUV.

"What's wrong?" Bull asked, his facial expression and voice tone mirrored his concern.

"Can we get out of here? I'll tell you while you drive," Chaise answered, still rattled from the events of the day. "I just want to get as far away from this place as possible."

Bull pulled out into traffic, his demeanor belying his thoughts and feelings. He knew from the fret in her eyes, the furrow of her brow, and the pitch of her voice that something was inherently awry. His first order of action would be to make sure she was safe. Second, he would find and kill anyone who threatened to bring harm to her.

"Tell me what happened," Bull stated calmly. "No one said they saw or heard anything out of the ordinary from our surveillance."

"There was a guy from the warehouse who was in the office all day today. He's never worked in the office before. But all day, he was everywhere I went. He watched me, listened to my conversations, and he just gave me the creeps! I just get a really scary vibe from him," Chaise explained.

"You can show me which one he is when we get to my house. I'll get Brad to pull up the feed and we'll identify him. Could be a good lead for the case," he reassured her.

"I hope you're right. I'm ready for this to be over! I don't know how you do this all the time."

"Training, babe. I've had a lot of training to prepare me for missions. It conditioned me and taught me how to deal with intense situations. You're doing great. You've been our eyes and ears all week," he replied with a smile that relayed how impressed he was with her.

"Now you're just being nice," Chaise playfully scolded.

"No one's ever accused me of that before," Bull laughed. "I need to stop by the store first, if that's all right with you?"

"Sure, that's fine with me."

Bull and Chaise strolled through the grocery store, picking out items together as though it had always been an everyday occurrence. Chaise genuinely enjoyed his company and getting to know Colton Lanier, the man behind the Bull façade. She found that he had a heart of gold and a protective streak a mile wide.

As they walked across the vast parking lot, talking, and enjoying each other's company, Bull wrapped his arm around her and pulled her close to his side. The casual movement was so natural but so intimate at the same time. Public displays of affection weren't in Bull's vocabulary, but he seemed to be making a lot of concessions for Chaise.

An alarming sound caught Bull's attention just in time for him to lift Chaise off the ground, roll across the front hood of a car, and duck between the parked cars. The all black, full-size SUV narrowly missed hitting them. The SUV came to a screeching halt several yards away and four men exited the vehicle, speaking in Spanish.

"Which way did they go?" the first voice called out.

"I saw them duck between those cars over there," the second guy responded.

"Spread out and find them. Kill him. Bring her to me—unharmed," the last voice commanded.

Over your dead body, Bull thought to himself. *There's still at least one more.*

Bull kept Chaise moving through the parking lot, winding between cars, and keeping low to stay out of sight. He kept the men trained in his sights, but there was still one missing. Four exited the vehicle but he only had eyes on three of them. As Bull and Chaise cornered another vehicle, he saw the fourth man.

Bull stopped dead in his tracks. All the years of training temporarily left him. He couldn't breathe. He couldn't think straight to make an intelligent decision when their lives depended on his skills and training. But he couldn't make his feet move. He felt Chaise beside him, holding his arm in her tight grip, furtively whispering to him but her words held no meaning.

When the man turned around, Bull stood up in plain sight and openly gaped at the man. Within seconds, Bull was knocked to the ground as gunfire erupted around him. A large body was lying on top of him, yelling something at him that he couldn't understand. He struggled to get free, but it was useless.

"Bull, damn it! Be still! What the fuck are you doing? Trying to get yourself killed?" Shadow screamed at him.

"Get the fuck off me, man!" Bull yelled back, finally finding the capacity to speak again.

"Don't do it, man. I'm warning you," Shadow growled back.

Chaise had no idea what "it," was, but Shadow's words penetrated Bull's anger. He finally nodded in agreement and relaxed his coiled muscles.

Rebel came running up at that moment. "They got away, but I got the plates. May be stolen but I have a feeling it's not. Let's go find out who we're going after."

Bull stood and looked between his two brothers. His jaw was hard set, the muscles ticking and bunching in his attempts to keep his anger reined in. His face was beet red, and his eyes were fierce—in a scary way.

"What the hell are you guys doing here anyway?" Bull snapped.

"You mean other than saving your ass? We're doing our fucking jobs," Shadow replied with his voice deceptively calm and low. "You nearly just got yourself and Chaise killed. What happened?"

"Nothing," Bull lied.

"Don't bullshit us, man. We saw the whole thing while we were getting into place to back you up. If you hadn't stood up, we could've had these assholes," Rebel admonished him.

"Fuck! You're right—you're right, okay? I fucked up. Let's get out of here." Bull moved back to his vehicle when he heard sirens in the distance.

Someone surely had called the police and he wasn't ready to talk to them. He decided he'd have someone from the Steele Security office call and apprise them of the situation. He had more pressing matters to handle first.

Bull drove them back to his house, keeping both hands firmly gripped to the steering wheel. His body was rigid, and his sunglasses shielded his eyes. But from what Chaise could tell, his eyes never veered in her direction. He was definitely in his own world and didn't want to be disturbed. Chaise gave him some time and space, knowing that he would have to answer for everything soon enough since Shadow and Rebel were following them.

When Bull put the truck in park, he exhaled loudly and turned to Chaise. His face was stoic, but she knew if she could see his eyes, they would be full of turmoil. Slowly reaching up to his face, she removed his sunglasses and what she saw broke her heart. It wasn't anger. It wasn't vengeance. She knew pain when she saw it—and Bull was hurting. Badly.

"Talk to me, Colton. Tell me what happened out there," Chaise asked softly.

"I could've gotten you killed because of what I did. I'm sorry, Chaise. If you want Rebel or Shadow to take over your security detail, I won't blame you," Bull answered.

"Wh–*what*? Of course I don't want either of them to take over." Chaise tried to contain the confusion, frustration, and pain his statement caused. She knew that he wasn't in the right frame of mind to realize how his words sounded. She didn't want to add to it with her insecurities. It was definitely not the time.

"Colton, whatever happened back there, I'm not leaving you. I don't trust anyone else like I do you. Besides, they would probably think something was really wrong with me if I tried to sneak into bed with them at night because I'm afraid to sleep alone." She tried to add a little levity to the moment to get Bull to smile and realize he wasn't alone.

Her plan worked—he gave her a small, half-smile as he rubbed his calloused fingers across her cheek.

"Over *their* dead bodies, Chaise," he countered.

"*There's* my Bull," Chaise laughed. She wasn't accustomed to using his nickname, but it seemed to fit and help remind him of his tough side.

He smirked. "I'll give you *your* Bull later tonight."

"*And* he's back, ladies and gentleman!"

Smiling, he shook his head from side to side. Bull couldn't believe how quickly and thoroughly the relationship between him, and Chaise had changed, but he had to admit that he was grateful for it.

She was his breath of fresh air in his stale world. After realizing how dull and lifeless his existence had become, he suddenly wanted no more of that life.

Since his father had abandoned him and his mother when he was just a young boy, he had kept personal attachments to a minimum. He had his mother, his brothers, Brianna—and that was it. He hadn't let any other woman in until Chaise. He knew without question that she was firmly seated in his heart and his life. Her support and belief in him, even though she had no idea what had just happened, solidified her place in his small band of trusted people.

Shadow and Rebel were waiting on the front porch of Bull's large, suburban home. It wasn't as big as Noah's palatial home, but it was big enough to have all the amenities he needed. His eyes cut to Shadow and Rebel as he nodded toward the door. "Let's get this over with."

Once inside the house, Shadow immediately started questioning Bull.

"What the hell happened, man? And don't tell me 'nothing'. You and I both know that's bullshit."

Bull gave them a full rundown of what had happened from his vantage point. He described the three Latino men in detail and gave a word for word recount of their conversation, including needing Chaise alive and unharmed. Then he reached the point of the story where he had to explain his actions. Or rather, he had to explain his lack of action.

"Go on," Rebel prodded, knowing that Bull was stalling.

"The fourth man with them was ... my father," Bull stated.

Stunned silence filled the room. Chaise's eyes flew from one man to the next, trying to figure out this part of the puzzle without interrupting their debriefing session.

"Shit," Shadow blurted out.

"Holy shit," Rebel echoed.

"Yeah," Bull deadpanned.

"Um, can someone explain this to me?" Chaise thought she had held her tongue long enough.

"My dad abandoned my mom and me when I was a kid. Just left one day and never came back. That was him I saw today ... in the parking lot ... with those guys who were after you." Bull looked apologetic, as if he were responsible for his dad's actions.

Then he turned his attention to Shadow and Rebel. "I have to go to my mom's. I need answers from her, and I can't do this over the phone. I'm going back to Alabama."

Shadow and Rebel simply nodded their understanding.

"What about Chaise?" Rebel asked.

"What about Chaise?" Chaise repeated, irritation laced in her words. "She's right here. Maybe you can ask her."

Shadow smiled at Rebel. "I like her."

Bull was torn about what he should do with her. On one hand, he wanted to take her with him, to make sure she was protected and to get her out of the area. On the other hand, he wasn't sure what information he would obtain from his mother, or how he would react to that information. Perhaps leaving her with Shadow and Rebel would be the best-case scenario.

Then he remembered her words spoken in jest while they sat in his truck.

"Chaise comes with me," Bull responded, leaving no room for argument.

Chaise's responding smile conveyed she knew exactly what he was thinking when he made his decision. Bull smirked at her sarcastically and shook his head as he walked toward the kitchen.

"Beer?"

"Yeah."

"Sure."

Drinks in hand, the guys worked on their updated plan while Chaise put the remaining groceries away and started cooking supper. After a half-hour, Rebel appeared in the doorway to the kitchen.

"Damn, what smells so good in here?"

"Chicken tortilla soup, Panini sandwiches, and chips," Chaise answered as she stirred the soup.

"Bull, you go on to Alabama. I'm taking her home with me," Rebel teased.

"The hell you say," Bull challenged, positioning his body between Rebel and Chaise. Rebel grinned, knowing he'd hit a nerve with Bull.

"Let's eat," Chaise called out to no one in particular. She only wanted to quickly diffuse the tension in the room.

Brad walked in with the surveillance recording so Chaise could identify the man who'd been watching her all day. As they ate, the recording played, and she watched herself move around the office as if she were watching a movie.

"That's him," she said as she pointed to the screen.

Brad stopped the video, isolated the sinister man, and uploaded his image to the facial recognition software. The software used specific facial features, such as the width between the eyes, width of the nose, and depth of the eye sockets to connect subjects to people already housed in a database. Once a match was made, the system returned a name and last known address.

"This could take a while to identify him. I'll let it keep running and contact you when it returns a hit," Brad told Bull. "We can start checking him out while you're in Alabama."

Bull nodded. "Thanks, Brad."

When the soup and sandwiches were gone and the guys had left, Bull sat on the couch with the phone in one hand and his head in the other. He had to make the dreaded call to his mother to let her know he was coming home. But he didn't want to tell her why just yet. He wanted to see her face when he told her he'd seen his father.

The couch dipped beside him when Chaise sat down and put her arm around him. She lightly stroked the back of his neck and he let her touch help ease the dread inside him.

"Do you want to talk about it before you call her, Colton?" Chaise asked supportively.

He didn't move other than to shake his head no. Her touch helped to calm him, her presence gave him strength, and he could feel her unconditional support. Without raising his head, his hand found hers and he lightly squeezed it, thankful that she was beside him. He brought her hand to his mouth and kissed her palm.

Chaise moved closer to him, aligning her body with his and wrapped her other arm around him. She kissed his cheek and then nuzzled her face against his. Inhaling the heady mixture of his masculine, musky cologne and the all-male scent that was inherently Bull, Chaise had to willfully fight the impulses he ignited in her.

Bull felt the change in the air and shifted his gaze to meet hers. He recognized the desire building in her eyes and knew his eyes mirrored hers. They'd slept together every night, but spooning had been the extent of their physical contact. With all the ambiguity in Bull's life at that moment, he wanted nothing more than to put it all behind him, take Chaise in his arms, and take her to his bed.

Bull tossed the phone onto the coffee table and pulled Chaise into his lap, straddling him so she was facing him. He crushed his mouth to hers, taking what he needed in a bruising, possessive kiss. There was no tenderness in it and he possessed no capacity for waiting. A voracious thirst had overtaken him, and Chaise was the only one who could quench it.

His hands hungrily and eagerly roamed over her body. He groaned into her mouth as his tongue swept over hers. Bunching her shirt up in his fist, he quickly yanked it over her head and threw it on the floor. Chaise pulled his shirt over his head, leaned into him, and ran her tongue over his chest. His hands threaded through her hair and gently pulled her mouth back to his.

"Chaise," he said between kisses. "I can't wait, baby."

"Then don't," she purred.

She instantly flew through the air and landed on her back on the soft, extra-wide couch, and he covered her body with his. As her arms moved to wrap around him, he grabbed them and pushed them above her head. While part of her expected him to maintain the distance between them during their most intimate moments, she couldn't stop the wave of disappointment that crashed over her. She'd hoped they'd turned a corner and had deepened their bond and trust.

While he was distracted, he released her hands from his firm grip. When she reached out to touch him, he captured her hands and moved them away from him.

"You're all mine, Chaise." His stake on her came out as a possessive growl.

His words were all she needed to push her over the edge. Her body's response felt like something akin to a tsunami. They rode the waves out together, until he had drained every drop of energy from her body.

When she moved her leg, he released her hands and fell forward on her body. She wrapped her arms around him, her body completely spent and sated, but her mind whirred and buzzed at what just occurred. They had agreed to take it slow, but the sizzling chemistry between them was stronger than a magnet to steel.

While she tried not to read too much into it, his apparent aversion to her touching him during intimate moments troubled her deeply. He didn't try to keep her at arms' length any other time. Like at that moment, as his body perfectly crushed hers into the couch, she gently stroked his back with her fingertips. But when they were at their most vulnerable, his steel walls were fully in place, and she felt like she was permanently on the outside of them.

Bull turned his face toward her and brushed sweet kisses on her cheek and jaw. He rose up on his elbows and gently stroked her cheek with his thumb. His eyes searched hers intently, but she didn't know what he was looking for yet.

"Did I hurt you?" he finally asked, concern laced his words and his expression.

"No, Colton, you didn't hurt me," Chaise whispered.

He lowered his forehead to rest on her shoulder. Chaise could feel the tension rolling off his body. The physical contact had only momentarily relieved his stress and it was coming back full force. Whatever he was dealing with, he wasn't sharing it with her.

With a deep breath, Bull stood up and pulled Chaise up with him. Wrapping his arms around her, they stood in the living room, stark naked, and just held each other for several minutes. Chaise felt the tears welling up in her eyes and fought to hold them back. She had no doubt that she was in over her head with him. There was no going back, no taking it slow, and no living in denial.

She had strong feelings for him, and she was afraid of getting her heart broken. Or more accurately, of breaking her own heart when she finally told him the truth about her true identity. Every day she berated herself for not telling him sooner. Every day she knew she was a day too late in telling him the truth.

"We'll leave tomorrow on the Steele Security jet and go to my mother's. I just can't deal with calling her tonight." Bull spoke into her hair, but he felt a million miles away.

"Okay."

That was the only word Chaise could choke out without risking a total breakdown. She had to remain strong to help Bull with the turmoil in his life. He'd protected her and saved her life, and it was the only way she knew to help him in return. At least, that was her rationalization.

Bull released her from his embrace and led her with his hand on the small of her back, as he always did, down the hall to his bedroom. She knew the moment he fell asleep, curled up with his front to her back, his arm protectively and possessively draped over her as he held her close. His breathing was deep and steady, his body relaxed, and she felt the tension seep from his muscles to be replaced with peacefulness.

Chaise silently cried herself to sleep.

12

CHAPTER TWELVE

The Steele Security jet was celebrity worthy. It had every opulent amenity anyone could possibly want, including a full-size bedroom and bathroom in the back of the jet. The front part of the Boeing Business Jet had one wall lined with soft-leather couches and small tables.

The other side was lined with cushioned leather captain chairs arranged in sets of four, positioned around a small table that was perfect for in-flight meetings. On the back wall, beside the hallway leading to the bedroom, was a large, flat screen plasma TV that was opposite a fully stocked bar. Chaise thought that Noah and Steele Security must have been doing very well to be able to afford such a luxurious asset.

Bull chose a small couch in the middle of the plane and patted the seat next to him, motioning for Chaise to sit with him. She took her seat and he immediately wrapped his arm around her, pulling her close to him. *He always does that*, she thought with a smile.

"What are you grinning about?" Bull asked.

She looked up at him, not realizing that she had an ear-to-ear smile plastered on her face until he pointed it out.

"I was actually thinking that you always do that—pull me into you when we sit down," she answered truthfully, then watched his face to gauge his reaction.

His smile remained in place. "I guess I do. Huh. How about that? Does it bother you?"

"No, it doesn't bother me at all. I like it. It's almost like I was made to fit next to you." Chaise blabbered before realizing that had just vocalized the very thought she meant to keep to herself.

Surprise registered in his eyes, but she didn't see any sign of panic. Nothing that indicated he was ready to parachute out of the jet to get away from her and her reference to them being made for each other.

"Maybe you were made to fit with me," Bull said, partly teasing and partly serious.

Chaise desperately wanted that to be true. Bull was not the type of man who would try to feed her a line just to string her along. But she didn't think he was the type of man who wanted long-term committed relationships, either. His tone of voice and the softness in his eyes when he said that made her think that something more could come of their relationship. It made her hope that she wasn't just a temporary distraction for him that would be tossed aside as soon as the case was closed.

"What if I was, Colton? Would you keep me?" she asked with bated breath.

The flight attendant saved him from answering her question. "The pilot has indicated we are ready for departure. Please buckle your seat belts until we are at cruising altitude," she politely instructed.

Chaise moved out from Bull's arms to secure her seatbelt. Bull's first instinct was to pull her back to his side. She did fit him perfectly. Her body fit perfectly with his. He thought about how well they got along—their playful banter, their deeper conversations, and their red-hot bedroom trysts. Chaise was the first woman Bull could see himself with for the long haul. That fact alone should have him running as far in the opposite direction as fast as he possibly could go.

In less than two hours, they would reach the airport in Mobile, Alabama. While there were special circumstances, Chaise would be the first woman he'd ever introduced to his mother. The implications of that fact were enormous to Bull. It signified that he cared enough about her to take her with him instead of leaving her with Rebel or Shadow. It meant that he had to share his most private life with someone he didn't fully know. It meant that he had to let her see him when he was at his most vulnerable.

For the first time in many years, his head and his heart didn't agree. His head told him there were still too many things he didn't know about her. His logical reasoning and training told him it could never work and that she was bound to betray his trust. He still didn't know her last name, despite the intimate moments they'd shared.

Did that make them less real?

Not according to his heart.

His heart said there was more to them than their physical compatibility. When his mind said to walk away and leave her behind, his heart made sure he knew that wouldn't work. He couldn't say he was in love with her. He didn't believe in love at first sight. He believed love took a lifetime to cultivate and nurture.

But somehow, she had found a way to break past his defenses and securely root herself deep inside him. When he looked at her now, he couldn't remember what he did with his free time before she came into his life.

Just a few weeks ago, in fact, he thought.

And there was his rational mind again, raging a war inside him and making him question what he thought he always wanted. He sat silently on the jet, arguing with himself over what he should do next. She was still beside him, oblivious to his entire inner monologue.

When his hand reached up to caress her cheek, he knew the instant he touched her that he wouldn't walk away. The battle had been decided and the war had been won. He walked into the situation knowing that she had secrets she was afraid to tell him. But he was a good judge of character, and he could read people like a book.

At his touch, she leaned her face into the palm of his hand. She closed her eyes and hummed in pleasure at such a simple touch. He could see it on her face, he saw it in her eyes when she looked at him, and he could feel it in her every touch. He knew she felt it, too.

She was the culmination of exactly what he thought he would never want, the very thing he could never have, and now that he'd had a taste of it, he didn't think he could give it up. She trusted him, she believed in him, and she made him feel protective and possessive like no other.

Bull leaned over and placed a chaste kiss on her lips.

"Mmmm, you taste so good. I don't think one kiss is enough," he murmured against her lips.

"By all means, Colton, if you're still hungry ..." she intentionally let her voice trail off so he would fill in the rest with whatever he wanted from her.

"You'll be ruined for anyone but me."

Chaise knew that was already true. He knew her body's needs and desires before she even realized. He navigated her body like he owned its sole road map. And she was sure that he would completely own her heart and break it just as thoroughly ... eventually.

"You've had a long, rough week. There's a bedroom in the back of the plane. If you'd like, you can take a nap until it's time to land. We have plenty of time before we arrive," Bull offered.

"We? Does that mean you're Are you going to nap with me?"

Bull smiled appreciatively. "If that's what you want."

"I do." Chaise leaned over to kiss him before walking back to the bedroom.

As she stretched out on the bed, she thought about how the conversations between them came much easier as each day passed, and their compatibility was undeniable. She'd tried to keep her distance, tried to keep her heart out of the situation, especially knowing what was still to come. But the ways he showed how much he cared, big and small, had completely wrecked her plans of maintaining her space.

She knew, without a doubt, she was unequivocally his.

The bed dipped as Bull took his spot behind her. His arm reached around her and pulled her securely to him. They lay with their bodies perfectly aligned, close enough to be one, as Chaise cherished the feeling that only snuggling with him could give her.

CHAPTER THIRTEEN

Stepping off the plane in Mobile, Bull and Chaise were immediately hit with the stifling heat and humidity of southern Alabama. While Mobile Bay afforded their accustomed ocean breeze, the airport was located outside the bay area and didn't have the same attributes. Their clothes immediately clung to them as the beads of perspiration popped up and glistened in the hot sun.

The vehicle rental was much like Bull's truck in Miami minus a few of the extra amenities he had personally added. Chaise took in the sights as Bull mindlessly drove to his old home. She asked a few questions about the area and about his family but gave up after his one-syllable answers returned.

She could feel the tension radiating off him. After everything he'd done to help her, she wanted to do something, anything, to help him in his painful situation. Chaise unbuckled her seat belt and moved across the center console and to the backseat. Bull looked at her quizzically, but she proceeded with a smile.

Once she'd positioned herself, she reached her arms around the seat and began massaging Bull's shoulders and neck. His all-male groan reverberated through the truck and through her body as she felt the tense muscles begin to relax. Working out the kinks and knots she found in his muscles, she could feel his tension lighten.

After several minutes of expertly massaging, kneading, and rubbing the sore areas, Chaise knew she had successfully helped him. When she climbed back into the front seat, Bull took her hand in his, lifted it to his mouth, and kissed it. But this time, he didn't let go. He laced their fingers together and held her hand in his lap.

It felt like another turning point to Chaise. Another sign that the solid steel walls constructed around Bull may just be bending to allow her to enter.

She squeezed his hand a little as she asked about him. "Did that help any?"

Bull smiled and replied with a wink. "Yeah, if I'd known you were a secret masseuse, I would've put you to work before now."

Chaise laughed. "I'm not a secret masseuse, but anytime you need the stress worked out of you, just let me know."

The heated look Bull gave her revealed he'd intentionally twisted her meaning in his mind. She laughed and corrected her statement. "Okay, let's try that again. If you need your neck and shoulders massaged, just let me know."

Bull laughed heartily. "I think I like my interpretation better."

The rest of the ride to Sandy Bay, Alabama was in peaceful silence. Bull continued to hold on to her hand, occasionally pulling it back to his mouth to kiss it. He had a far-away look in his eyes, as if he was remembering his time spent in the area but wasn't quite ready to share his thoughts.

He stopped the truck outside of a single-story, sprawling ranch-style house with lush green grass and shrubbery in the front yard. Bull sat motionless as he stared at the house. His stoic, emotionless mask was securely in place again.

"Colton, are you okay?" Chaise softly asked.

Bull nodded. "Yeah, let's get this over with."

"I can help get the bags," Chaise offered.

"We're not staying here. We'll stay at my place," Bull replied.

"Your place?" Chaise asked, confused.

"I have a small place here where I stay when I come to visit," Bull explained.

"Oh, all right."

Bull's mother, Michelle, met them at the door as they approached. She pulled Bull into her arms for an embrace as she squealed. "My baby boy's home! I didn't know you were coming. You should've called me."

Bull hugged her back but didn't verbally respond. He pulled away and dropped his arms from around Michelle. Her face instantly changed, sensing something was wrong.

When Michelle's eyes met Chaise's, she smiled genuinely and extended her hand. "Hello, I'm Michelle Lanier, Colton's mother."

"I'm Chaise. Colton's ... friend." She cut her eyes to Bull for a second.

She wasn't sure how to label what she was to him and asking him in front of his mom wasn't an option. She also noticed the tick in Colton's jaw and immediately knew he was thinking about her last name—or lack thereof. She quickly continued. "It's nice to meet you. You have a lovely home."

"Thank you, dear. Come in, come in."

Michelle showed Chaise around her house, including Bull's old room where she'd kept things much as they were when he last lived there. His pictures from his youth and some that were more recent hung on the walls and sat out on display. It was obvious that Michelle was very proud of her son then and the man he'd become.

When they finally sat down in the den, Bull cleared his throat and started. "Mom, we need to talk."

"Do you want me to leave?" Chaise politely interrupted.

The look Bull gave her made her instantly regret asking. From the look in his eyes, it was obvious he wanted her there with him and he was disappointed that she would even ask. Chaise moved closer to him and covered his big hand with her small one. "I'll stay," she whispered.

"What's this about, Colton?" Michelle asked.

"It's about Dad."

Michelle's eyes and mouth simultaneously flew wide open in surprise. She stuttered and stammered, trying to form coherent words, but none came. She quickly averted her eyes from Bull and Chaise. Her face was bright red, and her breaths suddenly increased.

"I saw him, Mom. He was with some really bad guys who shot at us, and were trying to kidnap Chaise," Bull continued without remorse. "I saw the letter he left, the one that said we were better off without him. Now, I need to know the truth about him because it's Chaise's life in danger now."

Michelle stood and walked over to the end table. She stood with her back to Colton and Chaise for several long minutes before opening the base of the table and retrieving the letter.

"I wish you'd told me you'd seen this a long time ago." When she finally turned to face them, she had the letter in her hands, clutched tightly to her chest.

"What difference would it have made if I had? He *abandoned* us without a second thought, and you just pretended it was all fine instead of facing the truth," he spat out in anger.

"No, Colton, that's not entirely true." She sighed heavily as she weighed her next words. "I was wrong to not tell you when you were old enough to understand, but he didn't want me to say anything. He was afraid it would put you in more danger."

Michelle took a deep breath. "He didn't *abandon* us, Colton. He had to leave to *protect* us. But he's always kept watch over you and me. All these years, he's never stopped loving us."

"You're not making any sense," Colton growled.

"Your dad works undercover with the DEA, Colton. That's why he traveled so much when you were young. He was deep under-cover on a very dangerous case, and his cover was about to be blown. This letter you saw was our secret code, should that day ever come. His case was big and had he been discovered, they would've killed us all.

"That's why we moved here. That's why you went to the military boarding school for high school. That's why I let you, and everyone else, believe he had just left without a word. It was the only way to keep us all alive."

Colton stood and started pacing the room. His hands were drawn into fists. The emotionless mask was gone, and full fury had replaced it. His muscles were tightly wound, like a rattlesnake ready to strike. He looked lethal and he was only getting started.

"You really expect me to believe that all this was for *our* benefit? He could've moved with us. He could've taken on a new identity and stayed with us. He didn't have to *leave* us."

"Those were different times, Colton. He had to make it look like we were dead, so we'd have a chance at a life without looking over all our shoulders all the time. We both did what we thought was best. That's all we could do." Her voice was rich with grief, regret, and remorse.

Chaise watched Bull intently to try to gauge his reaction. The whole conversation was a huge bombshell and she felt like she was still running to catch up to them. The silence was uncomfortable, and the room felt stuffy.

"Do you still talk to him?" Bull's eyes narrowed and he crossed his arms across his huge chest.

Michelle drew in a deep breath and Chaise had a very bad feeling about what was about to occur. "Yes, Colton, I still talk to him. He's still my husband. That's why I've never remarried. It's always been only him for me."

"How can you still be married if you never see him?" Bull growled.

"I do see him but not as often as I'd like at the moment. He's finishing up this current case and then he's retiring. He'll move here to be with me, or we'll move somewhere together." Michelle explained the situation with a shrug of her shoulder, showing she'd grown accustomed to their lifestyle while Bull reeled from learning the truth.

"I don't fucking believe this. He's been absent my whole life and you just take him back like what he did is nothing?" Bull's anger was reaching a scorching hot level.

"I love him, Colton. I knew what he was when we married, and I knew this was a possibility. We did the best we could with what we had. He watched over you your whole life, Colton. You didn't know, but he's always watched over you and your career. He's so proud of you."

Bull paced the floor, his hands on his head and threading through his hair in frustration. There were just too many lies, too many things that were kept from him, and a lifetime of regrets caused by an absent father. The same father who had always been proud of him and would be stepping back into the family like nothing happened at all.

"Chaise and I are going to my place. I need some time to think this through." He stopped and looked her in the eye. "You shouldn't have let me find out like this. You should've told me."

"I know, son. I'm so sorry. We were only trying to protect you. I love you, Colton."

Bull nodded but Chaise had the distinct impression that he wasn't really listening to what his mom was saying. His mind was a million miles away in that moment.

In the truck after saying their goodbyes, Bull was still very quiet. He answered Chaise when she spoke, but other than that, he was very distant. Chaise reached over and put her hand over his. Without looking at her, Bull closed his hand around hers and squeezed it lightly. That was his way of thanking her for her silent support.

Bull pulled into a secluded driveway that was barely visible from the road. The shrubbery and coconut trees partially blocked the view of the drive, giving the illusion that it was an old, abandoned road. Obviously, that was just how Bull wanted it to appear to keep unwanted visitors out.

At the end of the driveway sat a small house. It was immaculately kept and looked like an island oasis. The front yard was covered with lush, green grass and the backyard was the beach and ocean. Bull parked, grabbed their bags, and escorted Chaise into his home away from home.

The house was small and simple, not nearly as elaborate as his

Miami home. But it was the simplicity and the back view that was the true draw. The house consisted of three bedrooms, two baths, a den, dine-in kitchen, and a large wrap-around covered porch. The back yard held the typical manly-man essentials—a grill, a fire pit, and an oversized hammock.

Chaise had always loved the beach and the ocean. She had grown up living around the water and she loved it. She was strong swimmer. The sound of the waves and the feel of the breeze was her Zen place.

She looked at Bull and quipped, "I call dibs on the hammock tonight."

Her attempt at humor at least earned her a smile—the first one she'd seen since they had arrived at his mother's house. She heard, "humph," just before she was suddenly picked up and thrown over his shoulder. She squealed with laughter, and he playfully swatted her ass.

"Don't even think you're sleeping *anywhere* without me, woman!"

"Oh, I do love the *'demanding Bull'* so much," Chaise teased.

"You're about to get all the 'demanding Bull' you can take," he warned with a mischievous sparkle in his eyes.

"Promises, promises," she replied sardonically. While he couldn't see the huge grin on her face, she made sure her voice conveyed her playfulness. That was all it took for Bull to want to prove her wrong. Her plan was actually working much better than she had anticipated.

Bull deposited her across the hammock and softly covered her mouth with his. He was unusually tender in his approach and Chaise felt every ounce of her body melting into the hammock. She felt his thick, rigged muscles bulge against his shirt. The vibrating sensation was new, however.

"Fuck!" Bull said as he pulled his phone out of his pocket. Glancing at the screen, he saw Rebel's name just before he answered. "Yeah, man."

A few clipped words later, along with no display of emotion one way or another, Bull ended his call. Chaise looked at him expectantly as he prepared to fill her in.

"We'll have to stay here for a few days. That was Rebel. The guy you identified on the surveillance tape is not part of the *Tres Sieses*. He's actually part of a much more dangerous organization and they are apparently after you," Bull explained.

Chaise gasped audibly and the color drained from her face. "Worse than that gang? What's worse than having a gang after me?"

Bull cautiously answered her. "This is an *international* organized crime group. They are very professional and thorough, Chaise. They have their hands in several different illegal activities, including human trafficking and drugs. They don't tolerate failure, either. The guy on the video has been found shot—execution style. My guess is he was killed because he failed to get you."

The shock and terror that Chaise felt was indescribable and over-whelming. They had killed a man because he failed to kidnap her. He was supposed to kidnap her because she discovered the missing girls. The mere question of what else they could be hiding was equally as frightening as what she'd already uncovered.

"Colton, what am I supposed to do?"

His eyes revealed that his response held an intentional double entendre meaning. "Anything I tell you to do, Chaise."

"I'm serious."

"So am I," he declared. "Just stick with me, baby. I'll keep you safe."

"Come on. I know this is more serious than what you're telling me," Chaise gently chided him. "I know I haven't been a pillar of stone, but I'm not stupid."

Bull smiled gently. "I never thought you were stupid, Chaise. Yes, it's dangerous but there's a reason why we're the best at what we do. You'll just have to trust me."

"I do trust you, Colton," she replied warmly as she stroked his cheek. Her face took a serious countenance as she continued. "I hope you know you can trust me, too."

"I'm learning that," he said sincerely as he wrapped his hand around hers. Chaise was happy to have earned that much faith from Bull in their short time together.

"So, what do we do now?"

"We'll stay here for the next few days. We'll keep off their radar and figure out our next move. Rebel and Shadow are gathering more intel on them. No one else even knows where you are."

"Let's just stay here forever, then," Chaise whispered while gazing deep into his eyes.

"That's the best plan I've heard in a long time," Bull replied. "I have all kinds of ideas for you."

"It's a good thing I have nowhere else I have to be then, isn't it? I don't even have to worry about going back to work Monday," she replied with a sultry smile.

"Come on. It's time to eat and I'll show you around," he said as he stood and helped her up from the hammock.

Bull took Chaise out to eat at an oceanfront restaurant. Tiny white lights adorned the trellis that covered the intimate patio setting, naturally creating a romantic ambiance. Large, exotic plants were placed strategically to avoid blocking the ocean view but also gave the guests a modicum of privacy.

Once the maître d' seated them, Bull emphasized his words as he leaned over the table. "You are stunning." His hooded eyes matched the bedroom quality of his voice and Chaise clenched her thighs in response. The low timbre of his voice seemed to have more control over her body than she had herself.

"You know, you said that when you tried to get me to stay home with you tonight. But, since a lady never tires of hearing how good she looks, I won't try to stop you from telling me again," Chaise flirted and teased Bull.

"I offered to feed you." Bull responded and laughed when Chaise's face heated from her blush.

The waitress appeared and saved Chaise from having to respond to his overt attempt to arouse her. Placing the menus in front of them, she recited the daily specials before taking their drink orders. Once she was gone, Chaise looked back at Bull who was still smirking.

"So, tell me something I don't know about Colton Lanier." Chaise challenged, trying to change the subject while knowing she was opening herself up to questioning as well.

"What do you want to know?" Bull leaned back in his chair and put his hands in his lap. His posture was relaxed and open. His face showed his amusement, though she wasn't sure if that was from her abrupt change in subject or her question.

"Have you ever been in love?" Chaise asked while trying to hide her hesitancy. While she wasn't naïve, she didn't know if she really wanted the answer to this question.

"Straight for the jugular, huh?" Bull asked with his panty-dropping smile. "I thought I was, once. But while I thought she was a good person, it turns out she was a lying, cheating skank behind my back. After that fiasco, I decided relationships weren't for me.

"I think, now, that it wasn't really love at all. I didn't know her like I thought I did. I ignored too many signs that were more like huge, blinking billboards. It's not a mistake I've made since."

What he didn't tell Chaise was that he had fast developed feelings for her. He wouldn't go so far as to say it was love, but he couldn't deny that he thought he *could* fall in love with her. She was the first woman who had made him feel that way—protective, possessive, and happy. For the first time in a very long time, he wanted to see how a relationship with Chaise could work.

"It sounds like you've already decided that's not something you want," Chaise replied. Bull noted that she kept her voice even and unemotional, but her eyes betrayed her and revealed her true feelings.

"For a long time, yes, it was that way. My mind isn't so set in stone now," he replied cryptically. "My turn." He immediately noticed the rigid tone of Chaise's posture and the flash of panic that crossed her face.

"Ask away," Chaise said, preparing herself for the one question she didn't want to hear.

Bull narrowed his eyes and contemplated his question. He had a visceral need to understand her connection to Reaper. He wanted to know why she reacted the way she did when Reaper's name was brought up in conversation. He wanted to ask her how she could trust him with her life and in his bed, but not with her real last name.

"Have you ever lied to me?" Bull asked.

Chaise's body relaxed and she reached her hand across the table, palm up in request for his hand. Bull complied but didn't move his gaze from hers.

"I have—but I tried to tell you I did, and you said you knew. Martin isn't my last name, Colton. My last name is-," Chaise was cut off by the waitress.

"Here are your drinks. Now, are you ready to order?"

Bull squeezed Chaise's hand and answered. "Yes, I think we are."

Bull ordered their main entrees and handed the menus back to the waitress. The band started playing and Bull stood, offered his hand to Chaise, and led her to the dance floor. He wrapped his arms around her waist, and she wrapped her arms around his neck. He pulled her as tightly to him as he could, just to feel her body pressed against his as they moved to the slow, melodic music.

Chaise looked up at him. "Colton, I want to tell you."

"I know you do. And for now, that's enough. It tells me you finally trust me enough. We can talk about it when we get home. Then you can explain why you had to keep it a secret."

Chaise stretched up and kissed his lips. Bull tilted his head down to meet her and deepened their kiss. The music played in the background, but it was of no consequence. They were in their own world, their own time, and dancing to their own music. Their fully clothed bodies, intertwined and moving as one, was as sensual, erotic, and intimate as anything Chaise had ever experienced.

When the song finished, Bull led Chaise back to the table with his hand placed possessively on the small of her back. She liked the feeling that small gesture gave her. It announced to the world that she belonged with him. They arrived back at their table just as the wait staff arrived with their food.

After their meals were finished, and Chaise had consumed several glasses of Moscato wine, Bull led her back to his truck. She was tipsy but not drunk, though her inhibitions were significantly lessened. The lascivious look she gave Bull left no room for misinter-pretation when she purred, "I can't wait to try out that hammock, Colton."

Bull's head whipped around to look at her, shock and complete surprise at her boldness registered on his face. It was quickly replaced by wanton need and heated desire. His foot pushed the gas pedal harder as he sped back to his house.

14

CHAPTER FOURTEEN

The breeze from the ocean cooled the night air. The wind swirled around them when Bull opened the front door, and Chaise immediately realized why. The entire back wall of the house was ceiling to floor sliding glass doors, and several were already open.

"Is someone here?" She glanced around nervously, knowing Bull wouldn't treat their security with such blatant disregard.

"No, it's just us. I had the cleaning service open the doors while we were eating dinner. The house has been closed for a while, and I prefer to let it air out with the sea breeze. No one could've gotten past the motion sensors inside the house. Don't worry, babe."

"Colton, this place is amazing. If I were you, I'd quit working in Miami and live here full time. With that awesome view of the beach and the gulf, I'd never want to leave."

"Believe me, the thought has crossed my mind more than once or twice. Why don't you slip into something more comfortable so we can take a walk on the beach? There's a full moon tonight. The way the reflection sparkles off the water is hypnotizing."

"That sounds amazing. I'll throw on some shorts and be right back. Don't leave without me."

"Wouldn't dream of it."

A few minutes later, Bull and Chaise stroll hand in hand off his back lanai and onto the powdery soft sand of the Gulf of Mexico. The houses were few and far between, leaving the light of the moon as their sole guide. The lack of neighbors was what drew Bull to the house in the first place. Without additional room to expand, he didn't have to worry about his little slice of heaven becoming heavily populated in his lifetime.

"We can't walk on the beach without at least putting our feet in the water. It's a law." Chaise cut her eyes up to Bull as a sly smile covered her face.

"Well, if it's a law, we'd better comply. You wouldn't lie to me, would you?"

"You know better than that. It's most definitely a law. It may be only *my* law, but that's still a law."

"Fair enough."

The waves lapped at their ankles as they strolled along the line where the water met the sand. Occasionally, a larger one would crash into them, sending water up their legs and soaking their clothes.

"I don't know why we didn't just wear our bathing suits." Chaise looked down at her soaked shorts and laughed. "Why do the rogue waves keep finding me and missing you? That's not fair."

Bull shrugged. "The ocean knows better than to mess with me. You haven't shown it who's the boss."

"You know, I really like this playful side of you. Can we keep this version of Bull around? Unless someone is shooting at me, following me, or otherwise trying to harm me, of course. Then Scary Bull can come out to play."

He threw his head back in laughter. "You've named the different aspects of my personality, huh?"

"Yes, I absolutely have. But I'm surprised you didn't already know this. There's Playful Bull, Scary Bull, Serious Bull, and Sexy Bull. Although, that last one is misleading because you're sexy regardless of anything else."

"I'm glad you think so." He leaned over and stole a kiss as they continued their slow amble along the water's edge.

"Tell me something I don't know about you. Something from when you were a kid. What did you like to do?"

"Let's see. What did I like to do as a kid? I loved playing baseball. When I was seven, I started playing on the recreation league. Even though I was young, I was good at it. So, I continued playing through high school. I could've made a career out of it, but something about how athletes are revered as heroes or demi-gods always bothered me. When I decided to serve my country, I knew joining the Army was the only way I could feel good about it."

"What did you do in the Army?"

"Took orders, like everyone else."

"That was a vague and unconvincing answer. Try again."

"I did whatever was required to become part of the special forces division. Crawling on my belly through mud, wading through marshes and swamps with alligator and snakes, and endless hours of target practice made me a lethal professional at the top of the soldier ladder. When Reaper decided not to continue his commission when his time was up, Rebel and I made the same call so we could open Steele Security with him. We've been best friends since the day we met. There hasn't been a time when we didn't have each other's backs."

"Having a friend like that must be amazing. I've never had a close relationship that lasted the test of time. I've had plenty of friends, but when life pulled us in different directions, we lost touch. I often wonder how many other people are in the same boat with me and how many still have their best friend from kindergarten in their life."

"Well, I haven't known Reaper quite that long, but since the day we joined the Army and arrived at the same base for basic training. I watched him rise through the ranks, younger than everyone else, but I was one of the few who was proud of him for overcoming the obstacles in his way. Anyway, being a soldier fit me perfectly. The structure, the assignments, and the camaraderie of my squad made me who I am today."

"Do you have any brothers or sisters?"

"Yes, actually I have an older brother, but I don't really know him. He's twelve years older than me and attended a prestigious boarding school. By the time I was old enough to realize I had a sibling, too much time had created a distance between us, effectively making us complete strangers. To make things simpler, I usually say I'm an only child. What about you?"

"Yes, I have two older brothers, but I've lost touch with them. Our father wasn't the best man when we were growing up. When they both went their own way instead of taking the path he'd planned for them, he pretty much disowned them. Being left behind with that controlling man all those years was hell on earth. For many years, I blamed my brothers for abandoning me, especially the one who's closest to me in age. We were close at one time, but when he cut our father off, he cut me off too."

"What about now? Do you still blame him?"

"Yes, if you want the absolute truth, I still blame him most of all. But now that I'm grown, I can see both sides of the matter. Part of me still says he didn't have to choose to cut me out of his life too. I didn't do anything to him except love him. Maybe we weren't as close as I thought we were, though."

"That pain cuts deeply and it's difficult to overcome. I'm sorry that happened to you, Chaise."

"I know you understand it better than most. Not to bring up a sore subject, but do you want to talk about your dad? Seeing him again then learning the truth from your mom must have your mind reeling."

Bull stops walking and signals for Chaise to take a seat in the sand. He sits beside her and begins drawing concentric circles in the sand.

"My dad was my hero. He taught me how to play baseball, practiced with me all the time, and came to all my games. In fact, he was part of the reason why I loved the sport so much. He was so proud of me during every game, it made me want to do better. The main reason I kept playing after he abandoned us was because I hoped he'd show up at one of my games and we'd be a family again. You can imagine how conflicted I was a kid and a teenager when I was more depressed after winning a game than I was going into it.

"Anyway, you're right. My head and my heart are warring right now, and it's a full-on, take-no-prisoners assault. For the first time since I joined the Army, I have no confidence in my decision making abilities. I'm sure that's reassuring to you since I'm supposed to protect you, but you have nothing to worry about on that front. Being a soldier is so ingrained in me, I react mostly in instinct. If anyone is stupid enough to try anything here, my training will kick in and I'll kick their asses."

"I'm not worried about myself here, Colton. No one has a clue where we are. I'm concerned about you and how you're dealing with this blow. I mean, my father was a controlling asshole, but he was still there for me when I needed him. You've waited for your father to show up your whole life, and when he does, he appears to be the enemy. Then you find out it's worse than that—he willingly left you and never returned because he chose his job over his family. That has to make you question everything."

"I've never said this to another living soul, and if you tell anyone I did, they'll never find your body. But his disappearance made me believe I was the most unlovable person in the world. If my own dad didn't love me when I was only seven and innocent, how could anyone love me at any time in my life?"

"You already know what I'm about to say, but you still need to hear it and believe it. Your worth is not dependent on the mistakes your parents made in their lives. They did the best they could at the time when the choices were presented to them. We have the advantage of hindsight, but we both know circumstances are very different when you're living through the stress of the moment." Chaise cupped his cheek with her hand and nudged him to face her. When he did, she reached up to kiss him, their lips lingering in place for a heartbeat longer than usual as they gazed into each other's eyes.

"It's getting really late. We should head back to the house and get some sleep. We're safe and secure, but not quite out of the woods yet." He pushed a lock of her hair behind her ear, leaving a trail of goosebumps in his wake.

When they returned to his beachfront home, Chaise stopped at the hammock and raised her eyebrows at him.

"This looks so comfortable. It's such a beautiful night. Want to stay out here for a while?" Her eyes darted between Bull and the hammock, wordlessly signaling for him to agree.

"Whatever you want is fine with me." He deftly rolled onto the hammock without a hitch. "Climb on."

She hurriedly joined him before he changed his mind, claiming it wasn't secure enough. His fingers lovingly stroked her back as the hammock gently swayed. Both were unwilling to say it, but they both felt it—the shift in their relationship, the knowledge that it was more than a passing fling, and the unknown decision of what they would do about it.

Together, they fell into a deep slumber in the warm Alabama air. The rhythmic swaying of the hammock rocked them to sleep, and the warmth of their bodies cocooned them for the night. When the sun came up, the rays peeking through the canopy of the trees woke Chaise. She realized that somehow, she had moved to the protective crook of his arm and his other was draped protectively over her. He had removed his shirt and used it to cover her.

Titling her head up, she realized that he was watching her. "Did I wake you?"

"No, baby. I've been awake—just watching you sleep."

She smiled without responding.

"What is it?"

"You've started calling me 'baby.' I like it\" She snuggled in tightly to him. Her top leg moved over his as she wrapped her body around him. The hammock moved slightly, rocking them as it swayed in the wind.

His arm tightened around her as he lowered his lips to her ear. "It's a good thing you do, because I wasn't going to stop."

Chaise laughed jovially as she swatted his bare chest. "Now why doesn't that surprise me?"

"It really shouldn't," he teased.

After breakfast, Bull convinced Chaise to change into her bathing suit so they could enjoy a relaxing day at the beach together. It had been way too long since Bull had taken a real vacation. Work had always been his priority and he prided himself on giving it his all.

That day, his work and his vacation were one in the same. He had to keep Chaise away from Miami to keep her safe. There was nothing else pressing that he wanted to do. In fact, continuing the conversation with his mother was the very last thing he wanted to even think about, much less actually do.

While Chaise changed, Bull gathered all the beach supplies they would need and waited patiently on the patio. His low whistle of appreciation brought a smile to Chaise's face when she stepped through the door. Her tanned body and black hair accentuated her light pink bikini. Her curves on display made Bull's mouth salivate as if he'd never tasted her before.

Or maybe it was because he already knew exactly how she tasted.

Hand in hand, they strolled across the hot sand to where the waves rolled up on the shore. Placing the bag out of reach of the water, Bull removed two masks, two snorkels, and two sets of fins. Handing one set to Chaise, he asked, "Do you know how to use these?"

"Of course," she replied casually. "I grew up around the ocean and I love the water."

"There's a manmade reef several yards off the shore. We'll swim out and have a little fun out there," Bull said with a smile.

"Let's go!" Chaise sat in the shallow water to put her fins on her feet and to fit the mask to her face. Once she was set, she floated on the shallow water until the water was deep enough for her to turn and wait for Bull.

Bull had watched her with amazement that she was bold enough to don the equipment and swim out without waiting for him. Most women, in his experience, were afraid of what the water held. She seemed to relish in the discovery of it. He waded into the water to join her and they swam off to explore.

Hours later, they were both completely exhausted from their excursions as they headed back to Bull's beachfront home. They had first explored the manmade reef just off the shore. After a light snack on the beach, they walked along the shoreline, talking, and simply enjoying each other's company. Once they reached the house, Bull led Chaise to the bedroom and wrapped his arms around her for a mid-afternoon nap.

Over the next three days, they spent their time together in much the same way. After realizing how much Chaise loved the swimming, snorkeling, and the ocean in general, Bull made it a point to take her to new places each day. They explored new snorkeling spots, took long walks on the beach, and christened many new places with their lovemaking. In the evenings, he would take her to the boardwalk area to walk on the pier, shop in the beachfront stores, and eat in the local restaurants.

For brief moments, Chaise forgot that she was being pursued by a masterful criminal organization. She was in her own paradise oasis with Bull where she could happily stay. The time alone with him had given her a view into the real Colton Lanier—the man whom few seldom had the opportunity to experience.

And she knew without a shadow of a doubt that she'd fallen completely and undeniably in love with him. She never said the words, but she didn't try to hide the actions or feelings. The little things mattered to Chaise. He took such good care of her; she wanted to give what she could in return.

Every day, she rose early to cook his breakfast and make sure his black coffee was made just right. She dressed to the nines when he took her out to eat so that he would be proud to have her on his arm. When other men blatantly stared at her, she only had eyes for Bull. Lastly, she made sure that at any time he wanted her she was more than willing.

But with every time they joined, he kept her hands off him. Before or after they made love, he seemed to love the feel of her hands on him. He acted as if he craved her touch and couldn't get enough of her. Then in midst of their passionate encounters, he found a way to actively prohibit her from touching him.

Even with the intimacy they shared, she felt something was missing between them. She had tried to broach the subject of her identity with him a couple of times, but it never seemed to be the right time. She would catch him in deep thought, but she had a good idea it had more to do with his parents than anything else. They still hadn't ventured back to his mom's house to finish their discussion. She couldn't help but feel as if she was simply Bull's escape from reality. Nothing more ... nothing less.

On the fourth morning of their self-imposed beach exile, the uncertainty she felt from their relationship weighed heavily on her mind.

Did she feel she had a right to demand answers?

No.

Would that stop her from trying?

No, most likely not; especially not considering the doubt had continuously tortured her nerves. It was the 'not knowing' part that wreaked havoc on her emotions and had started to give her a complex.

Chaise had awoken early and left Bull sound asleep in the bed. She walked down the beach to where the waves were gently lapping on the shore and waded in ankle-deep water. She was slightly bent at the waist, looking for seashells in the surf, when she heard a male voice speak to her.

She jumped and looked up into a pair of unfamiliar brown eyes. He looked to be around forty, still handsome and fit, and slightly graying at the temples. His goatee also had light speckles of gray mixed in that gave him more character than age. His smile was easy and his demeanor was laid back.

"I'm sorry. Did you say something?" Chaise asked.

The man laughed and looked slightly embarrassed. "I just asked how the fishing was this morning."

Chaise laughed in response to his attempt at humor and struck up an easy conversation with him about nothing in particular. They looked for shells and sand dollars together for several minutes. When he didn't find any, he wished her a good day and walked away down the beach.

"Who the hell was that?" she heard a familiar voice bark at her from behind.

"That was one of your neighbors, Colton. His name is Gene Castleberry," Chaise answered without looking up from her task.

"What are you doing out here alone? What if he had been one of the men sent to grab you?" Bull's menacing voice was in full effect.

"You said they didn't know where I am. So how could he be?"

"Anyone can be traced, Chaise. You could hide at the South Pole, and I could find you with the right resources," Bull retorted.

"Well, I'm still here so I guess he's not one of the bad guys," Chaise replied nonchalantly.

The eerie silence forced Chaise's eyes from her search. Looking up, she recognized the storm brewing in Bull's eyes was not from concern of her safety. It was pure jealousy emanating from his eyes. She felt a twinge of satisfaction from knowing that she had somehow worked her way through his tough exterior. But that wasn't enough— she had to make him admit it before there could be any hope for them.

"Are you jealous, Colton?"

"Why would I be jealous, Chaise?"

"Oh, I don't know. Because I was talking to another man, maybe?"

"What you do with another man is not my concern. What is my concern, however, is your safety. For as long as you're my client and I'm responsible for your safety, you will not leave my side."

Chaise dropped the shells she held in her hand and stumbled backward in shock at his abrupt and cold answer.

"That's all I mean to you?" Her voice was soft and low, but full of unmistakable pain. She looked away from him as her hand flew to her face to whisk away the tears that were already falling.

She questioned herself. *How could I have been so wrong?*

She heard his exasperated sigh, but she refused to look at him. She'd seen her opening to talk about what was happening between them and she took it. It wasn't his fault that he didn't give her the answer she wanted. But damn if it didn't hurt, anyway.

15

CHAPTER FIFTEEN

Bull watched as Chaise walked away from him and back toward the house. He'd hurt her with words he didn't mean and didn't really feel. When he woke and she wasn't in the bed, his first thoughts were that she was cooking breakfast for him again. She'd spoiled him over the last few days and made him feel loved and cared for more than he'd felt in a very long time.

When he reached the kitchen, she was nowhere to be found. Breakfast hadn't even been started. There was nothing to even indicate she had been in there. He instantly felt a rush of adrenaline from thinking that someone had gotten to her.

He rushed outside and immediately froze in his tracks. She was in ankle deep water, and she was searching for seashells with another man. They were talking and smiling. They were obviously enjoying each other's company and he didn't even warrant a second thought from her.

The man walked off before Bull was close enough to speak but the damage had been done. Chaise continued to search for shells until Bull spoke. His tone of voice shocked even him, but he just kept plowing through the situation like he normally did. When the last words escaped his mouth, he only wanted to retaliate—first, for making him feel jealous, and secondly, for calling him out on it.

But he took it too far. He made her think that he didn't care about anything but the job. He basically told her she meant nothing more to him than a menial task. He called her name as she walked away from him, but she ignored him, walking briskly into the house instead.

Bull gave her a few minutes to calm down and then walked into the back door.

"Chaise?" he called out as he walked into the kitchen. He heard sniffles coming from down the hall. He walked silently toward the sounds until he found her. His heart pounded in his chest when he saw her—packing her suitcase.

"Are we going somewhere?" he asked softly.

"I am," she answered. "You are free to do whatever you want with whoever you want. I'll be gone in fifteen minutes."

He walked up behind her and wrapped his arms around her. He bent his head so that his mouth was at her ear. His lips brushed against her as he spoke.

"I don't want you to go anywhere, baby," he said earnestly.

She stopped folding her clothes as she replied with a watery, strained voice. "Don't call me that. I'm just a job to you."

"No, you're not. I was worried when I couldn't find you. Then I was mad when I saw you outside with another man." He tightened his grip on her a little more.

"Why would you be mad about that?"

"You were right—I was jealous. But I didn't mean what I said. I could never share you with anyone else, Chaise."

"Tell me something, then." She started to ask, but decided to wait for his nod of agreement. When he did, she continued. "Why can't I touch you when we make love?"

She felt his entire body go completely rigid. His hands stilled their gentle movements on her body. His breaths hitched in his chest. She had a fleeting thought that she shouldn't have asked, but right then was as good a time as any to find out the whole truth.

His arms slipped away from her, and she felt the immediate loss of his comforting body heat. He was pulling away again. She dropped her head forward, shook it in disbelief, and started folding her clothes yet again. No matter how badly she wanted to stay, she would never stay with him under those pretenses.

"You remember I told you I thought I was in love once?" he asked. His voice didn't hold the normal self-confidence and she knew she was about to hear something she wouldn't like.

"Yes," she said softly, without turning.

"I told you she cheated on me, right?" There was so much dread in his voice that she could feel herself cringe for him. "Well, one night when we were making ...having sex ... she called me by his name. Ever since that night, I just couldn't allow anyone to touch me like that again."

"Anyone? Will that always include me?" This time, she turned and faced him. She had to know if it was something they couldn't work past. She had to know if he would always keep her—literally— at arms' length.

They stared at each other for what felt like an eternity. Chaise could see the wheels turning in Bull's brain, trying to determine how to best answer her question while being truthful at the same time. She knew he was struggling with what to say. Bull's difficulty with giving an answer unfortunately told her everything she needed to know.

Chaise couldn't hide the sadness and disappointment from her expressive eyes. Her proud shoulders dropped, and her head dropped forward. She closed her eyes and fought back the tears that threatened to overtake her again. She turned her back to him while she finished packing her suitcase.

In an instant, his muscular arms whirled her around to face him. They enveloped her as he lifted her from the floor and deposited her in the center of the bed. His body covered hers as his mouth claimed hers. His kiss was fervent and needful. She let him take everything from her. Everything he needed, everything she had, everything she could give—it was all his anyway.

His hands wandered across her body, removing her clothing and his, until their bodies lay pressed together. Her hands were in his hair and then moved slowly down his back, lightly scraping his skin with her nails. He moaned into her mouth with anticipation and desire.

Bull halted his movements and peered into her eyes, the words on the tip of his tongue but he was still unable to say them. His eyes spoke volumes to her without him ever saying a single word.

He asked her not to betray his trust.

He told her he was giving her a piece of him that he'd only given away one other time.

He said he trusted her with his guard down.

Tears of joy and love slipped from her eyes and ran down her temples. She made love to every inch of his head, neck, shoulders, and his back with her fingers. She memorized the sinewy muscles, the striations they made, and how they contracted and relaxed with his every movement. She poured every last drop of her heart and soul into loving him with her entire body.

His mouth reclaimed hers in a sweet, gentle kiss. Each languid kiss into her brought them one step closer to bliss. One step closer to love. One step closer to becoming totally and completely lost in each other.

Bull's hands were cupped around Chaise's face as he peered lovingly into her eyes. Her fingers dug into his back, her fingernails scratching him in response to the intensity wracking her body. His name escaped on her breath as she rode out the last wave of pleasure.

The words were not spoken aloud. The newly formed bond was still fragile but there was no doubt they both felt it. Bull stayed fully seated inside Chaise, relishing in the feeling that was uniquely hers. His back bore the scratches from her as a badge of honor. He had allowed her inside his sacred space. He'd afforded her the privileges that others were denied. He was starting to feel whole again.

He bowed his head and kissed her lips, cheek, and neck before moving to her side. She groaned her disapproval and he lightly chuckled. "I know I was crushing you, Chaise."

"No, you weren't. I love the feel of your body covering mine."

"Come on, baby. I will cook breakfast for you today."

"If you don't mind, I'm going to shower first. I'll be quick." She kissed before sashaying off to the bathroom.

"Damn, I love that view," Bull called after her and gave his best catcall whistle.

Fifteen minutes later, Chaise exited the shower and towel dried her hair. When she walked into the bedroom, she realized all her clothes were in the suitcase that she had just finished packing. Rather than waste time unpacking again, she grabbed one of Bull's extra-large t-shirts from his drawer and slipped it over her head.

Bull heard her bare feet padding down the hallway. "It's about time you finished in there. I thought I would have to eat all this food myself," he teased.

Chaise turned the corner and came to a sudden halt. She blanched white as all the blood drained from her face. All the air was sucked from the room, and she could not breathe when she saw that they were not alone. Her towel was slung around her shoulders, she wore nothing but Bull's t-shirt, and she stood there facing all the main operators of Steele Security.

Including Noah.

Chaise knew that Bull was at the stove intently watching her every move. She also knew that Rebel and Shadow sat at the table, though their eyes followed everyone else in the room like a tennis match in progress. Another woman sat close to Noah, and from her slightly protruding stomach, she could only guess the woman was Noah's wife, Brianna.

The anxiety welled up inside her and threatened to overtake her. She hadn't told Bull the truth yet and there she was face to face with Noah. After the advancements in their relationship that they had made that morning, she could see everything crumbling before her eyes.

And she had no one to blame but herself.

"*Sierra*? What the hell are you doing here? And. Why. The. Fuck. Are you wearing Bull's shirt?" Noah suddenly stood, knocking the chair backward until it fell over.

Brianna looked up at Noah like he'd lost his mind. She clearly felt that Noah had a lot of explaining to do to Chaise—not the other way around.

"Noah, calm down and let me explain. I'm in trouble and needed help. I showed up at your wedding to ask you, but I couldn't get close enough to talk to you. Besides, you were leaving for your honeymoon." She gestured toward Brianna, reminding Noah he'd been away for quite a while. "Bull, Rebel, and Shadow stepped in. I explained the situation to them, and they agreed to help me."

"Oh, they agreed to help you, huh? Tell me something, Sierra. If you were in trouble, why aren't the police involved?"

"Because I don't know who to trust, Noah. These people have the police on their payroll and an effective method of making people disappear. I didn't want to be one of those people." Chaise's eyes and tone pleaded with Noah to listen to reason, but that clearly wasn't happening.

"So, they've kidnapped people, huh? And this wasn't something the Florida Bureau of Investigations, the FBI, or any other of the numerous government agencies you could've and should've contacted would've handled? It had to be my security company instead of the actual police agencies?"

"Noah, I've been terrified beyond my wits. I came to you for help."

"You know what I think? What I really think is going on here? You concocted this entire story to cover up some shady shit you're into, then dragged my friends into your mess to clean it up for you. Or you're using my friends to get close to me because you want something. Why else would you come around suddenly after all these years? Since I wasn't available to call you on your bullshit, you used and manipulated my friends."

"No, that's not true, Noah. Ask Bull what we've been through over the last couple of weeks. He'll tell you."

"Yes, that's a good idea. Let me ask Bull." Noah swung his fiery gaze toward his best friend. "*What in the fucking hell* is going on, Bull? What are you doing with Sierra—my little sister?"

Chaise's mouth gaped open at Noah's continued outbursts. She grabbed the hem of Bull's shirt she was wearing to hold it down in modesty. She unconsciously took a couple of steps backward out of the hostile room. She could feel daggers flying at her from both Bull and Noah as her brother continued his tirade against her. The others stared in open confusion, their eyes darting around the room as they attempted to gauge the entire scene..

"*Sierra?*" Bull asked in his accusatory tone, his eyes darting back and forth between her and Noah.

"Yes! *Sierra!* What the fuck have you been doing with my little sister, Bull?" Noah yelled as he advanced on Bull.

Bull's head snapped to Chaise. "*Sierra?* Your real name is *Sierra?*" He walked toward her pointing. "You fucking lied to me about *that?*"

"No, Colton, please—just give me a minute..."

"*You're Sierra Steele, Noah's sister? You're his little sister?*" Bull wasn't even looking at her anymore as he yelled. His hands were in his hair, pulling and raking through it.

Her anxiety attack was only being held at bay by the thought of what she would lose if she couldn't keep herself together at that very second. "Colton, please just let me talk to you. I can explain everything," she begged him.

Bull's face became hard. His eyes became cold. His voice was low and unemotional. "No. No explaining this away, *Sierra*. This," he motioned between them, "is finished. You should have told me from day one."

Tears slid down her cheeks as her hand flew to her mouth in an attempt to hold in the sobs. Noah stood stock still, his face displaying his disgust and disapproval. Bull wouldn't even look at her. The only camaraderie she felt in the room came from Brianna's eyes. There was depth and understanding in them, but Chaise couldn't focus on that yet.

She turned and ran down the hall to their bedroom. To *Bull's* bedroom. She quickly unpacked the clothes in which she needed to change. Once she'd dressed, she opened the door and heard shouts coming from the kitchen.

"Are you fucking kidding me? First of all, even if she wasn't my little sister, you know better than screwing a client," Noah yelled. "But the fact is, she is my sister. That's a line best friends don't cross."

"Reap, I had no idea she was your sister. You're right, I knew better than fucking a client. There's no excuse for that, but you don't know how everything went down. I'll swear an oath on my life that it'll never happen again if that makes you feel better," Bull replied.

His words speared Chaise's heart. She felt it shatter into a million pieces in her chest and knew it would never be the same again.

"You're both over-reacting." Brianna attempted to reason with the two men. "Noah, you need to calm down."

"Calm down? He didn't even know her last name. This is basic information that we collect on any client. The fact that he didn't bother honestly concerns me," Noah replied to Brianna, but with a softer tone than he used with Bull.

"Noah, babe," Brianna continued. "You weren't there. You don't know everything that happened and why. Don't jump to conclusions."

"He's right, Sunny," Bull replied. "I let him down."

Rebel and Shadow remained quiet, opting to choose their battles on another day. Chaise was completely heartbroken and drained. The anxiety attack was bubbling just under the surface, like a volcano about to erupt. She heard the resolute tone of Bull's voice. She heard the anger in Noah's voice.

There was no turning back now. She gathered her things, picked up her cell phone, and made a couple of phone calls. After she finished with her hair and makeup, she re-emerged from the bedroom with her possessions in tow. The conversation had returned to normal volumes, but it was obvious that they were still talking about her when she entered the room.

Bull watched as Chaise positioned her suitcase by the door and removed something small from her purse. She walked over to stand directly in front of Bull, but he wouldn't meet her gaze. She sat down on the coffee table in front of him and took a deep breath.

"You're right, Colton. I should've told you before now, and I tried to several times, if you remember. I wanted to. My name is Sierra

Chaise Steele. I haven't gone by Sierra for many, many years now." She cut her eyes at Noah as she stated the last part.

She handed Bull the business card that she had pulled from her purse. He glanced down at it long enough to verify that it did, indeed, say *Chaise Steele*.

"When I graduated college and started doing contract HR work, I changed my professional name to Chaise Steele. Too many people knew me as *Sierra-Steve-Steele's-daughter*. I told you how overbearing he was and that bled over into my professional life. I have gone by Chaise ever since then.

"As far as being Noah's sister, it's true, I am. I wanted to tell you—and I tried to tell you—but I take the full blame for that."

Turning to Noah, she explained. "Noah, he didn't know you were my brother. I gave him a fake last name so he couldn't have known. Don't blame Colton for this—blame me."

Chaise hated having the conversation in front of everyone, but there was no time and no other way to handle it. "Colton, this doesn't have to change anything between us. It doesn't change anything for me. I didn't lie about my name—it *is* Chaise. Please talk to me."

She was met with a painful, stoic silence.

"This is exactly what I thought would happen. I'm sorry I didn't tell you sooner, but I'm not sorry for anything that happened between us, Colton. I don't regret one minute of it," she said through her tears that were freely flowing down her cheeks.

She swallowed hard and stood on shaky legs to move away from Bull. She knew he would react in that way. She knew she didn't matter enough to him for him to hear her out. What they had between them wasn't enough for him to look past his pride. She'd known all along, deep down, that he would pull away from her as soon as she told him she was Noah's little sister. Noah had just beaten her to the punch.

An eternity passed as she made her way across the floor with all eyes burning a hole in her.

"And just where the hell do you think you're going?" Noah brazenly demanded.

"Noah Steele!" Brianna chastised him.

Chaise gave Brianna a small smile of appreciation before moving her eyes to meet Noah's. "I'm leaving."

"Like hell you are!" Noah's voiced boomed through the house. "The Cordova family is a major international drug and human trafficking organization. If they are really after you, *as you claim they are*, and if you leave here now, you may as well go turn yourself in to them. Besides, you don't even have a car here."

Chaise kept her voice calm and professional, as if she were addressing a group of executives. "Before I came in here, I made two phone calls. The first one was to Steele Security headquarters. I've paid your retainer fee. Any additional expenses I've incurred can be billed to me."

Bull still refused to look at her, but she could see how hard he had clenched his jaws. She couldn't even venture a guess about what he was thinking, but at that point it really didn't seem to matter.

"The second call was for a cab. It will be here any minute now. I had no doubt everything would turn out exactly this way, so I've already made travel arrangements. I had hoped it would be different, though. At any rate, since I'm the customer and I've paid for the protection I've received, I am now relieving you of your duties. I no longer require your services," she stated flatly.

The room erupted in arguments—regarding her ability to make decisions, of her ability to protect herself, and of her sanity. Noah's voice boomed and cut through the fog of dissension

"If you leave now, then I have no choice but to believe this whole thing has been a ruse and you were never really in any danger. How dare you try to play me and my brothers like that?" Noah accused.

Chaise's back was to him, and her hand was on the doorknob. The shock from his words hit first, then the pain, then the anger—the full-fledged, red-hot anger that that been building deep inside her. She whirled around, fire flashed in her eyes, and marched up to face Noah head-on.

"Let me fucking remind you of something, Noah. *You. Were. My.*

Brother. First. You want to live by the military code of never leaving a man behind? You want to talk about honor and loyalty?"

Her entire body was shaking but there was no stopping her. The entire room watched with bated breath as she tore into Noah.

"*You* left *me* behind. Without a second thought. Without a backward glance. You left me behind when I needed you the most! You were *my* big brother! You were supposed to look out for me! But you didn't. *You. Left. Me.*

"So, you just stay here with '*your brothers*' and pretend you're the one who has been wronged here. Keep telling yourself that and, maybe one day, even you will believe your own bullshit.

"Oh, and by the way, you're fired!" she yelled.

With that, Chaise stomped across the floor, yanked open the door, and hurried out to her waiting taxi. The driver put her bag in the trunk as she climbed into the backseat.

The taxi driver got in and looked at her in his rearview mirror. "Where to, Miss?"

"The airport, please."

16

CHAPTER SIXTEEN

The slamming door left everyone inside the house in complete silence. Bull's eyes stayed glued to the door as if he expected Chaise to walk back in at any second. The sound of a vehicle pulling away drew Noah's attention and he raced to the window.

"Son of a bitch!" he yelled when he watched as the taxi drove away. Raking his hands over this face, Noah stood rooted to the floor, deep in thought of what their next move should be.

"Why would you think this was a ruse, Reap?" Bull finally spoke.

"What?" Noah said as he spun around. His face was contorted in confusion at Bull's question. He had already moved on to other scenarios and Bull's question pulled him back from his own world.

"Reap, you said you thought she made all this up so we'd help her out of trouble she created for herself. Or that she was using us to get close to you again. Why would you think anything like that about her? She hasn't given me any indication she's been in trouble for anything. Also, the questions she asked about you weren't anything out of the ordinary. I'm not following your line of thinking." Bull quizzed him because his own thoughts strayed to whether Chaise had used him, played him, and then walked away.

"That's because he's not thinking logically." Brianna walked over to stand beside her husband. "Your judgment is skewed as far as your family is concerned, my love. Your sister has never done anything to you for you to treat her that way."

Noah sighed loudly in exasperation. "You're right, Bri, and I shouldn't have said any of that to her or even thought it about her. I wrote my entire family off a long time ago and moved on with my life without them. Then when she walked in, I was so shocked I couldn't think straight.

"The day I left my father's house wasn't my best day. Today is the first time I've seen or heard from her in years. The first thought I had was I'd be the last person she'd contact if she needed help. Plus, I've always expected my dad to send one of my siblings to guilt me into going back home. He's so manipulative—I just don't put anything past him, including using my sister." He turned back to the window as he continued, more to himself than anyone else. "I took out my anger toward my father on her. I shouldn't have done that."

"Reaper, you should know that she's really in danger. The men took shots at us, and I heard them say they had orders to take her alive and kill me. If they get to her, her fate will be much worse than death," Bull continued to speak with no emotion. He could've been repeating a grocery list for all the lack of empathy his voice portrayed.

Shadow rubbed his jaw line with his hand, his thumb and middle finger meeting at his chin as he took in Bull's demeanor. Rebel sensed it, too, because he leaned forward in his seat and pierced Bull with his gaze. They knew that Bull sensed their intense gazes, but he rebuffed their attempt to engage him.

Noah wasn't as easily denied. He took a couple of steps toward Bull and narrowed his eyes at him. "You sure sound concerned, Bull," Noah spat out sardonically. "So, my sister is good enough for you to fuck but not care about her wellbeing? Just another one of your whores?"

Bull was on his feet, in Noah's face, and had the front of Noah's shirt twisted in his fists in a heartbeat. He growled out, "Don't *ever* talk about her like that again."

Noah smiled at a very pissed off Bull. "Now, that's more like it."

Bull released Noah's shirt and took a step back, realization registered on his face. "You did that shit on purpose just now?"

"I did. I had to see where you really stood with her, man. That was the best way I knew how to get you to admit it," Noah replied.

"I honestly don't know where I stand with her, Reaper. I don't want anything to happen to her, but I don't trust her. I can't trust her," Bull stated matter-of-factly.

"You are so full of shit, man." Bull's gaze shot to Rebel, glaring menacingly at him after that outburst.

"What the hell is that supposed to mean?" Bull shot back.

"It means, *Bull*, that over the past several days, you haven't had any problems with trusting her. Today, you just turned your fucking back on her with no warning and for no reason. You should've taken up for her when Reaper was running his mouth about her. I'd expect no less from you if he was talking shit about me," Rebel replied.

"Whose side are you on, anyway?" Bull asked.

Rebel and Shadow replied simultaneously. "Chaise's."

Bull gave them both the middle finger salute.

Brianna stood and cleared her throat. "Can you boys excuse us, please? I'd like to talk to Bull alone."

Noah grinned from ear to ear, knowing Bull was about to get the ultimate tongue-lashing. "I don't know why you're smiling," Brianna said flatly. "You're next."

Noah's smile dropped and his eyes widened in surprise. "Me?"

"Oh yes, *you!* Now get out."

Brianna took Bull's hand and led him back to the couch as the other men filed out the back door to wait on the patio. She knew Noah's tactic to get Bull to admit his true feelings was brutish and would only work in the interim. Now that Bull realized what Noah was really trying to accomplish, it would be harder for Noah to get him to talk.

"I won't sugarcoat anything for you, Bull. You know as well as anyone that things between Noah and me haven't been easy. We've had to work hard at rebuilding the trust between us. It wasn't easy for

Noah to forgive me, Bull. He wanted to stay mad at me. His *male brain* even told him not to believe me. But where would we be today if we hadn't worked through everything?

"The most important thing is that we both *want* this relationship. We *want* to be together because we love each other. We *forgive* each other almost daily because neither of us is perfect. It's worth all the trouble because we can't live without each other.

"You can't berate her for not telling you she's Noah's sister. She was in trouble, and she needed help. Would you have helped her if you knew she was Noah's estranged sister? Sometimes the lesser of two evils is the hard road. You can't blame her for that. So, you need to answer this question for yourself. *Is Chaise worth it to you?*"

Brianna stopped talking and watched Bull's reaction. He didn't verbally respond but he did nod his head once in acknowledgement.

"I'm going to leave you to think about that while I go have a little talk with my husband."

Half an hour later, Brianna, Noah, Rebel, and Shadow entered the house. Bull was standing at the front door with his bag in hand. Everyone looked at him expectantly, waiting to discover what he had decided to do.

"Let's go get her," Bull stated.

"That's what I wanted to hear," Noah replied with a brotherly slap on Bull's back. "Don't think I don't still owe you an ass-kicking for sleeping with my little sister, though."

Bull, Rebel, and Shadow laughed while Brianna gave Noah a stern look in her attempt to admonish him. He smiled and winked at her. She responded with an exaggerated roll of her eyes at him.

Boys will always be boys, she thought.

"Go on to the airport without me. There's something I need to take care of here before I leave," Bull told them.

"What's up, Bull?" Reaper asked.

"I need to go talk to my mom. My dad was one of the guys after Chaise, but she says he's undercover DEA. I'll find out how to get in touch with him in case we need his help," Bull explained.

Shadow fished his vibrating phone out of his pocket and saw Brad's name on the screen. "Hey, man. Did you find her?" A few clipped sentences, a couple of 'yeahs' and 'uh-huhs' later, Shadow hung up and found all eyes on him.

"That was Brad. He found out that the cab company took Chaise to the airport. Let's get a move on in case she gets lucky and gets on an early flight."

Reaper looked at Bull and raised his eyebrows. "What do you want me to do when I find her?"

"Just try to keep her from boarding the plane until I can get there," Bull answered. Noah nodded and they all left in a race to the airport.

Several minutes later, Bull drew in a deep breath as he parked in his mother's driveway. He couldn't bring himself to turn off his truck yet. Sitting alone, he reflected upon everything he thought he knew about his life. He thought his father had abandoned his mother and him. He had accepted that his mother had lied to him, but then he'd learned it wasn't for the reasons he had originally believed.

Then, with Chaise, he was facing a similar conundrum. He knew from the beginning that she had lied about her last name, and he had allowed her to keep it from him all this time. Even when she said she wanted to tell him, he was in no hurry for it. Just the fact that she admitted it and wanted to tell him was enough at that moment.

The feelings he had experienced over the past few weeks were new to him. He was just beginning to learn how to deal with them when the shit hit the fan. He was just so relieved to learn that she wasn't one of Reaper's past lovers.

In retrospect, and knowing what he knew now, her questions and interest in Reaper made sense. Bull knew that Reaper hadn't seen his family in years and Chaise must have been a pre-teen when Reaper left home. Then, to find out Reaper was married and had a baby on the way must have really hurt Chaise, thinking she would never be the aunt she wanted to be.

Finally, Bull had to examine his own actions as closely as he had examined others'. For all his blustering of being the eternal bachelor, even he had to admit he started playing house with Chaise very quickly—and it all came so very easily. He had to face the truth and admit, mostly to himself, that he didn't want to lose her. He didn't want to go back to how his life was before he met her.

Bull finally left the sanctity of his truck and walked up to the front door of his mom's house. He rang the doorbell and waited, taking time to really look around at his childhood home. He finally allowed the memories to resurface and realized his mother had given him a great childhood despite the absence of his father. He realized there were plenty of fond moments and fun times. Growing up without his father in the home wasn't the constant turmoil he'd built up in his mind over the years.

The door opened and Michelle looked at him, her eyes hesitant and fearful.

"Hi, Mom," Bull said softly, pulling her into his arms. "How are you?"

Michelle wrapped her arms around Bull and held tightly to him. "So much better now."

They walked inside and sat down. Bull smiled at her and squeezed her hand in his way of telling her everything was fine between them. He'd always questioned her about why she never remarried. It never occurred to him that she was still married to his dad, John, or that she couldn't imagine her life with any other man.

"I need to know how to contact Dad," Bull started, knowing that his mom would be shocked at his declaration. "I may need his help with Chaise."

"Well, you can start by turning around, son," a friendly male voice boomed from behind him.

Bull jumped up from the couch and whirled around to see his father standing in the doorway. He wore an old, ratty robe, had a towel around his neck, and his hair was still wet from his shower. He had a slight smile on his face, but Bull knew his father was trying to gauge his reaction.

"I know this is awkward, son. I wanted our reunion to be under better circumstances. Your mom told me about her conversation with you and everything she said is true. I am so damn proud of you. You were always a great kid and you're a damn fine man," John said with his voice full of emotion and pride.

"I appreciate that. Maybe we can spend some time together, to get to know each other and be a family again. But, right now, I have to focus on the case. I need to know why they're after Chaise," Bull said earnestly.

"Where is Chaise?" Michelle asked.

"We had some complications. She left for the airport," Bull paraphrased.

"What?" John's mouth dropped open. "You have to go get her, son. Now."

"Tell me what's going on," Bull demanded. The urgency in his voice matched his rising blood pressure.

"I'll change and tell you in the car on the way. We have to get to her first." The worried look on John's face ate away at Bull's confidence.

I never should have let her leave, Bull thought solemnly and with a silent prayer that she was safe.

***

At the airport, Chaise approached the ticket counter to purchase her one-way ticket back to Miami. Coming in on the private company jet had been a completely different experience than flying back in the coach section of a heavily crowded commercial airplane. They had left from Steele Security's private airstrip so she didn't have to jump through all the hoops required by the major airlines.

With her boarding pass and driver's license in hand, Chaise approached the TSA agent at the first security checkpoint. After verifying her credentials, she walked to the conveyor belt, grabbed a bin, and dropped her shoes and purse inside. Then she waited for the next agent to instruct her to step inside the full body scanner.

After she'd passed the scanning procedure, she waited at the end of the conveyor belt for her purse. And waited. And waited. Another agent walked over, took her purse out of the machine, and turned to her. "Ma'am, is this your purse?"

"Yes, it is. Why? What's wrong?" she asked.

"We need to scan it again. Sorry for the delay," the agent explained vaguely.

Chaise shrugged and continued to wait as the agent put it back on the conveyor belt and sent it back through the x-ray machine. The agent at the monitor stopped the belt and closely examined the screen. Within a few minutes, a plain-clothed agent, wearing a suit and tie, walked up behind the seated agent, and started at the monitor.

"There's nothing in there. You're welcome to look for yourself," she told them, aggravation lacing her tone.

"We're not allowed to, ma'am," one agent stated.

"What? What are you talking about?" she asked.

Other uniformed agents started grabbing luggage off the conveyor belt and putting it on the next machine. Everyone in line eyed Chaise suspiciously as her lane was shut down and everyone was moved away from her purse.

She was mortified and thought, *What the fuck is going on?*

The plain-clothes agent approached her and apprised her of the situation. "It appears there are two live rounds of ammunition in your purse. Do those belong to you?"

Her hand met her head as she dropped it forward. "Yes, those are mine. I completely forgot about them."

"Do you shoot guns a lot?" the agent asked nonchalantly.

"Yes, I do. I have my whole life," she said defensively.

"Do you have a concealed carry permit?" he continued to politely interrogate her.

"Yes, I do, actually. It's a Florida license and it's in my purse. But I can't get to my purse to show you." The people walking by, openly gawking at her, were really starting to annoy her.

"Do you know that you can't bring live ammunition through a TSA security checkpoint?"

"Yes, I know that. I just forgot they were even in there. I went to a shooting range and just dropped the extra rounds in my purse," she explained.

"Where are you headed today, ma'am?"

"Back to Miami," Chaise answered as she watched a police officer approach them. *Are you freaking kidding me?"*

"I just need to search your purse. I understand there are live rounds inside. Is that correct?" the officer asked.

"Yes, go right ahead," she answered with a wave of her hand. Everyone else had gawked at the contents in her person so the police may as well have their go at it now.

The officer removed the two .357 rounds and she watched as they measured, photographed, and wrote their reports. The plain-clothes agent took her driver's license and said he had to run an NCIC report to check for any warrants for her arrest.

"How long is this going to take? I have a flight to catch. This was a simple mistake. I thought you were having a fit about a bottle of lotion in my purse!"

"It shouldn't take too long," he replied as he continued to complete the paperwork. Twenty minutes later, Chaise had her purse back, minus the .357 rounds they confiscated, and the agent advised she would receive a letter in the mail that advised she couldn't bring live ammunition through the TSA checkpoint.

Yeah, I got that part, she thought sarcastically.

Four hours and one connection in Atlanta later, Chaise walked out of the Miami International Airport without a clue of where she should go. She hailed a taxi to take her to retrieve her car from Bull's house. That plan at least gave her a little extra time to figure out where she was staying for the night.

She considered staying in his house since some of her stuff was still there but quickly decided against it. His entire place was meticulously guarded and monitored by Steele Security so there was no way she could get in undetected. She decided she didn't need any additional reminders of Bull, anyway. She'd had enough heartbreak for one day.

Cranking her car, she fought back the tears and her anxiety

threatened to take over her mind. The dark feeling of foreboding was like a living, breathing presence in the car with her. She had effectively compartmentalized her day so that she could function; however, she had already decided that as soon as she checked into a hotel room, she was having a complete and total mental breakdown over a bottle of Moscato wine.

Thanks to her shitty day and equally shitty mindset, Chaise decided to splurge on her hotel room and stay at Loews Miami Beach Hotel in South Beach. She requested an oceanfront suite so that she could soak in a jetted tub. She had stopped on the way in to purchase two bottles of her favorite wine.

The clerk swiped her credit card, handed her room keys to her, and had the bellman take her bag up to her suite for her. Once she was settled into her room, with the door securely locked, she filled the garden tub full of hot water, turned on the jets, and sank down into the luxurious tub.

Then, she opened all the doors of the compartments she'd created over the course of the day and let the tears flow unchecked. Her whole body convulsed with sobs. She mourned losing Bull. Even with their short union, she had foolishly let herself believe she had found a good man who would stand by her through the hard times.

Her heart had shattered when she sat in front of Bull, in front of everyone, and tried to explain herself only to have him completely ignore her. Her eyes begged, her tone of voice pleaded, and her body implored. She already knew what his answer would be—she knew before she left the bedroom—so she made the call to arrange a taxi to take her away from them.

She mourned losing her brother, Noah, again. She had purposely sought him out at the beginning of the whole debacle with two intentions. She missed her brother and wanted him back, and she needed his help and protection. Then, when he accused her of engineering everything solely to manipulate him, he had hurt her more than she imagined he ever could. It was as if he had told her he didn't care that her life was in danger.

Once the water turned cold, she wrapped herself in one of the thick robes, took her chilled bottle of wine to the terrace, and decided it was well past time to get plastered. All the problems of the day would still be there the next day and she would face them when the time came. For the time being, she thought she had earned some self-pity time.

CHAPTER SEVENTEEN

Brad stayed in constant contact with Shadow as he tracked Chaise's movements via her credit card transactions. He mused to himself that people on the run would never learn that every time they used their card, the exact location was tracked, logged, and catalogued for future use against them.

Bull's thoughts never strayed far from what John had shared with him about the case while they drove to the airport. He wanted to kick his own ass for the way he'd treated Chaise. What was really killing him was knowing he allowed her to leave after he'd witnessed the extreme level of danger surrounding her. His lack of compassion was downright cold and heartless, and he knew, without a doubt, she would've never reacted to him in the same way.

"Keep your focus on the case, son, not on your feelings. Your mind needs to be clear to be able to see the next move, to be the one calling the shots, *then* you can get her back." John attempted to comfort and impart his wisdom at the same time.

Bull nodded. "I know. We wouldn't even be in this predicament if it weren't for me. I've royally fucked this up, but I plan on making up for it. She has to be all right."

John's recount of his case had Bull on edge. The Cordova family was worse than Noah knew. Their alliance with the *Tres Sieses* gang was a new development but a familiar modus operandi for that organization.

The Cordova family had recently acquired Viboro Distributing and used it mainly as a front for their illegal activities. Chaise's contract was negotiated and signed before the Cordovas bought the company. Since they didn't want to draw attention to their acquisition, the Cordovas kept her contract in place as originally agreed. Once she started identifying the missing girls, and asking about them, she became a liability.

Bull's phone rang, pulling him from his thoughts and forcing him to focus again on their current predicament. "Yeah, Brad, what do you have for me?"

"She was detained at the security checkpoint for a while and they ran an NCIC on her," Brad chuckled.

"They what? Why?" Bull didn't understand how a casual traveler, who fit no dangerous profile, could suddenly warrant having a National Crime Information Center report run on her.

"She had two .357 rounds in her purse and tried to go through security with them. They frown on live ammunition on the plane." Brad was openly laughing now.

"She didn't even have a gun on her. What was she going to do? Throw the bullets at them as hard as she can?" Even Bull had to laugh at that visual.

"Yeah, well, you know how tight security is now. But they eventually let her go and she's already on route to Miami. She had a connecting flight in Atlanta, but that flight has already departed," Brad advised.

"Have them get the company jet ready, Brad. We're almost to the private airstrip now," Bull ordered.

"Already called them. They're fueling up and doing their pre-flight inspection. I'll keep you updated on her whereabouts," Brad promised.

Bull hung up with Brad and called to inform Reaper, Shadow, and Rebel of the current plan. They had gone ahead to the airport to try to stop Chaise, but they had just missed her fiasco at the security checkpoint.

The group met Bull and John at the private airstrip. Reaper looked as bad as Bull knew he looked. They had both fucked up their relationship with Chaise and they both wished they could go back and do it all over again. Now, they had to confront the grim possibility that they wouldn't get to her in time to prevent the Cordova family from getting to her.

Reaper looked at Bull with haunted eyes and asked, "What did she mean that I left her when she needed me the most? What happened?"

"I don't know, Reap. She told me her father was more than over-bearing and she had to get away from him. That was the reason why she couldn't go back home when all this started. She showed up at your wedding to ask you for help, but we wouldn't let her near you and Brianna," Bull explained.

Reaper drew his arms up and balled his hands into tight fists. "That man probably put her through hell when I left. We were close back then. I never thought he would take my leaving out on her, but it sounds like he did. *Motherfucker!*"

Reaper looked tortured at the thoughts of Chaise enduring the wrath intended for him. Brianna wrapped her arms around him and Bull watched him instantly relax from her touch.

"Noah, she's *your* little sister—give her some credit. She's strong and she has obviously made a good life for herself away from your father. It took strength to walk away and live alone. She knows she's in danger, so she'll take precautions. Let's just get to her as soon as we can. Okay?"

"Brianna, have I told you today how much I love you?" Noah wrapped his arms around her, and his big hand rested protectively on her baby bump. "You always know how to make me feel better."

"She has anxiety attacks," Bull interjected. "What if she gets in a situation she can't handle and has an attack?"

Brianna looked him dead in the eye and responded. "Bull, it's not about how many times she gets knocked down. She shows how strong she is just by the mere fact that she gets back up *every time.*"

"You're a lucky man, Reaper," Bull said while looking at Brianna with admiration in his eyes.

"Damn straight, I am. Sounds like you are, too, Bull." Noah's tone of voice both stated and asked at the same time.

"I was. Even if we beat the Cordovas and reach her first, she has no reason to forgive me for how I treated her," Bull replied somberly.

"Love is reason enough to forgive, Bull," Brianna answered. The resulting expression on Bull's face made Brianna laugh out loud. "Oh yeah, big guy—you got it bad! May as well admit it to yourself now and accept it."

Rebel called out to them and motioned with his hand. "We're boarding now. Let's get a move on, people!"

Bull made a beeline to the private jet and took his seat. The flight time for the private jet was barely over two hours but she had a big head start on them. He tried to relax and find a comfortable position in which to sit, but his thoughts kept straying to the last time he was on the plane. He was with Chaise in the plane's bedroom, and he would give anything to be there with her again.

"Bull—relax, man. We haven't even taken off yet," Shadow joked. "White knuckle flyer."

"I'm not afraid of flying, Shadow. I'm just ready to go, dickhead," Bull deadpanned. Shadow and Rebel both laughed heartily at their friend's expense.

Bull made it through the two-plus hour plane ride of ridicule from his friends. He knew them well enough to trust them with his life and not question it, so he knew it was all good-natured ribbing. He had screwed up royally and he knew it. He would take his lashes like a man. But he would also wait for the day to repay the favor to both of the bastards he called brothers.

Exiting the plane in Miami, Bull immediately called Brad for an update.

"Hey, Bull, she showed up at your house, got her car and left. She stopped to buy two bottles of Cabernet Sauvignon wine, and I haven't seen a swipe of her card since then. That was just over two hours ago," Brad explained.

"Text me the address where she got the wine. Check on any past purchases that shows a pattern, a place she goes to frequently, or anything like that. Let me know what you find ASAP," Bull directed.

"You got it. Call you back in a few," Brad said before disconnecting.

"Reaper, would she go back home to your dad?" Bull asked.

"No way."

Bull updated the team on what Brad had found from Chaise's credit card usage. He knew she had to find somewhere to sleep that night—unless the Cordovas had found her. But he couldn't allow himself to follow that line of thinking.

Bull's phone pinged with the incoming text from Brad with the address of where she purchased the wine. "She bought wine in South Beach. Let's check the hotels around the store and see if she's checked in."

Bull called Brad and had him double check any charges from all the hotels around that location—just in case something showed up late. The team, minus a pregnant Brianna, canvassed the area hotels in South Beach looking for Chaise. Noah refused to let Brianna tag along in case they ran into trouble. Brianna informed him that if she wasn't already so tired from all the traveling they'd done, he wouldn't have won that argument. She reluctantly went home and let the men take the night shift.

After checking several high-end hotels with no luck, Shadow approached the clerk at Loews Miami Beach Hotel with his dashing smile securely in place. The clerk batted her eyes and openly flirted with Shadow, who was using his good looks to his advantage.

After a few minutes and few suggestive comments from the clerk, Shadow had the information he needed. He swaggered back to the waiting group with a smile that split his face in two.

"Who's the man?" he asked as he approached.

"She's here?" Bull asked excitedly.

"She is here. She's in a deluxe suite with an ocean view. She specifically told them she doesn't want to be disturbed tonight," Shadow explained, then gave Bull the suite number so he could go up and disturb her anyway.

"Do you mind if I go with you?" Reaper asked. "I have some making up to do myself. Then I'll leave you two alone."

"Not at all, man. I may need the backup," Bull joked.

Outside her suite door, Bull said a silent prayer and knocked on the door. When she didn't answer a couple of minutes later, he knocked harder and called her name. Soon, Bull and Reaper were both beating on the door and yelling for her to open the door.

"I'm not leaving until you let me in, so you may as well get it over with now," Bull yelled through the door. "I have things I need to say to you, and I'd rather not do it like this, Chaise. Please open the door."

"Sierra Chaise Steele—open this door right now!" Reaper yelled. Turning to Bull, he asked, "What if she's not in there?"

"Excuse me. Are you two gentlemen guests here?"

Bull and Reaper turned to find an armed security guard eying them suspiciously. "We've had complaints from customers on this floor about the noise level. They said men are in the hall beating on doors and yelling at someone."

"My sister is in this suite, and we're concerned about her. We're trying to get her to open the door so we can talk to her," Reaper explained politely. "So far she's not cooperating with us. We may have been a little loud. I apologize for that. I'm just really concerned for her."

"If you're not guests here, I will have to ask you to leave the premises. She may not be in there and if she is, she obviously doesn't want to talk to you. You're disturbing the other guests," the guard said as he extended his hand toward the elevators, indicating for Bull and Reaper to leave.

Bull stood firm. "I'm not leaving without talking to her and making sure she's all right. Can you at least go in the room and check on her?"

"No, I can't without just cause. You've given me no indication that she intends to harm herself. You can leave of your own volition, or I can have you arrested for trespassing. Your choice," the guard threatened.

"Let's go, Bull. We won't be able to help her if we're both in jail." Reaper sighed and turned toward the elevators.

Bull reluctantly left but felt something was very wrong. Chaise knew she was in danger and understood the severity of the situation. She wouldn't put herself in more danger by being out where she could be recognized.

"Know this," Bull said to the guard, "If anything happens to her, I'll be back to see you."

"Is that a threat?" the guard asked defensively.

"That a fucking guarantee," Bull answered before turning to follow Reaper out of the hotel.

Once they reached the sidewalk, Bull pulled out his cell phone and called Chaise's cell phone first. When it rolled to voicemail, he called her hotel room. He decided he would keep alternating between calling her cell and the hotel room until she answered.

***

CHAISE SAT in the warm Miami breeze, enjoying her terrace ocean view. She was still in the bathrobe, had her feet propped up, and was on her last glass of wine. Her second bottle was empty, and her body had run out of tears to cry. She downed the contents of her wine glass, stumbled through the sliding glass door, and made her way back into her suite.

She heard her cell phone ringing from the bedroom area but made no attempt to rush to find it. Within seconds, her hotel room phone started ringing. Thinking it may have been the front desk calling since no one else knew where she was, she snatched the receiver off the base.

"Hello?" she answered with a slur.

"Chaise! Are you all right?" Bull sounded frantic but he was just so glad to have finally reached her.

"I'm fine," she lied. "I'm just a *little* drunk," she said, emphasizing *little* a tad too much. She apparently found it to be funny because she couldn't contain her laughter.

"Chaise, I really need to talk to you," Bull said tenderly. "Can I come in? Please. We should talk face to face. I don't want to say this over the phone."

In the background, Bull heard a loud banging coming from Chaise's hotel room. His gaze swung to Reaper, who still stood beside him.

"Oh, is that you at the door? I need to tell you to fuck off in person." Chaise replied in a drunken, sing-song voice.

"No! Don't answer it, Chaise!" Bull yelled, but it was too late. She had already put the phone down and walked away.

He could hear Chaise calling out, telling the person on the other side to wait a minute. He waited for the sound of the metal deadbolt sliding open, but what came next was worse. The unmistakable noise of the door being knocked off its hinges immediately preceded Chaise's scream.

"What do you want?" The fear in her voice was palpable and made his heart jump out of his chest.

When he heard a scuffle, he thought he would go ballistic.

"She's in trouble!" he yelled to the other men as he ran back into the hotel.

Bull, Reaper, John, Shadow, and Rebel were met in the lobby by the hotel security team. Despite the fact that Bull insisted she was in trouble, the security team wouldn't let them pass. Splitting up, they watched the elevators and exits but Chaise was nowhere to be found.

Reaper called the general manager, explained who he was, and finally persuaded him to send his team to her room. When the manager returned with an ashen face and an aversion to making direct eye contact with them, he apologized profusely and said he'd called the police. The door had broken from the outside and Chaise was not in the room.

Reaper and Bull joined the other three men outside and were met with downtrodden faces.

"What? What is it?" Bull asked.

John pointed at the blinking lights in the night sky, "They took her to the roof and put her in the helicopter. The Cordovas have her now."

Bull's eyes followed the helicopter's movement as it disappeared into the night sky, flying out across the ocean. "Where are they taking her?"

"I don't know, son," John answered, knowing the question was directed at him. "I haven't infiltrated their organization to that level yet."

Bull felt ice run in his veins, much like his time on clandestine operations as a Delta Force member. The old training never really leaves. It may lie dormant for a while, watching and waiting for the right time. But when those killer instincts are needed, there's no doubt it reemerges with a vengeance.

And vengeance would be his when Bull had those men in his sights.

"I just talked to Brad. He tracked down the flight plan for that helicopter. It's headed out to a tanker a few miles offshore. We need to get her before they either put her on another helicopter or that tanker takes off somewhere else with her," Shadow informed them.

Rebel said, "Let me make a call. Be right back."

Reaper's eyes stayed glued to the black horizon as he imagined what would happen to his sister if they didn't get to her in time. He looked at Bull and saw the worry in his eyes, but he also saw the man he'd known while they served in the Army together. His razor-sharp edge made him lethal, his innate distrust of everyone made him naturally suspicious of anyone's intentions, and his training made him a killing machine.

It was during his assessment of Bull that Reaper had a revelation: Bull really was in love with Chaise. This was more than a job to Bull. The Cordovas had made things personal by taking Chaise. Reaper had known Bull for many years and knew him as well as any man could. He knew, without a doubt, if anything happened to Chaise, no man in the Cordova organization would be left standing.

"Let's go. I have a friend in the Coast Guard. We have enough probable cause for them to board the boat and search for her. He's letting us ride along but we have to stay on the Coast Guard cutter while they search the tanker," Rebel explained.

"I can't go, son. If they see me, my cover will be blown, and they would definitely kill her then. I'll see what I can dig up here—get the word from the lower-level guys," John explained.

"I'm going—I have to be there when they find her," Bull responded.

John nodded his understanding. "Son, listen. These guys won't hesitate to kill you and throw your body overboard. Watch your back out there."

"Always," Bull answered.

The men parted ways, with the guys from Steele Security rushing toward the docks and John strolling off to meet up with his local crew. John hoped some of the guys were loose-lipped and bragging so he could get more information about Chaise's whereabouts.

18

CHAPTER EIGHTEEN

As far as prisons went, the oceanfront presidential suite was the most luxurious her captors could've chosen. But regardless of how plush her accommodations were, it was still Chaise's prison.

She decided the attractive man sitting in front of her couldn't be the head of the Cordova organization. He looked entirely too young and refined to be part of any criminal activities. His smile was warm and inviting. His eyes were a rich, chocolate brown. His hair was slightly long, black, and was wavy on the ends. It was styled away from his face and gave him a polished but roguish look that was very appealing.

"Hello, Ms. Steele. I am Rico Cordova. Regretfully, we haven't had the pleasure of meeting in person before now. I apologize for the circumstances of our meeting, but I'm afraid there was no other choice." His choice of words was meant to reassure her, while the tenor of his silky-smooth Latino accent was intentionally intimate.

"You could've just invited me up for drinks," Chaise cooed in response. "This suite is amazing, and the company is infinitely better than what I had before you whisked me away from my hotel."

Rico smiled at her attempt to flirt with him. "I'm afraid that wouldn't have worked, Ms. Steele. I couldn't risk you declining my offer. I'm not so sure you would've accepted my invitation. So, here we are—together at last, as they say."

"You seem to have me at quite a disadvantage. I'm still in my bathrobe. I hardly think that's the appropriate apparel for any type of meeting," Chaise quipped.

"My men have brought your clothes. You may change if that makes you more comfortable. But I'm afraid you'll have to stay with me for quite a while now, Ms. Steele. You have been a tad too thorough in your research at Viboro Distributing," Rico explained. His voice was even and soothing but held the undercurrent of inherent danger and unmistakable warnings.

Chills ran down her spine, her heart palpitations increased, and she was breathing so fast she was sure she would hyperventilate. He was telling her, in his polite and inviting voice, she would never be free again. The panic attack that she had staved off earlier in the evening now threatened to rear its ugly head with full force.

Swallowing down her fear and anger, she met his gaze with hers. "I'm afraid that's not an option, Mr. Cordova. I have a previous engagement that I can't break. We can finish our conversation here and I will take my things back to my own suite at the hotel." She tried to project self-confidence and courage, but she was sure she had failed miserably.

Rico laughed and showed his genuine amusement. "You know, Ms. Steele, I believe we could've been good friends under different circumstances. Alas, it was not meant to be."

With a flick of his eyes, the two goons who had snatched her from her room picked her up and carried her screaming into the adjoining room. They left her with instructions to get dressed or go naked, but one way or another, she would leave the hotel with Mr. Cordova.

When they left, Chaise quickly dressed and searched through her things for her cell phone. It was missing, of course. They hadn't reached the pinnacle of the underworld organized crime ring by making careless mistakes like leaving their captives with a way to call for help.

Within minutes, someone knocked on the door and then quickly opened it without waiting for her to answer. "Ah, good. You decided to go with clothes rather than without. Less attention is drawn to us that way," Rico teased.

Chaise was not amused.

The two goons escorted Chaise out of the suite and down the back stairway. There were several flights of stairs to navigate, but Rico seemed to exert no effort. The limousine was waiting in front of the hotel and Chaise was promptly escorted into the backseat.

As they drove off, she wondered if she would ever see anyone she knew again. The thoughts of the last words she spoke to her brother rang through her head like a persistent echo. The regret of not settling the unresolved issues with Bull weighed heavily on her heart.

Chaise had been more than tipsy when Bull called her earlier. She had thought about simply hanging up on him but there was something in his voice that stopped her. Desperation. Hope. Love?

Truthfully, she had hoped Bull was the one who knocked on her door, waiting to see her, longing to hold her, and eager to make amends. But when the door flew toward her, she quickly sobered, knowing the very people she'd hidden from had found her within hours.

If only I hadn't left Bull's house in Alabama, she mused. *Although, they didn't exactly give me a choice.*

The limousine slowed to a stop in an area a posh stretch limousine had no business in. Chaise struggled to identify a familiar landmark, anything she'd seen before or could commit to memory to describe her location. But the surrounding buildings blended into one unremarkable locale. From the outside, the large, metal-gray warehouse appeared to be abandoned and in disrepair, a description that fit every other structure within sight. The driver pressed the button on the remote and the solid metal door began to move, sliding open only enough to allow the car to enter before closing again and locking them inside.

The interior section of the warehouse Chaise was in looked like a simple car garage. There were a several other cars parked inside, no doubt to hide their presence from prying eyes, but they were empty and appeared to have been there for some time. The dust had settled around them, leaving only the area underneath the cars untouched. An inner wall had been constructed to hide the contents of the rest of the warehouse. A single metal door connecting the two sections was in the far corner. Other than that, the room was intentionally nondescript.

The door opened and several more burly, scary men walked into the garage area. They escorted Chaise into the back area, purposely keeping her feet moving and her field of vision obscured by their presence. There were workmen milling about the area, putting up iron bars along one wall. The buzzing of machines and arcing of electricity echoed throughout the room with each metal bar they welded in place.

They were building a small prison inside the warehouse. The entire wall was being lined with prison cells, complete with locking doors.

The stench emanating from the dark, musty warehouse was putrid. She covered her nose and mouth and tried to regulate her breathing as much as she could. Chaise fought back the bile that attempted to rise in her throat—from both the smell and from the fear that was taking hold of her senses.

She heard sniffling and whimpers coming from the dark corner. She strained her eyes to see what she was walking into and gasped audibly when she made out the shapes. A sparsely furnished, makeshift cell had been constructed in the corner. The sounds came from any one of the numerous young girls who was crammed into the small space.

As she got closer, she immediately realized they were dirty and appeared to be barely fed. The stench that permeated the air seemed to emanate from their bathroom. The bathroom, which she quickly amended, was in reality only a five-gallon bucket that had been haphazardly placed in the corner of the cell. Chaise's stomach roiled at the thought of what the destitute young girls had suffered at hands of the monsters who held them against their wills.

As she passed by their cell, she mentally noted how the girls barely glanced up at her. Their will to live was almost gone and their fight to get out had long since vanished. Not one even tried to ask her for help. Chaise bit back the tears that stung the back of her eyes. She knew she had to keep her wits about her to have any chance of getting out of her own situation, much less in helping anyone else.

The men escorted her out the back door of the warehouse and onto a rickety old pier. The brackish water lapped at the sides of the waiting boat. An ominous feeling about the impending trip covered Chaise like a wet, thick blanket of fear. At least while she was on land, she believed she had a fighting chance to escape. She could run, hide, scream for help, and in Miami, someone was always within earshot.

But out on the open ocean, she would never be found or heard.

"Where are we going?" She raised her chin in defiance and stopped in her tracks.

The bigger man didn't say anything in response. He simply picked her up and placed her on the boat. He jumped onboard after untying the hitching line and nodded to the other man. The boat's engine revved as the propellers pushed them away from the dock. Chaise kept a cautious eye on the direction in which they were headed and made mental notes about landmarks.

After several minutes of traveling toward the horizon, the boat slowed, and Chaise saw their intended destination. A large, luxurious yacht was anchored offshore. The boat she was on idled up to the back boarding platform and two more men secured it with ropes.

Chaise was escorted into the main living quarters. Though riddled with fear, her eyes took in her surroundings and noted the opulence that the criminal underworld enjoyed while she worked hard for every dime she earned. They walked her down the narrow hallway and into the dining area.

The man sitting at the head of the table was no doubt the senior Cordova. He was older, more distinguished with his slightly graying temples and crinkle lines around his eyes, but there was no mistaking the likeness between that man and Rico. Chaise approached the table and when he saw them, he quickly stood, pulled her chair out, and motioned for her to sit with him.

He called for another plate for Chaise as he took his seat. His smile seemed so genuine—the laugh lines around his eyes were evidence of his penchant for smiling. Chaise couldn't reconcile the two men in her head—the kind, thoughtful host and the evil, underground empire ruler. He must have sensed her inner turmoil as his face took on a self-deprecating grin before he spoke.

"Ah, I see you have perhaps heard of me, no?" His Spanish accent was thicker than Rico's, but it fit him perfectly. He had thick, black hair with small speckling of gray scattered throughout. His eyes were almost black, and his skin was a beautiful shade of brown. He was most definitely a handsome older man.

"You must be related to Rico Cordova. He bears a striking resemblance to you," Chaise answered with a smile. She felt like the worst hypocrite, having food and drinks with the man who had effectively kidnapped her, but she thought this was her best chance at escaping. She needed to keep her enemies as close as possible.

"You are very kind to avoid offending me by assuming he is my son," he said with a smile. "Yes, in your culture, I would be known as Ricardo Cordova, Sr. In my country, it would not be so, but that is of no matter. You may call me Ricardo," he explained while pulling her hand to his mouth.

"Thank you, Ricardo. My name is Chaise," she said politely. "I see your son learned his manners from you, as well."

Chaise's plate was placed in front of her, along with a glass of water and a glass of wine. After drinking two bottles of wine earlier, she really didn't want more but she wouldn't rudely refuse him while she was still in his good graces.

"This looks delicious," she said while picking up her fork. The waiter took her linen napkin and placed it on her lap. Chaise nodded graciously at him and took a bite of her food. "Mmm—I love this! My compliments to the chef!"

Ricardo and Chaise finished their light meal with companionable discussions, though each intentionally avoided the subject of why she was there, for how long, or if she would ever be free again. Ricardo walked Chaise to the sitting area on the middle deck of his luxury yacht. The waiter brought their drinks out then left them alone.

"Chaise, I know you're curious about why you're here with me," Ricardo said, his voice maintaining his friendly host tone. "There are certain parts of my business I can't say I'm proud of running, but those components are a necessity in our world. You have stumbled into one such part of my business, unfortunately.

"This saddens me because I have truly enjoyed your company. I'm afraid we must part ways now, Miss Chaise. I had to meet you first, though, because you are truly one intelligent lady. It has been my pleasure," Ricardo stated.

"I don't understand what you mean. I haven't stumbled across anything." She hedged her bets by lying, but she had to take every opportunity to stall. She knew she had found something significant from the beginning, but she didn't know all the details of the operations. The how, the where, and the why were all vital factors, and without those answers, her word wouldn't convict the Cordovas of anything. She hoped to use her ignorance of the key details to her advantage. "I've only found some date discrepancies in your payroll and human resources documentation. That happens in every company. Why would you want to fire me over that?"

"Let's not insult each other's intelligence by pretending we don't both know the answer to your question. Our time together has been far too pleasant to taint it with that kind of ending," he said.

Two of his men appeared and pulled her up to standing. "Goodnight, Miss Chaise," he called as the men walked her back to the waiting speedboat.

***

THE CUTTER APPROACHED the tanker with Bull and Reaper pacing nervously back and forth in anticipation. Rebel's friend with the

Coast Guard had come through and they were fast on their way to boarding the other vessel. Bull's hands were locked in a permanent fist, and they were ready to pound the first man he came upon.

"No one but Coast Guard personnel leaves this cutter. Is that understood? We do this by the book, or we won't do it at all," Commander Harper ordered.

All the men answered affirmatively except Bull. Commander Harper gave him a pointed look, raised his eyebrows, and waited for an answer. Bull huffed and reluctantly nodded his head.

"But if she's on there, you get her off that ship before you do anything else," Bull commanded.

"You have my word," Harper replied.

The cutter slowed and a small motorboat full of men who would conduct a thorough search of the vessel was lowered into the water. Bull and Reaper watched intently as the men boarded. Bull snatched up a pair of binoculars, intent on searching for Chaise in any way that he could.

When he caught one of the men in his sights, he stopped on him and examined his face. The man appeared to be looking directly at him with a shit-eating smirk on his face. He was mocking them and laughing at them for wasting their time searching for her. He was helping waste time by not volunteering any information.

"Motherfucker!" Bull yelled loudly.

"What is it, Bull?" Reaper asked.

"She's not here. The whole crew is too calm and collected. The one guy on deck is pointing over here and laughing. They're making us waste our time because they've taken her somewhere else," he explained. "This has all been set up as a decoy."

"You don't know that," Commander Harper countered. "Now that we're here, we will conduct a thorough search and if anything turns up, we will haul them in."

Bull shook his head. He knew a decoy when he saw one. He knew they'd been duped, and the search of a tanker would take hours. He was stranded in the ocean on a cutter with no other way to get back to shore. He was positive he would have a stroke before he was able to get back to land.

Three hours later, the search of the tanker was concluded with the exact results Bull had predicted—Chaise wasn't onboard. They'd wasted all that time on a wild goose chase, and he was no closer to finding her than he was when he left shore. He stood on deck, feeling the wind whipping through his clothes, as he imagined how frightened she must be.

As soon as he was back on land, he stalked off while Rebel and Reaper thanked Commander Harper for his help. Bull held his cell phone in his hand and was conflicted on whether he should contact his father yet.

Even that thought alone was foreign to him. Contacting his father had never been an option before. He thought about all the strange turns his life had taken over the past several weeks. How his ties to Reaper led to his ties to Chaise and ultimately led him to his ties to his father. As a man who didn't believe in coincidences, he knew there was a higher power at work, bringing them all together at this stage of his life. He had to believe it would all work out in the end.

Putting his phone away, he decided he couldn't contact John just yet. He didn't want to chance blowing his cover and losing Chaise for good. He racked his brain, trying to decide the next move they should make. The idea struck him like lightning, and he grabbed his phone up again.

"Brad, it's Bull. I need you to pull a list of every piece of property the Cordovas own in Miami. Send that to us ASAP. Thanks, man," Bull said, ending the call and turning to his brothers.

"Brad is pulling the Cordova owned properties in Miami. She's here, Reap. They haven't taken her away yet. We have to find where they're keeping her," Bull explained.

"Sounds like a good plan to start. Let's see what Brad comes up with in his research. If there are too many, we can call in more men, divide them up and save some time," Reaper said. The stress and concern were infused in his voice, though he tried to maintain his edge and remain the fearless leader.

Bull's phone pinged with the incoming text from Brad. "There are twelve warehouses and two estates. The warehouses are all relatively close, but the two houses are pretty far away from each other," he relayed.

"Let's get to the office and get our gear. I'll call in Blake and Roman for additional recon help on the way there. We'll get our game plan together so that we're all on the same page," Reaper directed. "We need a coordinated front to make this work. We have no idea how many men Cordova has."

Bull agreed even though it was killing him to wait another minute. He wanted to storm in with guns blazing and take Chaise from wherever it was they had her hidden. He knew Noah was right —without a plan of attack, they would unwittingly put Chaise in more danger. He just hoped that she was being held in one of the known Cordova properties.

If not, Bull didn't know where else to look. He only knew that he would never give up searching for her or for the men responsible for taking her away from him. There was no explanation for how she had invaded his thoughts, his life, and his heart in such a short time. Bull only realized that he had strong feelings for Chaise, and he couldn't let her go.

He would've looked for her just because he was a good man, he was good at his job, and he had a duty to act. His heart, however, was more than involved in the case. It ruled him, it ruled his decisions, and it ruled his actions. A soft, loving woman turned the tough, stoic man inside out in a matter of days. It defied logic and reason but it was no less true.

They drove to the main Steele Security headquarters to change clothes and gather all the gear they'd need for an incursion. They dressed in all black and donned a variety of weapons in numerous locations throughout their attire. They spread out a map of the city on the table in front of them as\ they pinpointed the location of each warehouse and the private homes Brad had found.

The identical warehouses were spaced evenly apart, as expected, and in an old rundown section on the outskirts of Miami. One of the houses was in a completely unexpected area, however, and surprised glances were exchanged all around. The first house was in Key Biscayne, an influential island town that was connected to Miami by a bridge. While it was large enough to house guests held against their will, the proximity of the other houses on the island made the chances of it being the one they were looking for highly unlikely.

The second house owned by the Cordova family was on Seychelles Island, a small barrier island off the coast of South Beach that could only be accessed by boat or helicopter. Satellite images showed a single large home and several smaller structures scattered across the landscape. A sole dock extended into the shallow waters immediately offshore, and a helicopter pad sat squarely behind the main house, ensuring no one could land undetected. Bull and Reaper exchanged concerned looks. Any rescue attempt from that island would be very tricky with such limited access points.

"One step at a time, Bull. Let's check these warehouses first. The helicopter was a decoy, so there's a strong possibility she's still on the mainland." Reaper attempted to console his friend while bolstering his own confidence at the same time.

Looking around at the five men, Reaper continued with his pre-invasion instructions. "We'll split up and check every warehouse. If you find her," he stopped and pierced Bull with his gaze, "*do not engage* without all of us there unless you have no other choice. Understood?"

Four of the five men responded affirmatively. Reaper cleared his throat and waited for Bull to respond. "Understood," he finally answered, but his voice lacked conviction. Reaper shook his head, knowing it was a fruitless exercise to argue with him at that point. Bull's nickname may have been originally given to him because of his size, but it also described his personality.

Once they had parked in a covered garage, they moved on foot toward the warehouses. They were all heavily armed and experienced in covert operations. The urban warfare maneuver would be a walk in the park compared to the dangers the team had collectively faced.

The Cordovas had just created an enemy they could have never imagined, even in their worst nightmares. Bull parted from his friends to conduct his search of his two assigned warehouses for any signs of Chaise. His stride was swift and confident, and his determination was set in the hardness of his eyes.

After he rescued Chaise, he would unleash hell at the Cordovas' front door.

19

CHAPTER NINETEEN

haise was taken back to the warehouse and put in the small, crowded cell with the younger girls. Many of them looked emaciated and almost lifeless. Their eyes were dull, and their stares were vacant. Chaise had a strong suspicion that they were drugged to keep them compliant.

As she stepped over the bodies strewn across the floor, trying to avoid stepping on anyone while she looked for an empty space, she saw a familiar face. Her breath caught in her chest and her mouth gaped open. Tears sprung to her eyes, and she stumbled to reach the sleeping girl in the corner.

She quickly swallowed the ball of emotions in her throat that threated to overcome her. "Aura! Aura!"

The girl slowly opened her eyes and tried to force them to focus on the shadowy figure moving toward her. She heard the name Aura being called but she thought she had been dreaming. She had been in that shit hole for so long, she was beginning to forget what life outside it was like.

"What did you call me?" The girl visibly struggled to rouse from the exhaustion threatening to swallow her, but the shadowy figure calling her name finally came into focus.

"Aura, it's me, Chaise." She knelt beside the young girl, gingerly wrapping her fingers around the girl's gaunt arm.

Chaise had suddenly forgotten the stench and the filthy conditions of the cell. All she could focus on at the moment was the fact that Aura was in front of her. She was just so relieved that Aura was still alive.

"I'm not Aura," the girl replied weakly. "I'm Ana. Aura is my twin sister." A single tear escaped from her eye. From the looks of her, she was so dehydrated and malnourished, she didn't have many tears left in her to cry.

"Ana? Twin sister?" Chaise was repeating the words, but they hadn't quite sunk in yet. "If you're Ana, then where is Aura? Have you seen her?"

"No. Oh God, I hope they didn't get my sister." Ana's face contorted in pain, as if her heart were breaking in two and she wanted to sob. But no tears would flow, and she made no sounds as she curled into a fetal position.

Chaise easily lifted the girl's head and shoulders off the cold, concrete floor and slid her over until her upper body rested in Chaise's lap. As Chaise laid her back down across her legs, sharing the heat of her body to help warm the frail young girl, Ana's small hand grabbed Chaise's and held on as tightly as she could muster. Chaise stroked her dirty, matted hair as she uttered words of comfort.

"I'm sure she's fine, Ana. If she isn't here, she's probably hiding somewhere," Chaise reasoned. She was beginning to get a good idea of why Aura was so adamant to help with the research at Viboro Distributing.

Leaning forward as far as she could, Chaise whispered to Ana. "Did you work at Viboro?"

Ana simply nodded her head 'yes.' In that simple gesture, Ana confirmed exactly what Chaise thought was happening. They would hire young, attractive Latino women and then abduct them for their own nefarious plans. Chaise's thoughts then strayed to Aura and how responsible she'd felt for Aura's disappearance.

The young girl was trying to save her twin sister, Ana, whom she loved and missed. The poor girl who was lying in Chaise's lap, sound asleep, had obviously been mistreated and abused at the hands of her captors. Chaise wanted to ask Ana more questions but didn't have the heart to wake her again.

Chaise leaned her head back against the metal bars and fought back the panic attack festering just under the surface. The situation on the whole was too much to handle at once. She started breaking it down into bite-size chunks so she could deal with one issue at a time.

The first issue, obviously, was that she had been kidnapped and no one knew where she was. That thought alone threatened her last thread of sanity. A fleeting memory took root in her mind, and it suddenly calmed her and filled her with a sense of peace. Her thoughts created a temporary refuge from her reality.

Bull had called her hotel room phone just before they knocked on her door and eventually busted it down. He knew where she was, and he knew that she'd been taken. He wouldn't stop until he found her. Bull wouldn't leave her there. His internal code of never leaving a man behind wouldn't allow him to walk away from this situation.

Thoughts of Bull simultaneously broke her heart and gave her strength. Regret filled her over the way they parted, the way he found out who she was, and especially that she walked away from his house without forcing him to hear her side of the story first. The betrayal from Noah stung deeply, and his accusations stunned her into silence. But the thought of Bull believing those lies about her stole her breath.

In her drunken stupor on the phone with him, she had secretly wanted to punish him for rejecting her in front of everyone. She thought they had moved past that stage of their relationship when he relented and let her touch him while they made love. Thinking she had gotten through to him in a way that no one ever had before, she wanted to be *the one* for him—like she felt he was for her.

Suddenly, she realized the deeper meaning of his call. First, he was back in Miami and had searched until he found her. Secondly, his tone of voice was a mixture of relief and regret. That told her he still cared about her and that there may still be a chance for them to salvage their budding relationship from the mistakes they'd both made. And third, it gave her even more reason to fight, to live, and to escape the situation with as many of the girls as she could take with her.

Chaise realized she must have fallen asleep at some point. She was already completely exhausted by the time she reached her hotel room, and several more hours had passed since then. The adrenaline dump after being "escorted" to Rico's room and then Ricardo's yacht had her running on all cylinders for several hours. When she crashed, she did so sitting on the uncomfortable concrete floor, leaned against the hard iron bars, with a scared, young girl in her lap.

Her legs were asleep, and the painful pin-prickling sensation ran through them like lightning bolts. Her back and neck ached, and her backside had moved past numb into almost excruciating pain. From the small holes near the ceiling, she could tell it was still dark outside. The approaching male voices awakened her and put her nerves on high alert.

Chaise turned her head to the side to get a glimpse at who was approaching. She tried to hide her surprise when she saw a familiar face. It was one of the men who had shot at her and Bull in the parking lot. A glimmer of hope began to bloom in her chest. One of those men was Bull's father. He was there with the Cordova family members, walking with the men who had taken her from her room and talking to them like he was one of them.

When he looked at the girls in the cell, his face registered no emotion. She knew if what Michelle had said was true, then John was trained to keep his emotions locked away deep inside where they wouldn't blow his cover. His eyes raked over the bodies in the cell until they met Chaise's eyes.

The flash of recognition and concern was so quickly masked that Chaise would've missed it had she not specifically been watching for it. She didn't know if John could get word to Bull fast enough to help her. He wouldn't blow his entire case just for her safety, but maybe he could find a way to help.

"We need one of these *putas* to make a run before daylight. We have to make a stop by Rico's house, too," the tall, thin thug told John in his thick Spanish accent. Together, they walked to the cell to choose who would go out next.

"Diego, these girls look bad. Are you feeding them, man?" John asked.

"They eat sometimes," Diego replied nonchalantly. He opened the door and walked around the cell, not bothering to avoid stepping on anyone who was in his way. He approached Chaise and Ana and kicked Ana with the toe of his boots.

"*Puta*, wake up. It's your turn," he said cruelly.

"She's not a *bitch*," Chaise spat out at him, venom lacing her voice as she spoke. "And she's in no shape to go anywhere. Leave her alone."

Diego smiled at her bravado and then he backhanded her across the cheek. Her head jerked violently to the side, clashing against the metal bars, and sending her toppling over onto her side. Her cheek immediately swelled, and she felt a small bead of blood roll down her face from where his ring cut her skin.

Ana fell to the concrete when Chaise was knocked over. She woke and rubbed the side of her face where it had hit the concrete. Diego kicked her again with his boot and told her to get up. Ana tried to push herself up but couldn't muster the strength to finish her movement.

Chaise jumped up, faced Diego, and took a step toward him to block his access to Ana. "I said she's not going anywhere. I'll go in her place. Just tell me what I need to do."

"Well, aren't you a brave little *puta*? Maybe I should teach you some manners. You need to know who *el jefe* is around here," Diego said with a snide smile.

He started to reach for Chaise when the shorter, but stockier, man's words stopped him cold. "Diego, don't touch her again."

"Okay, Manuel," Diego replied, sounding like a whipped dog. Looking at Chaise with anger and disgust in his eyes, he said, "Follow me."

Diego led her out the door that led to the docks. John and Manuel followed close behind them. Diego, Chaise, and Manuel got into the speedboat. John untied the mooring line and threw it into the boat. Manuel looked up at John and issued his command. "Stay here and watch the girls. We'll be back sometime tomorrow."

John watched until the boat disappeared into the blackness hovering over the ocean. He had to find some way to contact Colton and let him know he'd seen Chaise. He needed a way that wouldn't call attention to him and blow his cover before he was ready to close the case. There were still questions that had to be answered and people who had to be arrested before he could walk away.

The deplorable conditions the girls were left in turned John's stomach. He could easily take the men out and turn the girls loose, but that wouldn't give him what he needed to stop the Cordova family from doing it again somewhere else. His rationalization weighed heavily on his conscience, and he couldn't wait to retire from the insidious underworld life.

John had already given up too much in his life under the guise of justice and protecting others. The nagging issue that kept him up at night was the injustice he'd committed toward his own family. He was young and impetuous when he made the decision to leave for the sake of his wife and son.

Looking back, he decided if he could do it all over again, he never would've left them. He would've built his life around them instead of chasing the whims of a young man, bent on intrigue and adrenaline. As soon as the present case was finished, he resolved to retire and move back home to Alabama with his wife. If Michelle wanted, they could even move to Miami and be close to Bull. One way or another, the case had to wrap-up soon because John wasn't sure how much more he could take.

As he looked at the pitiful creatures in the cell, part of him rejoiced that he had moved up in the Cordova ranks. Another part railed against himself for being such a good undercover agent that he could pull it off. Unable to stand it any longer, he brought the girls food and water from the kitchen. Though he may face repercussions from his cohorts later, he couldn't pretend he didn't see their pain and suffering. With any luck, Chaise's connection to the case would help bring it to a close sooner than he could alone.

John's entire purpose behind going with Diego and Manuel was to keep an eye on Chaise, even though that very act put his life in more danger than usual. The conflict he felt when strangers were involved was a heavy enough burden. But playing the part when someone so dear to Bull was in the middle muddied the waters where his duty to his country and his duty to his son were concerned. Watching them take Chaise away was one of the hardest things he'd had to do as an agent—right behind leaving his family.

His inner turmoil boiled down to one question. *Will Colton ever forgive me?*

***

BULL MOVED around the darkened warehouse and instinctively knew it was empty. The dust covered the floor was untouched. Cobwebs stretched from the long fluorescent lights above to the metal walls. Discarded cardboard boxes littered the floor. That wasn't the location where they were holding Chaise, but he could see the Viboro Distributing label on boxes still stacked on pallets. Rows and rows of boxes reaching almost twelve feet high lined the interior of the rundown building. No reputable company would use such dilapidated buildings.

That made him want to know what was inside those boxes even more. Every bit of intelligence he could collect on the Cordova empire would help solve one more piece of the puzzle. Anything that helped him locate Chaise was worth whatever he had to do. Bull crept inside, keeping low and in the shadows, until he had cased the entire inner perimeter and verified no one was there.

All the boxes were exactly the same height, width, and depth. Bull opened one of them and removed a wooden box with a hinged lid. It was marked with the *Blue Cypress Casino* logo on the top. Bull opened the lid and stared at the casino chips inside. They appeared to be genuine, high-quality clay chips that were used by the higher-end casinos.

Bull picked up one of the multi-colored chips and immediately noticed the weight was wrong. He closed his fist around it, squeezed with minimal pressure, and felt it collapse under his grip. Underneath the colored outer shell, a white, powdery substance crumbled in his hand. He looked around again at the rows and rows of boxes that were ready to be shipped. He walked through the warehouse, looking at the shipping labels, and noted they were being sent to casinos across the country.

"Holy shit," he uttered under his breath in disbelief.

He unpacked one package and counted twenty wooden boxes. Each wooden box contained one thousand chips. The amount of illegal drugs passing through just one warehouse was staggering.

Bull took pictures with his phone, capturing the names and addresses on the shipping labels. He also snapped pictures of the contents and the compressed, white powder inside the chips. He rushed back the way he entered and on to his next destination as he continued his search for Chaise.

The next warehouse search was fruitless. It obviously hadn't been used in quite some time. Dust and dirt covered everything, with no tracks or anything else to indicate anyone had been there in months. "That explains why they have so many warehouses," he said aloud to himself. "They're alternating between them to avoid getting caught."

Bull texted the others to let them know his search was complete and there was no sign of Chaise in either of his warehouses. Within a few seconds, he received texts back from all the others relaying the same information, except one. Receiving no response from Shadow, he decided that was where he needed to go next.

As he silently walked through the darkened streets, he heard voices coming from behind one of the vacant buildings. He slowed his pace and listened for any sign his position had been revealed. The number of voices increased, and he was able to identify six distinct voices. They were speaking in Spanish and talking about the beautiful new Cordova girl.

"Jorge, you think she'd want you, *ese*? You're crazy, man!"

"Yeah, Marco, she is hot! She'd definitely pick me over you, homes."

"You two losers don't have to worry about it. Manuel already ordered everyone to stay away from *Senorita Chaise*. If I catch you near her, I'll cut your dick off myself." An older voice cut into the conversation, chastising the younger boys with both his tone and threat.

"We were just fucking around, man," Jorge responded, clearly offended that he had been put in his place.

The voices trailed off, so Bull moved into position to follow them. They had no clue he was close behind them, monitoring their moves and waiting for them to take him to Chaise. He listened to their boasting from the shadows and gave them all the rope they needed to hang themselves at the end of the line.

Bull sensed a change in the air, a sudden spark of energy, and the distinct feeling of being watched. He skirted around the corner of the building, still hidden in the shadows, and silently unsheathed his knife. Holding it firmly in his grasp, he readied himself for the man moving along the side of the building toward him.

When the other man reached the corner, Bull's arm flew up in a split second and stopped just short of the man's neck. "Shadow, what have I told you about sneaking up on me?"

Shadow's deep chuckle rumbled through his chest, "Are you getting rusty in your old age? The Bull I knew would've known the very second I moved into his range."

"Fuck you, man. Old my ass—I made you as soon as you stepped on my block," Bull said with a smile.

Shadow's tone became serious as he replied. "Come with me. They've taken Chaise to Rico's house. I couldn't get to the boat before they left. John is at the warehouse with the other girls."

Bull's blood turned to lava in his veins at just the thought of what Rico planned to do to Chaise. "Lead the way," he responded.

Shadow and Bull jogged to the waterfront warehouse where they'd held Chaise. Bull swore under his breath when he saw the girls locked up in the cell. Looking at his father, Bull asked, "You're just going to leave them in there?"

"I have no choice until I can close this case and bust the Cordova family," John answered. "I have to figure out their trade route so I can shut them down or they will just go somewhere else and start this all over again."

"This ends *tonight*, one way or another," Bull responded. "I'm not leaving here without Chaise."

John walked over to the cell and asked one of the girls to follow him. She eyed him wearily, but she did as he asked. Once he had her out of earshot of the others, John and Rebel sat down with her to decipher Cordova's plans.

"What's your name, sweetheart?" Rebel asked in a calm, reassuring tone.

"Consuela," she answered meekly.

"Consuela, my name is Rebel. I won't hurt you. I promise. I'm here to help you. Can you tell us what's going on here? Why do they have you locked up in here with these other girls?"

Her eyes darted between Rebel and John and then over to the other men who were waiting a few feet away. "They send us to their contacts in other countries to pick up the drugs for them. We bring them back here and I don't know what they do with them after that."

"So, they're using you as mules. That way they won't get caught trafficking," John stated. "How do they send you?"

"In the bottom of a big, dirty ship. The men on the ship are mean, too," Consuela replied with sadness permeating her voice. "Once the ship reaches US waters, it stops. We have to take the drugs the rest of the way in a small boat. It is very dangerous with the waves and the weather. They tell us if we don't come back, they will kill our families.

"And, sometimes, we take the small boats far out into the ocean and meet another boat that looks like a submarine with a snorkel sticking up. They throw the packages in the water for us to get," she finished explaining.

"How do you know where to go?" John asked.

"The boat has a GPS device that shows us where to go. The men put the information in it and then send us out. We just follow the direction it shows."

"Do you know what kind of drugs they are sending you to pick up?" Rebel asked.

"Sometimes it's meth, but usually it's heroin. I've heard the men talking about it," she answered. "They have radios, and someone calls out a bunch of numbers. Every time we hear that, we know they're about to send one of us out."

John looked up at Rebel. "Now we know where they're getting the coordinates to put in the GPS. If we can get one of the radios, we can monitor it and be there to trap them."

"Diego left his radio. He forgot about it after he hit the pretty lady," Consuela said as she pointed to a radio that sat on a shelf littered with garbage.

Her statement immediately caught Bull and Reaper's attention. Bull walked over to where they sat, turned a chair around, and straddled it. He smiled at Consuela as he asked, "What did the pretty lady look like, sweetheart?"

"She had long black hair, pretty green eyes, and she was so nice. She saw Ana and thought she was Aura, her twin sister." She pointed to Ana. "She helped Ana when Diego was being mean. She took Ana's place for the run tonight."

"She took her place?" Rebel asked.

"Yes. But I heard Manuel say they are going to *Rico's* house first. That is not good," Consuela said.

"Why is that not good?" Bull asked.

"The girls who are taken to Rico's never come back," she whispered, as if she thought he would appear just by mentioning his name. Her eyes were wide with fear and her bottom lip trembled with the thoughts of what Rico would do with Chaise.

Bull swallowed hard to keep his thoughts and feelings under control. He didn't want to frighten the poor girl with his tirade, but he was going to kill the men who took Chaise. Every one of them would soon face him and he vowed to be the last person they would ever see.

CHAPTER TWENTY

The boat slowed in the blackness of the night and Chaise sat up straighter, trying to get her bearings on where she was. Diego was at the helm and Manuel sat beside him. They put Chaise in the back of the boat so she couldn't see the modified GPS or hear what they were saying over the engines.

As the boat came to a stop, she thought she saw something approaching from the right. There was something sticking up out of the water, but her eyes could not make out the form in the darkness surrounding them. Diego pulled out a spotlight and shone it across the water just as a small, semi-submersible watercraft fully surfaced.

The pipe sticking up out of the water acted as a waterproof snorkel for the craft that allowed air in, but a special valve kept the water out. The top hatch opened, and a man threw several large packages out into the water. The packages were strung together with a thick cord and floated in the water between the two vessels.

Diego turned to Chaise and snidely ordered her. "Go get them, *puta*. I hope you can swim."

When Chaise didn't move, Diego pulled his gun and leveled it at her. "*Ahora*." *Now*.

Chaise stepped up on the side of the boat and dove into the deep, black water. She quickly swam to the packages, grabbed the cord, and towed it back to the boat. Manuel reached down and took the cord from her hand and pulled the packages into the boat.

"Get back in the boat or drown out here, *puta*. Your choice," Diego taunted.

Manuel shot Diego a look that made him sit back down and look away. "You know we have orders to take her to Rico, Diego," Manuel chastised.

Looking at Chaise, Manuel commanded her. "Get back in the boat."

Chaise swam to the back of the boat and hauled her body out of the water onto the small platform. Once she was back in her seat, Diego gunned the engines, and they took off across the choppy waters. Chaise noticed the winds picking up and the waves getting higher. It was the middle of hurricane season in Florida and apparently another storm was brewing in the Atlantic Ocean.

Diego kept the bow straight to run headlong into the waves so the boat wouldn't capsize as the wave height increased. The noise from the boat's engines, the whipping wind, and the splashing waves made it nearly impossible to hear anyone speak. Chaise could see Diego and Manuel talking but couldn't hear most of what they were saying. When she made out part of Manuel's sentence, her heart dropped to her knees. Even though she was wet, and the night wind was cool against her skin, she broke out into a cold sweat from her fear.

Manuel had just told Diego that they were to kill Chaise when Rico was finished with her. She knew they were taking her to Rico, but she had no idea what he planned to do with her. She only knew she wasn't going to stick around and find out. While they were busy battling the wind and waves to keep the boat straight, Chaise eased up to sit on the back of her seat.

When a high wave rolled underneath them, Chaise leaned back and intentionally fell off the side of the boat. She let the surge of the wave propel her forward as she swam as hard as she could away from the boat and her captors. She knew there were other barrier islands that were close to Seychelles Island. She just hoped she was going in the right direction.

The sheer terror of being out in the open ocean at night was enough to render her immobile but the threat of being caught and tortured overtook her. She swam harder and faster until her foot brushed against the sandy bottom. Breathing hard, she slugged through the breaking waves until she reached the beach. She fell flat on her stomach, exhausted from the exertion and the nearly debilitating fear. Within moments, she had passed out from the toll swimming in the rough seas had taken on her.

The sound of a speedboat engine woke Chaise from her slumber. She pushed up to a sitting position and tentatively looked around to get her bearings. She was momentarily lost until she remembered she swam up on the beach to escape Diego and Manuel. The sound of the motorboat caught her attention and she scrambled behind the cover of the vegetation behind her.

As the boat passed by, she recognized the outline of Bull as he stood in the middle of the boat. He was with several other men, and they were headed toward several lights that appeared to be just across the channel from her. From the look of the area, she decided she was on Lauren Key, and they were going to Seychelles Island.

From the northwest tip of the barrier island, it was only about a hundred yards across the channel. She was exhausted, not thinking clearly, and only wanted to reach Bull. She jogged along the shoreline until she reached the island point then swam across the channel on pure adrenaline.

In the distance, she could see the boat coasting to the shore. They had obviously cut the engines before they got too close. Chaise started to run toward them when she was suddenly grabbed from behind and yanked backward. A menacing voice growled in her ear.

"You caused me a lot of trouble tonight, *puta*."

Diego twirled her around to face him. The sound of his hand hitting her cheek made a loud *thwack* and sent her flying to the ground. She grabbed her already bruised cheek and cried out in pain. He yanked her up by her hair and then dragged her behind him.

When she stumbled, her hair was painfully yanked by his tight grip. Diego turned and kicked her several times in the back and legs while telling her to get up. She struggled back to her feet as he grabbed her upper arm to push her toward a mansion that was partially hidden by the beach foliage.

When they reached the door, Diego shoved her up against it as he ground his erection into her abdomen. "You are mine now, *puta*," he hissed in her ear. Chaise fought against his hold, pushing him with all her might. He stumbled back a step or two but was instantly back against her with even more force. She was just about to scream when she heard a familiar voice.

"Diego, what the fuck do you think you're doing?" Rico asked coolly.

Diego quickly jumped away from Chaise to put distance between them, but he knew he'd been caught. He looked down at the ground in shame and embarrassment. He didn't dare try to give Rico a lame excuse, so he kept quiet.

Rico looked at Chaise and his face registered his surprise. His eyes grew wide at first and then narrowed as he inspected the damage to her face. "Who did this to you, *mi amor*?" Rico gently eased his hand across the angry bruise and swelling on her cheek.

His fingers brushed down her arm and stopped at the bruises in the shape of fingers that were forming on her upper arm. His eyes narrowed more but he said nothing as he continued his perusal of her body. Rico took Chaise's hand in his and gently twirled her around to find the bruises beginning on the back of her legs. He lifted her shirt just enough to see the marks on her back from Diego's kicks.

As he turned Chaise back around to fully face him, his voice was calm and reassuring as he spoke to her. "Chaise, I'm very sorry for the way Diego has treated you. I promise you, *mi amor*, he will never touch you again."

Before Chaise could respond, Rico drew his gun from its holster and shot Diego in the head point blank.

Rico didn't bother to look at Diego as his body fell limp onto the lanai. Chaise screamed and backed away from Rico in shock. "Shhh, *mi amor*, I said he would never touch you again and I meant it. Come inside with me." He took her hand in his and forced her inside his beachfront mansion.

"You've been very hard to keep up with, Chaise. If I didn't know better, I would think you've been intentionally avoiding me." Rico continued flirting with her as he led her to a beautifully adorned kitchen. He stopped at a large island with bar stools and motioned for her to sit.

"What do you want with me?" Chaise asked with more courage than she felt.

"You will be my consort for the foreseeable future. I've chosen you and you should feel honored," Rico explained. His tone of voice indicated she should be happy about his decision as his eyes held a glimmer of insanity mixed with pure evil.

Chaise shook involuntarily as a shudder ran down her spine. Just the thought of him touching her turned her stomach and made her long for Bull even more. She had to keep Rico talking for two reasons: to keep his hands off her and to give Bull more time to storm the house.

She knew Bull and Noah were outside somewhere, along with several other linebacker-sized men. She could picture them drawing a map in the sand to plan their attack. Stalling sounded like her best option since Rico had already shown how fast he was with his gun.

"What does being your consort entail?" she asked, feigning interest.

He smiled warmly at her, and she had the fleeting thought that he was pleased with her question, as if he believed this is what she wanted. "Anything and everything that pleases me, Chaise. Don't worry—I will make sure you are pleased as well. But first, we need to get you out of those dirty, wet clothes and into something more suitable."

Pulling her up from her seat, he led her up the stairs and into the guest bedroom. He pulled out a thigh-length, satin nightgown, and matching robe before escorting her to the bathroom. After giving her a towel, he instructed her to shower and dress and then join him in the den. Before he left her alone, he turned and gave her a pointed look before issuing his warning.

"Don't bother trying to run, Chaise. You can't outrun a bullet."

She stayed in the shower as long as she could to stall and give the guys time to put their plans into action. Dressing in the nightgown Rico had given her, she tiptoed into the hall. None of the upstairs lights were on but she saw the glowing light filtering into the foyer below her.

The storm was rolling in stronger than before. The sheets of rain had started coming down, and lightning flashed across the sky. If the thunder rumbling in the distance was any indication, the storm would get much worse before it passed. The wind whipping outside blew the light rain sideways. The raindrops sounded like pebbles tapping against the windows.

As she slowly descended the stairs, she strained her ears to listen for any sounds—voices, movement, or even gunfire—but there were none. Rounding the corner, she saw Rico sitting on a large, sectional sofa with a drink in his hand. He smiled lasciviously at her as he raked his eyes over her body.

"You are so beautiful, Chaise. I think you may be my best choice yet. Come sit with me."

"Your glass is almost empty. Can I refill it for you first?" she asked, trying to buy more time for herself and for her rescuers.

"That would be nice," he said as he extended his arm to hand the glass to her. When her fingers grasped it, he intentionally dragged his fingers across hers and his eyes darkened with desire. Keeping her face neutral as much as she could, she asked what he was drinking.

"Evan Williams Bourbon," he responded as he watched her. "Pour yourself a glass as well."

Chaise turned toward the bar that sat to the side of the picture window. As she approached the window, her eyes landed on Bull's who sat crouched outside. He put his finger over his lips, telling her to be quiet, before giving her a single, slow nod. In that gesture, she knew he was telling her everything would be all right.

Chaise poured two drinks and walked back to Rico. Though she knew Bull had probably already moved, she couldn't help but use her body to block Rico's view of the window. She fought to keep her nervous energy under control as she handed Rico his drink. She took a small sip of hers to keep her hands and mouth busy.

Rico's laid his hand on her knee, drew lazy circles on her skin, making each one bigger than the last. His eyes were glued to her legs and where his fingers met her skin. Chaise couldn't keep her breathing under control. Her chest heaved from the ragged breaths she drew in. Rico no doubt thought she was affected in a good way when all she wanted was to claw his eyes out and bleach her skin clean.

The shrill sound of Rico's phone filled the room. Rico looked at the display and it showed a blocked number. His eyes, full of lust, met Chaise's as he apologized. "I'm so sorry, *mi amor*. I said no interruptions tonight. This must be an urgent matter for my father."

Chaise nodded, happy for the interruption. Rico answered the phone and within a minute he suddenly shot to his feet. His face contorted in anger as he started spewing curse words in Spanish. Pacing back and forth, his tirade ended with, "Come get me then, asshole. I'm waiting."

***

BULL WATCHED Chaise walk into the den wearing the flimsy nightgown and robe. His eyes shot to Rico and his hand instantly went to the Glock .40 on his side. Reaper stilled Bull's movements and slowly shook his head from side to side. Bull wanted to kill the man for the blatantly lustful way he looked at Chaise. When she didn't sit down, Bull took a huge risk by letting her see him, but he had to let her know he was there.

He noticed she wasn't overly surprised to see him and kept moving toward the bar as if there was nothing out of the ordinary. The team had already made all their preparations to enter the house and search for Chaise. Seeing her had confirmed their suspicions and made their Plan B go into effect.

That was exactly what Bull wanted.

When Rico put his hand on Chaise's leg and kept moving his fingers up her thigh, Reaper and Shadow had to physically restrain Bull to keep him from going through the window. After they convinced him to stick to the plan, the team moved into position and Bull used the secure phone to call Rico's number.

"You took someone tonight. *She. Belongs. To. Me.* Let her go now and I will *think* about not taking everything in your life away from you." Bull issued his offer to Rico in a low, menacing voice.

Rico's response was to curse at him in Spanish and pace around the room. When Rico told Bull to come and get him, Bull smiled as he replied. "I was hoping you'd say that. You just wait right there for me." Before Rico could answer, Bull disconnected and nodded to the other guys.

This was the part of the job Bull loved the most. The thrill of the covert operations, the excitement of one-upping the bad guys, and the success of a job well done were his rewards. But this time, it was much more personal. It was more than a mission where he followed orders, had his brothers backs, and toasted their success with a simple clink of their beer bottles. This time, his heart was involved and, even though that was foreign territory for Bull, he had to admit he wanted Chaise for himself.

The storm building around them couldn't begin to match the rage that Bull had inside him. He moved into position to cover his assigned area of the house. He still had eyes on Chaise and wouldn't hesitate to take Rico out if he touched her again. Bull smiled to himself, knowing he had effectively killed Rico's libido with his phone call.

Rico was yelling into a two-way radio, calling out several names and demanding they come to the house, but no one was able to answer him. The team of Steele had dispatched of Rico's men on their way to the house. Bull watched as Rico's apprehension rose to astronomical levels and chuckled to himself. While Rico questioned what happened to his personal protection detail, the man had no idea what terrors awaited him.

Whispers through Bull's earpiece told him that all the men were in position and ready to finish what they had started. While Chaise had stalled Rico, the men from Steele Security had already infiltrated the house, disarmed the security system, and made the appropriate adjustments to the house to carry out their plans.

Bull's muscles contracted and he prepared for a fight to the death when he saw Rico snatch Chaise up by her hair and drag her toward the stairs. He angrily whispered into his communication device. "He's hurting Chaise. It's time to move *now*."

Reaper gave the word and each man stealthily moved into the house. Bull rushed in toward the same direction he saw Rico dragging Chaise against her will. Slowing only to check around corners, Bull took the steps two at a time until he reached the landing at the top.

He heard Chaise's screams and his blood turned to ice in his veins. The indestructible destroyer inside him was activated, and only a blood offering would satiate him.

21

CHAPTER TWENTY-ONE

The intense pain and stinging in Chaise's scalp were sudden. Before she realized what was happening, Rico had yanked her from her seat in a fit of anger and was pulling her up the stairs by her hair. She tried to fight back but he only further twisted his hand, increasing the pressure and his grasp.

"He says you belong to *him*. We'll see who you belong to by the time I'm finished with you." The disdain dripped from his words as he spat them out at no one in particular. He was mumbling, swearing under his breath, and spouting various obscenities as he ignored Chaise's cries.

Once inside his bedroom, he tossed her on the bed while he paced back and forth across the floor. As if he suddenly remembered she was there, he stopped and gave her an evil smile. Chaise instinctively scurried backward as he advanced on her. He crawled across the bed, grabbed her by the ankle and roughly pulled her toward him.

Chaise screamed and kicked him repeatedly with her free leg. With all the fear and adrenaline coursing through her veins, she didn't feel any pain as she kicked him with her bare feet and punched him with her fists. Blinded by rage and fueled by fear of what he planned to do to her, she didn't even realize the moment when Rico went flying across the room.

"Chaise, baby, calm down for me." Bull called her name several times, trying to soothe her.

Rico roared as he scrambled back to his feet. He rushed toward Bull and tried to tackle him. Had Bull not been so close to the edge of insanity, he would've laughed at Rico's pitiful attempt to assault him. However, when Bull walked in the bedroom and saw Rico attacking Chaise, and how hard Chaise fought to keep him off her, Bull saw red.

Simply throwing Rico across the room didn't quench his rage. Bull clenched his fists and drew his right hand back. The loud *thwack* of flesh pounding flesh echoed through the room. Chaise seemed to come to her senses and gawked at Bull in amazement.

Rico fell to the ground as his eyes rolled back in his head. Bull was tackled a second time but this time he welcomed it as he felt a soft, female body meld with his. He wrapped his arms around her and kissed the side of her head. He whispered soothing words into her ear, telling her he was there, she was safe, and he would take her away.

When he pulled back and looked at her face, his lips formed a thin line and fire burned in his eyes when he saw the angry bruises on her cheek. He attempted to keep his anger controlled so he didn't appear to be upset with Chaise, but he had to know. "Who. Hit. You?"

"Diego did this," she said, pointing to her face. "Rico shot him."

Bull gently wiped the tears from her eyes and pulled her back to him. She turned her face to the side, pressed her body against his and wrapped her arms around his waist. Just as she hugged him tightly, she caught movement from the corner of her eye.

"Look out!" Chaise screamed.

Bull whirled around and pushed Chaise behind him, using his body as a shield to protect her. Rico had his gun drawn and aimed at Bull. An ugly sneer was plastered on Rico's face as he mocked Bull. "Not so tough now, are you?"

"I'm still as tough as I was when I knocked you on your ass a minute ago," Bull retorted sarcastically.

"Step aside, I want to make sure Chaise has a good view of your death," Rico ordered.

Chaise was hidden behind Bull and stood as close to him as she possibly could. She felt a bulge in the back of his waistband. Bull's arm still held Chaise safely behind him. He felt her careful movements as Chaise eased his shirt up and placed her hand on his gun. The cold steel brushed against his skin as she quickly removed it and placed the butt of it in Bull's hand.

"Whatever you want, man," Bull responded casually. He faked a step to the side, quickly raised his arm and fired two shots in rapid succession. The bullets hit Rico once in the chest and once in the head. His limp body once again hit the floor but there was no way he would get up this time.

Bull pulled Chaise in his arms again and when he finally looked up, he saw his entire team in place. Bull smirked at them. "Thanks for the help, guys."

"You had it under control," Rebel answered with a shit-eating grin.

"Yeah, you *needed* to handle this yourself, man," Reaper replied.

The thunder boomed and the strikes of lightning crackled outside the window. Bull couldn't take his eyes off Chaise—even for the howling wind or horizontal rain beating against the windows.

"We need to get you out of here," Bull said as he pulled the blanket off the bed and wrapped it around her. The flimsy material of her nightgown would look like a second skin on her if she wore it in the rain. Bull wasn't about to share *that* view with any of his brothers.

"We need to get moving before the storm gets worse or we'll be stuck on this island until it passes," Shadow said.

Bull wrapped his arm around Chaise and led her out. "I know we still have things to talk about, but I'm not letting you go."

Chaise nodded but was so overwrought with mixed emotions she couldn't respond coherently. The main emotion she felt was an overwhelming joy of getting out of the whole sordid affair alive. She snuggled in close to Bull's side and allowed him to lead her out the front door and toward the dock.

As they moved past the outer perimeter of the property, a bolt of lightning struck close to the house. The popping and sizzling of electricity hung in the air for a few seconds before the house they had just left exploded into a huge fireball. Within seconds, the entire place was engulfed in flames and smaller explosions fired in sequence.

Chaise gasped and jumped out of Bull's embrace. His hand was fast but not as fast as her eye. He nonchalantly slipped a remote detonator into his pocket and gave her a feigned innocent look.

"Did you do that?" Chaise asked, pointing at the raging inferno behind them.

"I don't understand the question," Bull answered, telling Chaise all she needed to know.

They made it back to shore despite the choppy seas and whipping wind. An uncomfortable silence settled between Chaise, Bull, and Reaper as they stood on the dock, facing each other, not knowing exactly what to say or where to start.

Chaise broke the silence. "I don't know how I can ever thank you for everything. You saved my life." Her voice cracked on the last word when everything that had happened suddenly caught up with her. Tears fell from her eyes and rolled down her cheeks.

She tried to quickly wipe them away, but Bull pulled her into his embrace before she had a chance to regain her composure. He wrapped his thick arms around her and nuzzled his face in her hair. The bass timbre of his whispers made her weak in the knees and temporarily helped her forget where she was.

"I've got you, Chaise. You're mine and I'm never letting you go again. I was a fucking idiot for not stopping you before. Never again, baby," Bull promised in a hushed tone.

Chaise stayed glued to Bull for what felt like an eternity. She felt rather than saw that Noah was still standing beside them. She reluctantly pulled away from Bull's embrace but smiled up at him when he took her hand in his. He literally didn't intend to let her get far from him.

Chaise turned to Noah and searched his eyes for a few moments before speaking. "You came for me. I don't know what to say except 'thank you,' but that's not enough. I'm so very grateful and forever indebted to you."

Noah's emotions raged in his eyes and in his heart that was about to beat out of his chest. His initial estrangement was from his over-bearing, controlling, and domineering father, but he'd never consid-ered the serious impacts his absence had on his siblings. Looking at his sister, he saw the one person who had always idolized him, imitated him, and loved him with her whole heart. The searing pain he felt in his chest was like someone had stabbed him with a hot knife.

She was right—he had reneged on his duty as her brother. He had left her behind. Even though he thought it was best for her at the time, he had let her down. She was thanking him for coming to find her. The brutal truth was she was somewhat surprised that he didn't leave her behind again.

And he couldn't blame her.

Noah shook his head, took a deep breath, and stepped toward Chaise. He opened his arms and held them out to his sides, inviting her to hug him. That same gesture was what he used to do when she was little and would run out of the house to meet him after school.

The tears she had managed to hold back escaped as she flew into his embrace. He wrapped his arms around her and picked her up off the ground. "I'm sorry, Chaise. I'm so fucking sorry for leaving you behind." Noah's voice pleaded with her for forgiveness.

Chaise shook her head and responded through her tears. "I've missed you so much, Noah. So much. I'm just so happy to have you back. I was afraid you wouldn't want to see me."

Noah crushed her to him as his heart broke from her words. "I've missed you every day, baby sister."

Bull watched them together, brother and sister reunited after so many years apart, and a nostalgic memory from long ago resurfaced.

He remembered wishing he'd had a brother or sister close to his age when he was young. Then when he joined the Army and his best friends became his brothers, he felt the missing piece of his life had been found.

As he watched them—the man he loved like a brother and the woman with whom he had fallen in love—he knew his life was complete. There wasn't one event that he could pinpoint that had given him that feeling.

It was a culmination of all the nights Chaise spent in his house and in his arms. It was the laughs they shared and the light she brought into his life. It was the possessive and protective part of him that only she summoned. It was in the way she gave all of herself to him—even when she tried to tell him the truth and he stopped her.

Had he been honest with himself at that point, he really didn't want to know the truth. He was truly happy for the first time in a long time, and he didn't feel the need to know anything about her that he didn't already know from just being with her. He didn't want anything to ruin the good thing he had with her.

Noah released Chaise from his hold as John joined them in the covered area of the docks. John nodded at Chaise as he introduced himself as Bull's father. John's voice held genuine warmth when he added, "I'm glad to see you all made it back safely." Then, he looked around and asked, "Where's Rico? Did he get away?"

"Lightning struck twice in the same place. Damnedest thing I've ever seen," Bull said with a straight face and his Southern drawl securely in place. "Whole damn place went up like kindling. He didn't make it out."

John eyed him suspiciously for a moment, but Bull kept his face neutral. John cut his eyes to Chaise, but she quickly looked away and saw agents swarming around the warehouses. She pointed toward the action and asked John, "What's happening over there?"

John turned and looked toward the direction she pointed. From his profile, Chaise could tell his thoughts were already on something else. She had effectively changed the direction of the conversation and avoided any questions of what had occurred on the island. She knew the questioning would come later regardless, but she needed a momentary reprieve.

"After Colton left to find you, I talked to a few more of the girls. They had some solid information I called in to my team to investigate. We were able to gather enough hard evidence to start making arrests. The girls are being taken to the hospital and their families are being notified," John explained.

"What about Aura? Ana's twin sister? I never found her!" Chaise exclaimed.

John chuckled lightly. "Aura is fine. You really gave me a run for my money over her, Chaise."

"What do you mean?" Reaper asked.

"Aura knew something had happened to her sister at Viboro Distributing—that's why she went to work there. But she got too close to the truth, and they were about to take her too. So, I moved Aura and her mother to a safe house. We erased their existence from the servers. We had to work fast, because while we were busy trying to hide them, someone else was busy finding the other girls' missing persons posters."

Shadow and Rebel cleared their throats nervously, knowing that they had accessed confidential, secure servers illegally. Neither of them would ever actually admit to it since their computers were secure and untraceable. John tried to hide his knowing smile but failed miserably.

Bull shot Chaise an apologetic look, knowing she had tried to convince him that she wasn't lying about Aura, but he didn't believe her. He leaned over to her ear and asked, "If I promise to never doubt you again, would that make up me for not believing you?"

"It's a start," she countered. "But I have more imaginative ways of making you pay."

"That's a deal!" Bull's smile lit up his face and Chaise was again reminded of how he made her heart flutter. He suddenly turned serious as he asked, "Did they hurt you? Do we need to go to the hospital? I won't leave you."

Chaise stroked his cheek and jaw line as her heart melted at his offer. "No, nothing like that. Diego hit me but that was about the extent of it." She moved in close to him again, comforted in the crook of his arm. Her arms wrapped around his waist, and she hugged him tightly.

Daylight began to break on the horizon, reminding Chaise that she'd only had a few minutes sleep in too many hours. She felt the tiredness creeping in and overcoming her. She yawned loudly. "Since I know the girls are being taken care of, I need to get some sleep."

The full meaning of her statement didn't dawn on her until she'd said it aloud. She had nowhere to go—she had been staying with Bull for the past couple of weeks. She couldn't go back to the condo Viboro had supplied her. Her last hotel room stay didn't end well, and if she admitted it, she was afraid to be alone again. But she wouldn't reveal that to anyone.

"Am I free to go now?" Chaise asked John.

John nodded. "For now. You'll have to come in and answer some questions later." John took Chaise's cell phone number and promised to contact her later. Chaise thanked him and John left them to return to help the other DEA agents.

"I will take you ... home," Bull's low, bedroom voice whispered in her ear. The promise inherent in his voice and in his words made her weak in the knees but not from lack of sleep. She was suddenly very awake.

Noah's voice held concern and regret. "Get some rest, little sis. I'd like to talk to you later if that's okay. I have a lot of making up to do, too."

"I'd like that," Chaise replied sincerely. "I've missed you, Noah." Without a second thought, Chaise's arms wrapped around Noah's neck, and she kissed his cheek. "I love you, big brother."

"I love you, too," Noah replied as he squeezed her to him. Before releasing her, he pinned his gaze on his friend. "Take care of my little sister, Bull."

"You don't have to tell me twice, Reap," Bull replied.

Once Bull and Chaise arrived at Bull's house, the sun had fully risen behind the dark, black clouds. The continuous torrential downpour continued with the occasional boom of thunder and crackle of lightning. Bull pulled his truck into the garage, and gathering her into his arms, carried Chaise into the house.

She shifted in his hold just enough to wrap her arms around his neck. She nuzzled her face against his neck, inhaling his masculine scent. All the events seemed to catch up with her all at once. She felt strong and weak at the same time. She was happy and sad, guilty and unashamed, calm and irate—and she had no way to explain any of it.

But being back in Bull's arms felt ... *right*. It felt like she was home, where she belonged, where she wanted to be, and where she was welcome and safe. She could blame it on extreme circumstances, and most people probably would anyway. But she knew that when she was away from him, he was all she thought about. When she was taken, she knew he'd come for her, and she put all of her faith in him.

I love him, she thought as the realization hit her like a runaway train.

Raising her head to look at him as he carried her to the shower, she kissed his cheek.

"Bull?"

"Yeah, baby, we're home. I'll help you shower then we'll take a long nap," he replied.

"I love you."

Bull stopped in mid-stride. He drew his face back to look at Chaise, his face twisted in bewilderment and his eyes narrowed to mere slits. Chaise didn't know what response she expected to see, but that clearly wasn't it. He looked like he wanted to tell her she misunderstood his intentions, that he didn't feel the same way about her, or simply that he didn't return the sentiment.

"I just wanted to tell you. After everything that's happened, I don't want to take it for granted that I'll have time to say the things I want to say," Chaise continued.

Bull put her feet down and stood fully facing her, studying her in his way that used to make her feel like she was a freak science experiment. Now, it just felt like her heart was shattering into a million pieces, splintering inside, and cutting away at her. She refused to back down—she meant what she said regardless if he felt the same.

Chaise met his gaze and lifted her chin in an act of defiance. Bull had constructed a wall around his entire life, barely letting people in, but she knew she had penetrated that wall. He was too afraid to admit it, but their ties ran deeper than a casual acquaintance.

"It's okay if you can't tell me you love me," she said, choosing her words carefully.

Bull shook his head, placed his hands on his hips, and looked down. Chaise watched as he took a deep breath, his massive chest contracting and expanding with air, then he blew it out in a huff. He was wrestling with something internally, but she wasn't going to let him off the hook that easily.

"Colton, look at our lives. We've both been guarded because we were hurt at a young age. You've been with *my* brother all these years. *Your* father has been investigating my employer. Our families are back together because *we're* together. We have so many common ties between us. Are you fighting it? Or do you really not feel anything for me?"

"Chaise," Bull's voice was full of need, desire, longing, and just a hint of unease. His one-word statement called to her—bidding her to touch him, feel him, and to make him feel her in return.

Chaise answered his request by stepping into him, aligning their bodies, and slowly raising her lips to meet his. She ran her fingers through his hair until she reached the back of his head. She placed soft, chaste kisses on his lips until his arms wrapped around her and held her. She slowly licked the part in his lips, asking for permission, until he opened his mouth and granted her entrance.

He tasted even better than she remembered. Her fingers gripped his collar, and she quickly pulled his shirt up and over his head, breaking their kiss for only that split second. Shirtless Bull was a wonder to behold, but she allowed her fingers to memorize every muscle striation, every groove, and every line on him.

While they stood in the middle of the living room exploring each other as if for the first time, the intensity and depth of their feelings became a living, breathing being. With every breath, every kiss, and every touch, she surrendered more to him than she had any man in her entire life. The love she felt for him became all-consuming, pushing her to be bold and take the lead, surprising him with her ministrations.

"You're killing me, babe. I love what you're doing, but you have to stop because I have far too many plans for this to end so soon."

"Promises, promises."

Bull picked Chaise up, threw her over his shoulder and marched toward the shower. She squealed in laughter and Bull playfully spanked her ass cheek. Then he added, "The other side is jealous," as he spanked that cheek.

He undressed her, taking his time as he kissed, licked, nipped, and caressed every inch of her body. The bathroom was filled with steam from the running shower by the time he guided her into the tiled shower stall. The showerhead was large, and Chaise felt like she was standing in the pouring rain. She let the hot water pour over her body, washing away the tension and the events of the past few days.

While Chaise stood under the waterfall with her eyes closed, Bull soaped up a washcloth and began washing her. She opened her eyes with the initial contact of his hand, but then closed them again and let him thoroughly pamper her. When he was finished, she let out a deep, contented sigh.

"Chaise," Bull stated.

"Yes," she replied with her standard answer when it came to Bull.

"I need to hear you scream my name now."

His hot breath fanned out across her core just before his tongue found her sensitive nub. He flicked his tongue across it before lightly scraping it with his teeth. Wrapping his arm around one leg behind her knee, he carefully lifted it until he placed it across his shoulder.

"Better hold on, Chaise," he said with confidence.

Moisture flooded to her already heated center in anticipation of his intentions. Chaise grabbed onto the top of the shower door just in time as he reclaimed her, owned her, and devoured her. When the pressure built to incredible levels in her abdomen, she cried out in pleasure.

"Not enough, Chaise. I said I need to hear you scream my name," Bull demanded. He continued his attentions until he heard the sound that was like music to his ears.

"*Colton!*"

22

CHAPTER TWENTY-TWO

Chaise was like putty in his hands. Her body responded to him like no other's had before. It was as if she were made especially for him—to be adored, worshipped, and thoroughly sated by only his touch. He'd fought the feelings she evoked when she told him she loved him. Part of him wanted to respond, to tell her she was the best thing that had ever happened to him, and that he loved her, too.

But another part, a deeper part, told him to back off. The part of him that shut down in emotional situations and allowed his logic and reasoning to take control told him to let her go. His mind warred over the best course of action—take a chance by telling her the truth or keep it to himself and let her go?

"Don't think you're getting off that easily," he said to Chaise with a wicked grin as he turned off the water. "Pun intended. I'm not finished with you by a long shot."

Bull grabbed a towel and dried Chaise off first and then he led her into the bedroom. He placed her on the bed and covered her body with his.

"If you weren't so tired, this would be much different," he whispered in his bedroom voice. "I'd have you bent over this bed, watching in the mirror as I make you mine all over again. But for now, you need to feel me, and I need to feel you."

Bull felt her eyes searching his, looking for answers and hoping for a different one than he'd previously given her. Dipping his head, their lips met with urgency. Their tongues danced, caressed, and melded together. Bull memorized her taste, her scent, and her sounds.

He knew every part of her body and mind. Still, he didn't think he could get enough of her even if he had more than one lifetime to spend with her. She had ingrained herself in his life, his head, and his home.

One lingering doubt remained in his thoughts. *Can I give her my heart?*

As he continued to kiss her, invading all her senses, and making her crazy with desire, his fingers lightly brushed across her ribs, hips, and legs.

"Chaise, do you want me?"

"Mmhmmm," she answered.

"That wasn't an answer. I asked you a question. Do you want me?"

"*Yes*, I want you, Colton," Chaise replied with a more urgent, demanding tone.

With a sudden, fluid movement, Bull fully entered her, gliding inside her to the hilt. Stretched and filled, Chaise cried out in response to his sudden intrusion. Bull pushed into her over and over, loving every time she screamed out his name or clawed his back. The feel of her hands on him again after what felt like an eternity apart was heaven.

"That's my baby," his voice rumbled low in her ear. "You are mine, Chaise. Mine. And I don't share. Your body knows it belongs to me now."

His words made her blood turn to red-hot lava in her veins. His declaration of ownership of her body confused her. Questions of why he would say she was his if he didn't love her crowded her mind. She wanted to be his, but she wasn't so sure he wanted to be hers.

"I need to hear you scream my name one more time before I'm done," he said. "Are you ready?"

"Mmm, yes!"

Their bodies were tightly pressed together, their eyes locked on each other's, as he made good on his promise. The sensations he created in her were overwhelming. The dull pull that started low in her abdomen became strong spasms, pulling her closer and closer to the edge. She felt the sweet tension building more and more, knowing that her body could only take so much before she completely exploded.

And that was exactly what he wanted.

His eyes stayed glued to hers, daring her to even try to look away from him at that moment. They were both on the edge, holding on by a bare thread that would break at any moment. He knew all too well how to make her body hum.

When she couldn't take anymore, he felt her tighten around him. As her body quivered beneath him, the ripples in her muscles caressed, stroked, and brought him to the brink with her.

"Wow," Chaise gasped, drawing the one syllable word out to five or six. "That just never gets old."

Bull chuckled as he placed sweet kisses on her face and his thumbs stroked her cheeks lovingly. Those intimate moments weren't all that made Chaise think Bull was hiding his feelings from her and from himself. He had been a rock for her through the whole ordeal. Even when he had messed up and let her leave, he came after her and saved her.

As he continued lovingly lavishing attention on her, she felt him invading her heart just a little more. And a little more. She pushed away the doubts that tried to enter her mind. Her body was well spent, and completely sated, thanks to Bull. She needed sleep to be able to function in any reasonable capacity.

Bull rolled to her side, pulled the covers up, and positioned her to spoon her from behind. He draped his arm over her body, pulling her close to him as he nuzzled his face into her hair. Sleep overtook them and, for the next several hours, Chaise had only good dreams, safe in the arms of her Bull.

The next morning, Bull awoke to an empty bed where Chaise should have been. He sat up and strained his ears to listen for voices. Hearing a faint murmuring, he put his shorts on and walked to the kitchen. Chaise, Brianna, and Noah were sitting at the table drinking coffee. He immediately noted that Chaise was fully showered and dressed. Her suitcase sat on the floor beside her.

"What's going on in here?" Bull asked, intentionally keeping his voice calm, but his eyes told of the storm that raged inside. He spoke to the group, but his question was undeniably directed at Chaise.

"Just having breakfast with my sister," Noah replied as he squeezed Chaise's hand. "It's been way too long."

"We were just talking about Chaise coming to stay with us for a while until she can find her own place nearby. We thought that would give Chaise and Noah some time to reconnect. What do you think about that plan, Bull?" Brianna asked, fully aware of what she was doing. She was blatantly testing him and making him test himself.

"I think that's great for Chaise and Noah. They need to reconnect," Bull replied as he stared a hole through Chaise. "Does she really need to live with you to do that?"

"Well, we're closing the case. The arrests have been made. They have Ricardo Cordova in custody along with the rest of his crew. Rico is dead. She doesn't need constant protection any longer." Noah ran through the list of accomplishments on the case as if it should be simple to understand.

From the corner of his eye, Bull saw Brianna attempting to hide her smile. He couldn't remove his gaze from Chaise long enough to shoot Brianna a dirty look. Bull moved toward Chaise, like a tiger stalking his prey. He moved with lethal stealth and his sights were set on her.

"Can you two excuse us for a minute? I need to talk to Chaise. Make yourselves at home," Bull said as he pulled Chaise up from her chair and out of the kitchen. He didn't slow down until he reached the bedroom. He physically sat Chaise on the bed then turned to close the door.

He paced the floor in front of her, his face showing the turmoil he had tried to hide in front of their company.

"Colton, talk to me," Chaise finally said.

He suddenly stopped pacing and fully faced her. His face was red, and his eyes were narrowed in anger. "Why are you leaving me again?"

"I'm not leaving you, Colton," Chaise answered calmly. "I will still see you. What exactly did you expect would happen? Did you think I would just move in with you permanently?"

"No. I don't know. I don't know what I expected. I know I'm not ready for you to leave," he answered truthfully.

"You don't love me, Colton. I think we both know that. We haven't been together long and the time we have been has been under extreme circumstances. I think it's best that I find my own place now and we can still see each other. We'll just see where it goes," Chaise said quietly.

Bull had to concede that it was way too soon for them to consider living together. What he couldn't figure out was why he felt like she was abandoning him by getting her own place. It made sense for her to live at his house when she was in trouble, and he had already gotten accustomed to having her there with him. He rationalized that simply enjoying her company was not a basis for a permanent address change.

So, why couldn't he shake the feeling that their relationship would drastically change when she left?

Unable to come up with an alternative plan, Bull sighed and conceded. "Well, it'll be good for you and Reaper to spend some time together. You and Brianna can get to know each other and look at apartments together."

Chaise swallowed hard and simply nodded her head in response. She knew it would be hard, but she never imagined that it would be nearly impossible for her to willingly leave his house. A small part of her had hoped he would be more receptive to the idea and give her a reason to leave. No such luck with that.

"Well, they're waiting so we should get back in there," Chaise finally said. They walked out of the bedroom in silence. They both carried a heavy heart and a lingering doubt that their relationship would survive the regular day-to-day grind.

When Bull rounded the corner into his kitchen, the breath was knocked out of him. Brianna was sitting in Noah's lap. Noah had his one arm wrapped around Brianna and the other hand was on her slightly rounded stomach. They were whispering to each other, their faces nearly touching, and the smiles on their faces conveyed their deep love for the other.

Bull finally had to admit to himself that he wanted that kind of relationship, too. He wanted someone to call his own. Someone with whom to share his life, to give his love, and have a family. He knew he wanted it, but he didn't know if he could actually go through with it.

Noah had his heart ripped out when he thought Brianna was dead. His best friend didn't really live for the three years she was gone. Bull's mother never really went on with her life after John left. Michelle waited for John, much like Noah seemed to wait for Brianna. Those couples had found their once-in-a-lifetime love and had their hearts broken for it.

Bull had been disappointed, hurt, and scarred when John left him. He'd never really gotten over that feeling of giving all his love only to have it discarded like common trash. He seemed to be the only one holding on to old hurts, though.

Noah was so happy that Brianna was still alive, there was never any other option but for them to be together. Michelle loved John so much that there was never any other choice but to wait for him to be in her life full time.

Bull was pulled from his thoughts when Noah and Brianna sensed they were not alone. When Noah looked up, he caught the look on Bull's face, saw Chaise's long, gloomy face, and instantly knew what had occurred. He whispered into Brianna's ear and smiled warmly at her. She nodded and stood up to face Bull and Chaise.

"Ready to go, my new sister?" Brianna asked cheerfully.

"I think so," Chaise answered, uncertainty prolific in her words.

"Let's go get you settled in," Noah replied, excited to have his sister back in his life. "I had your car taken to my house."

"Thank you," Chaise replied but couldn't take her eyes off Bull.

The tension between Bull and Chaise was thick in the air, depleting the oxygen in the room and making it harder and harder for her to breathe. She felt the panic welling up inside her again, threatening to cripple her where she stood.

Chaise thought she'd managed to put it behind her when she was in the warehouse cell. She realized she had focused on the young girls and how they needed her to be strong for them. She had no choice but to push down her own fears and do whatever it took to help them. She wasn't feeling that strength inside her at that moment.

"Colton, I don't know what to say other than thank you for everything you've done for me. You took me in, protected me, helped me, and saved my life. I didn't give you any reason to help me, but you went out of your way to do it anyway. You're a good man—you have a good heart," Chaise said, fighting back tears and trying to keep her panic from consuming her.

She was really leaving the safe haven she'd found in Bull's home. Safe in his arms.

Chaise lifted on her tiptoes and wrapped her arms around his neck. His arms wrapped around her waist but the look on his face remained pensive. Covering his mouth with hers, she kissed him like she would never see him again. She poured all her heart, all of her love, and all of her feelings into the kiss, willing him to feel it and return it to her.

When she pulled away from him, the only sign that the kiss had affected him was the furrow in his brow. Not knowing how to take that, she picked up her suitcase and turned to follow Noah and Brianna out the front door.

Bull walked them out and watched them drive away. When they were out of sight, he walked back in his house, wandered around, and recalled all the moments he'd spent with Chaise. He walked to the bedroom and stared at the bed. He still smelled her sweet perfume scent, heard the echoes of her moans of pleasure at his hand, and felt the love she had given him. Walking back to the den, he punched a hole in the drywall.

CHAPTER TWENTY-THREE

Three days. Chaise hadn't seen Bull in three days, and she was going mad. She'd tried to ask Noah and Brianna about him in a roundabout way, but neither of them gave her any real information about him. She had a suspicion they were both acting and avoiding telling her what they knew she wanted to know. He hadn't called or come by to see her and she was miserable. All they would tell her was that Noah had sent him off on an assignment as a security escort for some corporate CEO.

Noah had to go into the downtown office of Steele Security for the day and Brianna had hotel business to attend to for her father. Chaise couldn't stand being cooped up in the house any longer. She grabbed her keys and left a note on the kitchen counter letting them know she had gone out.

Just getting out and driving around in the warm, Miami air made her feel better. She had been avoiding going back to the luxury condominium Viboro Distributing had set her up with but decided she couldn't put it off any longer. She had to pack the rest of her belongings and start looking for her own place. She already felt like a third wheel in the home of the newlyweds.

"Hi, Paul," she called to the security guard as she pulled up to the gate.

"Hello, Miss Steele! Long time, no see," he smiled warmly. "What brings you back here?"

"I have some personal belongings left in the condo, Paul. I just need to run up and finish packing. Can I drop my keys off with you when I'm finished?"

"Sure thing," he replied genially as he opened the gate for her. "Let me know if you need any help with anything at all."

"Thank you. I appreciate that," she replied as she pulled through the gate.

Chaise had been in the condo for almost an hour, packing her clothes and various other items, when the hairs on the back of her neck suddenly stood at attention. She felt the electricity in the air change and knew she wasn't alone. Turning quickly to look behind her, she shrieked as she took a few steps back.

"What are you doing here?" she demanded, fear and anger mixed in her voice.

"I'm here for you. What else?" the suave, Spanish accent answered.

"They arrested you. How did you get out?" Chaise asked.

"It's good to have many different kinds of friends, Miss Steele," he answered.

"Ricardo, you need to leave right now. The security guard knows I'm here and he will be here to check on me any minute now," she lied.

Ricardo smiled knowingly. "I don't think so, Chaise. You see, Chaise, Paul works for me. He called me the instant you showed up here."

Chaise turned and ran toward the door, leaving her packed suitcases behind. As she reached for the doorknob, two very large, very scary men grabbed her from behind. One of the men grabbed her upper arm and squeezed, tightening his grip on her, and leaving finger-shaped bruises in his wake. She twisted and turned, trying to break his hold, but that only made her arm hurt worse.

"I am going to allow you to leave here for one reason only. I want the flash drive with all the information you gathered from Viboro and you're going to bring it to me," Ricardo explained.

"Why would I do that?" Chaise asked.

Ricardo pinned her with a look of pure evil in his eyes. "Because I have Aura. If you don't show up, I will kill her and feed her body to the sharks. Then, I will do the same to everyone else you know. No one will be safe."

Chaise believed him.

"You will be followed. If you tell anyone else, or if anyone follows you ... Well, you know what will happen. Don't you, Chaise?"

"Yes," she replied meekly.

"Good girl," he replied sardonically, as though he were praising as dog. "Come back here when you have it."

Ricardo and his men watched her leave. She refused to turn her back to them again as she backed out of the apartment.

"You know she'll go get her brother and his team," one of the men said to Ricardo.

"I'm counting on it," Ricardo answered.

Chaise ran all the way to her car and shot Paul a dirty look as she tore out of the parking area. He had the audacity to smile and wave at her as she drove away. Taking a page from Bull's playbook, she flung her hand out of the window and gave Paul the middle finger salute.

Grabbing her cell phone from her purse, she called Aura and Ana's mother first. When Gabriela answered the phone, Chaise immediately knew Ricardo had told the truth. "Chaise! Chaise! Where is Aura? Where is my daughter?"

"Ricardo Cordova has her, Gabriela. I will get her back. I know what he wants," Chaise explained.

After several minutes of trying to console the frantic woman, Chaise disconnected and immediately called Noah.

"Noah, do you have my flash drive? The one with all the evidence against the Cordovas on it?" Chaise asked.

"No, John took it as evidence. Why?" Noah asked suspiciously.

"Are the files from it still on the computer?"

"Yes. What's going on, Chaise?"

"I need a copy of it. If I bring a flash drive, can you copy the files for me?" she asked, avoiding his question.

"Sure, come on by," Noah answered.

After an hour of Noah's brand of interrogation tactics, Chaise was finally leaving the Steele Security building with the data-packed flash drive. She was a nervous wreck just thinking about going back to that condo alone.

Chaise sat in her car, in the parking lot, for what seemed like an eternity. She played out every scenario she could dream up in her head, but they all ended in disaster. She knew it had to be a trap–Ricardo wasn't stupid enough to believe he could simply take the documents and his case would be dropped.

She leaned over and put her forehead on her steering wheel. Anxiety and uncertainty flooded her senses, so she just solely focused on breathing. Drawing from her memories, she imagined Bull's protective arms wrapped around her, his possessive voice telling her that she was his, and felt his masculine aura giving her strength. Lifting her head, she fished her cell phone from her purse.

"Noah? I need help," she confessed.

The deep, rumbling chuckled reverberated through her phone. "Yeah, little sis, I know. I'm waiting for you to leave so I can tail you."

"What do you know, exactly?" Chaise asked, her hackles now raised in suspicion.

"I know all kinds of things. But right now, I know you need my help and I'm not letting you go alone. They don't need to see me with you, though, so just do what you had planned to do and know that I'm with you," Noah reassured.

Chaise hesitated for a second too long, her mind asking where Bull was and why he wasn't protecting her.

"It'll be fine, little sis. No one will hurt you. You can trust me," Noah urged.

"I know, Noah. It's just difficult for me. I'm going now." Chaise hung up and pulled out onto the street, heading back to the last place she really wanted to go. She had some modicum of relief in the knowledge that the head of one of the best security firms in the world was close behind her.

Chaise repeatedly searched for Noah in her rearview mirror, trying to make sure she didn't lose him at a red light. She never found him in all the Miami traffic, though, and had to concede that if he knew what he was doing, she would never find him in the crowd of cars. Ricardo said she was being followed by one of his men, too, but she didn't see them, either.

She didn't even stop to talk to Paul when she entered the security gate. His sneer was enough to turn her stomach, and though she wasn't normally a violent person, she considered using torture tactics on him that would make waterboarding seem appealing. When she was past him, she hung her arm out of her window and flipped him off again—just for good measure.

Before exiting her car in the parking garage, Chaise searched her car for a tissue to wipe her eyes. She had held back the tears as long as she could but had lost the battle. Determined to not show her weakness, she wanted to hide any remnants of her mini breakdown before Ricardo saw her.

When she opened her glove compartment, she gasped in relief. Bull must have hidden the Ruger LCR .357 she used at the shooting range in her car because it was staring her in the face. She grabbed the low profile, concealable revolver and slipped it in the back band of her pants.

She wiped her palms on her pants and made the lonely walk to the elevators. She still hadn't seen Noah anywhere, but she had to trust him to handle the situation the way he knew best. Chaise tried to keep her thoughts on Aura and the possibility of saving her.

Once she reached the condo door, she took a deep breath and tentatively opened the door. The foyer opened into the large living area, giving her a good vantage point to see where the enemy was waiting. She quickly slipped the gun out of her waistband and slid it behind a large flower vase on the table just inside the entrance.

"Ah, Chaise. So nice of you to join us," Ricardo's smooth voice called out. His men chuckled at Ricardo's sick joke. Aura was sitting in a chair that had been moved from the dining room. Chaise realized Aura's hands and feet were taped to the chair arms and legs. She also realized that without Noah's help, neither of them would get out of the situation alive.

"You didn't leave me any choice, Ricardo," she replied sarcastically. She reached into her pocket and removed the flash drive. "Here, take this and let her go," she said, extending her palm to offer the evidence.

Ricardo laughed heartily. "I love that you are so trusting. I don't need that, Chaise. I have you—that's all I need."

"I don't understand," Chaise stalled. "What do you mean?"

Ricardo smiled at her, but his eyes held no mirth. They were black, cold, and void of compassion. "I think you know exactly what I mean. You're very clever."

"Ricardo, you asked me for the data I found at Viboro Distributing. I got that for you, and I came back here on my own. Now, take what you asked for and let Aura go," she replied with a stern voice.

"No. Neither of you are leaving here alive, Chaise. You will pay for what you did to Rico. Your boyfriend will pay, too," he hissed.

Ricardo seemed to have suddenly snapped. He started rambling nonsensical words, muttering to himself, and pacing back and forth. Fire danced in his eyes, and he flexed and contracted his fists over and over. As he passed one of his men, he grabbed the gun from the man's side and pointed it at Aura's head.

"You can watch her die, Chaise. That'll be a good punishment for you since you care about her so much." Ricardo laughed maniacally.

"She hasn't done anything to you, Ricardo. I'm the one you want. Let her go and do what you have to do to me," Chaise bargained.

Ricardo studied Chaise for a moment before he apparently had an epiphany. His face lit up and a smile tugged at the corner of his mouth. He moved the gun away from Aura's head and signaled to one of the men to cut her bonds.

"You can go now, Aura. If you stay, you will be shot," Ricardo said dryly.

Aura gave Chaise a panicked look before Chaise assured her. "It's okay, Aura. Get out of here. Now."

Aura reluctantly left and Chaise exhaled when she heard the door click and knew that Aura was safely out of Ricardo's reach. He walked toward Chaise and grabbed her by her shirt. He shoved the gun against her temple and spat his intentions out at her.

"I'm going to shoot you. Right here. *Right in the fucking head.* Then, I'm going to hang your body off the side of the balcony. *Like a fucking beacon for your boyfriend to find you.* And when he finds you, I will give him enough time to cut your dead, broken body down before I shoot *him* in the fucking head, too."

Ricardo walked her backward toward the balcony. His gun hand was shaking with excitement and anticipation of carrying out his evil plan. When Chaise's back hit the glass door, she prepared for the worst. Noah hadn't made it inside yet and it would be too late for her.

All the things she wished she'd said to Bull suddenly rushed to the forefront of her thoughts. She was scared beyond the capacity of rational thought as she faced the certainty that she was about to die. Coping with that fact was more than overwhelming but adding unrequited love and longing for Bull to the equation was downright debilitating.

The tears rolled unchecked down her face as she watched the madness grow in Ricardo's eyes. "Can you give him a message from me first?" She didn't know where she found her voice, but there was something she had to say to Colton.

"Oh, please, let me deliver your final words to him. *Such poetic justice,*" he crooned.

"Tell him ... Tell him that I love him and I wish, more than anything in the world, that I had stayed at his house. I don't care that I only knew him a few weeks. I don't need more time than that to know he's the only one for me. I only wish we had more time together," Chaise said.

"Oh, that is so sweet," Ricardo said mockingly. "But I will gladly relay your message just before I blow his fucking head off."

"Say your goodbyes to me now, Chaise," Ricardo said as he opened the large, sliding glass door behind Chaise.

"You say goodbye, asshole." The deep booming voice came out of nowhere. The distinct sound of the gun clicking, indicating it was ready to fire, immediately followed. "Put that fucking gun down and face me like a real man," Bull challenged.

Ricardo's head jerked around and found his men on the floor, unconscious, and Bull had his gun leveled on his head. He spun around, pulling Chaise with him, and using her body as a shield from Bull's aim.

Bull kept advancing on Ricardo, his arm fully extended, and his deadly aim still fixed on the spot between Ricardo's eyes. There was no way Bull would allow Ricardo to hurt Chaise or to walk away from the scene alive. He knew Ricardo would never stop his cat and mouse game and there was no way in hell Bull would let him threaten Chaise ever again.

"Your choice, man. You escaped from jail and the Feds have been looking for you. They're on their way now. They can either take you away in handcuffs or in a fucking body bag. My choice would be the latter," Bull threatened.

"You won't shoot me with your precious girlfriend in front of me. You might miss and hit her. We can't have that now, can we?" Ricardo asked as he leaned his face into Chaise's.

His tongue darted out and licked the side of her face as Bull watched in disgust. "She's so sweet. No wonder you want her back so badly. Maybe I should have some fun with her before I kill her. I would let you watch, but I'm not into that. I will let you live long enough to hear her screams, though."

"Over *your* dead body," Bull said menacingly, taking another step forward as he prepared for his next move.

"Chaise, baby," Bull said soothingly, effectively getting her attention as he kept his eyes and gun trained on Ricardo. "Remember what I told you I'd do to you if you hadn't been so tired that day? I need you to do that right now."

Understanding dawned on her and she knew this was her best

chance at escaping without risking Bull being shot or killed. She jerked her body forward, bending at the waist with all the force she could muster.

The sudden movement caught Ricardo off guard, and he was momentarily dazed when she slipped out of his grip. He was left exposed, and Bull took the opportunity to end their standoff immediately. The bullets hit Ricardo in the chest before the sound of rapid gunfire registered in his brain. The blunt force of the bullets sent Ricardo flying backward, out onto the balcony, and over the railing.

Bull lowered his weapon and rushed to Chaise. He gathered her in his arms and held her tightly to him as she cried. Her whole body shook with an overdose of adrenaline and fear. She grabbed him with all her might and held onto him as if he were her only lifeline on a sinking ship.

"Well, looks like our work is done here," Noah said, appearing out of nowhere. "You did good, little sister. Although, next time, don't give up your gun so easily." He placed the .357 on the table beside Bull and Chaise before clapping Bull on the shoulder.

Rebel and Shadow were suddenly standing behind Bull, both with smiles splitting their faces in two. They seemed to be laughing with each other over some private joke.

"What's so funny, guys?" Noah asked.

"We're just being stupid, Reap. We were laughing about how it sounds when you sing, *'Chaise and Bull, sitting in a tree. F-U-C-.'*"

The look on Reaper's face stopped them cold for a split second and then they both doubled over with laughter.

"Shit man, I forgot she was your sister for a minute there. Sorry, dude," Rebel said between fits of laughter.

24
____

CHAPTER TWENTY-FOUR

It was dark by the time they finished with all the police questions and paperwork. Bull led Chaise to his truck and drove her straight to his house. He didn't ask her first. He didn't give her an option of going anywhere else.

And he had no intentions of letting her leave again. Ever. He had claimed her as his own.

Bull helped her out of his truck and walked her inside, his hand in his possessive spot on her lower back. Chaise expected him to lead her to the bedroom, as he normally did after an intense situation, and he couldn't express himself any other way. But he surprised her by steering her toward the couch instead.

This is new, she thought.

Bull sat down and pulled her down onto his lap. She fit perfectly in the bend of this arm and the crook of his shoulder. She inhaled his purely all-Bull, masculine and sandalwood scent. She had recently associated that scent with love and safety. It was Bull's unique aroma that she wanted to bottle and keep all to herself.

"Chaise, baby, look at me," he asked softly. She raised her head and met his gaze. The worry in his eyes melted her heart. He was concerned about her and was being as gentle as Bull knew how to be.

"What you did in the condo was so brave. I was amazed at your courage. I am so proud of you—you got Aura out of there and to safety. You willingly took her place," he continued.

All the intense feelings were building up inside her again. She was thankful that a panic attack wasn't one of those feelings. They never happened when she was in Bull's arms. She had a sudden feeling of alarm, however, when he narrowed his eyes and firmly set his jaw before he continued.

Through gritted teeth, he finished. *"Don't. Ever. Fucking. Do. That. Again.* I thought I was going to lose you, Chaise. I thought he was going to shoot you before I could get you away from him."

He crushed her to him as both of his muscled arms wrapped around her. Chaise could barely breathe under the weight of his embrace. But she wouldn't complain about it even if she were able to speak. She thought to herself, '*This is home. This is where I belong.*' She had already decided she would wait for Bull to love her in return. It was better to be with him and be the object of his desire and affections than to keep living without him at all.

"Promise me. *Swear to me* that you'll never do that again," Bull demanded. "I watched my mom lose my dad. I watched Reaper lose Brianna. It killed them both. Even though they kept going, the spark that gave them life died when they lost their true love. I don't know if I'm as strong as they are. I don't know if I could stand losing you and I never want to find out.

"I heard what you said to Ricardo—your message to me. You have no idea how fucking hard that was to stand there and listen to you say your goodbyes. Your final words would've been confessing your love for me, Chaise. I still can't believe that. You didn't ask for anything else," he said sincerely.

"I didn't want anything else, Colton. I knew he wouldn't let me go. I knew Noah had followed me, but I didn't see him anywhere, so I thought he would get there too late. I just needed you to know how I felt," she explained.

"How do you feel, Chaise?" he asked purposefully.

"I love you, Colton. I know it's too soon, but I meant what I said. I don't need more time to know there's no one else for me."

"I love you, too, baby," he whispered, his mouth hovering just above hers.

His lips lightly brushed against hers as he spoke, sending cold chills down her spine and an intense tingling feeling in other more important regions. His words finally caught up with her senses.

"You love me?" she asked hopefully.

"I love you," Bull answered resolutely. "I have never said those words to anyone outside my family before you. I will never say them to another woman. You're it for me, too, Chaise. I'm yours just as much as you are mine."

"Wait a minute. Noah said you were off on an assignment. Where have you been? How did you know I was even there?" Chaise asked, narrowing her eyes at him.

Bull cleared his throat before smiling mischievously at her. "Well, I was on assignment, but *you* were my assignment," he confessed. "We knew Ricardo had escaped from federal custody and it was only a matter of time before he came after you. I was right in thinking that something was wrong with that condo. They had security cameras hidden inside so they could watch everything that happened there. Brad happened to come across the feed—while he was surfing the Internet," Bull smiled as he lied. "So we were able to keep an eye on the place.

"When we received word that Aura was missing, we knew there was no way you wouldn't help her. So, we arranged to be there with you."

Chaise leaned into him, grabbed his face in her hands, and thoroughly kissed him. Straddling him, she moved her mouth to his jaw line and then on to his neck. She worked her way up to his ear and whispered seductively to him. "Remember what you said you'd do if I wasn't so tired?"

She felt his hands tighten on her back in anticipation of what she'd say next. The very thought of him being revved up over her gave her the courage she needed.

"What if it wasn't bending me over the bed? What if it was bending me over the couch instead? There's a mirror right there," she cooed.

Chaise screamed, as she was suddenly airborne while Bull hopped over the back of the couch with her in tow. "That is one thing you'll never have to ask me twice, my love."

Within seconds, Bull had them both stripped naked and the standing mirror positioned exactly where he wanted it. He stepped into her, pressing his front to her back, as he moved her hair to the side. "I will go slower next time, but right now, I just want to feel you."

"You're taking too long, Colton. We really need to talk about your lack of focus," Chaise playfully chided him.

His hand went to the center of her back, and he pushed her head down and over the couch. "Now I can see your face. You know what I want to hear, Chaise."

"Your name, screamed from the rooftop for all the neighbors to hear," she replied.

"Damn straight," he answered before he pushed into her without warning. She screamed with delight at the full sensation he created in her. "I don't think the neighbors at the end of the street heard you. I better up my game."

Before she could respond with something equally smartass, he made good on his promise. And so did she.

***

FOUR WEEKS LATER, the whole gang was at Noah and Brianna's house for a cookout. Brianna's tiny baby bump had grown into a more noticeable protrusion and Noah couldn't keep his hands off her stomach.

"Noah, if you don't let me walk without you being attached to my stomach, I'm going to scream," Brianna laughed.

"You are walking close to dangerous weapons. What if you hurt my baby?" Noah replied sincerely.

"It's called a spatula, Noah, and it's not a dangerous weapon." Brianna bent at the waist from laughter.

"Hmph," was Noah's only response.

Chaise watched the two of them together and tried to reconcile the story Bull had told her about Brianna's disappearance. She couldn't imagine those two not being together for three years. They were so obviously made for each other.

Bull had said that their spark had died when they were apart, and that reference just clicked as she watched her big brother with his pregnant wife. Anyone could see that Brianna was Noah's greatest strength and biggest weakness. And Noah was Brianna's as well. One didn't exist without the other.

Bull got up to get them both another drink and Noah sat down beside Chaise. "What are you thinking about, little sister?"

"About you and Brianna. Colton told me about what happened with you two. The three years apart," Chaise's voice trailed off when she saw the shadow cross his face at the memory. The spark was extinguished for that split second.

"I was gone from your life much longer than that, little sister," he said apologetically.

His voice held so much regret and remorse that Chaise's heart broke for him. She'd been so young when he left, and she had only focused on how hard it had been on her. That line of thinking had continued her whole life. She'd never even considered that he might not have wanted to be separated from her.

"I have you back now. That's what matters, Noah. I'm never letting you leave me again, though. Losing you was hard enough the first time. I can't do it again," she told him.

"Ditto."

"You and Brianna are perfect together. I love her, too," Chaise said as she watched Brianna playfully teasing Bull.

"We were meant to be. I firmly believe that," Noah said. "But it seems that you and Bull are pretty firm in your relationship, too."

"Yeah, I think we are. I love him. I can't imagine my life without him—as cliché as that sounds," Chaise laughed.

"It's not cliché if it's true. It is for me, and I had to live my life without her for three years. It was the worst three years of my life," Noah said as he looked at Brianna. It was as if Brianna could feel Noah's eyes on her because she looked over at him at the same time. Brianna smiled warmly and mouthed *I love you* to him from across the deck.

"Bull says he loves me. He shows it, too. I've never felt more at home than I do with him. He protects me, makes me feel safe and loved," Chaise said as she watched Bull with adoring eyes.

"You love him," Noah stated.

"I do, Noah. I love him very much," Chaise admitted.

"That's all I need to know," Noah said as he stood. "Better get back to cooking. My pregnant wife needs to feed my baby."

"I heard that," Brianna called from across the deck, causing Noah to laugh in response.

Chaise laughed and as she looked over at Brianna, her eyes met Bull's. The heated look he always had for her held something more that night. She couldn't quite put her finger on it, but she knew something was on his mind. She had already tried to get him to talk, but Fort Lanier was closed up tight.

Noah turned the outside speakers on, and soft music filtered through the air. The sun was setting, and the sparkling rays bounced off the rippling water of their expansive pool. Noah had strung small, white lights around the deck and the pool so that as the sun disappeared, the lights twinkled like stars and created a romantic atmosphere.

They talked and laughed as they ate, making up funny names for the baby, much to Noah's chagrin. At one point, he declared his baby as off limits for any conversation because they refused to keep their comments within his guidelines.

"Don't listen to them, baby. Daddy will kick their asses for you," Noah said to Brianna's stomach before cutting his eyes to the others.

Laughter erupted all around and Chaise watched them, longing for her own family one day.

Bull reached over and took Chaise's hand in his. She looked at him when she felt his lips on the back of her hand. She could feel the love radiating from his intense stare. It was more than the sexual, take-charge Bull that she knew and loved. It was the man behind the mask looking at her at that moment.

It had taken them a while to get to that point. She'd had to endure several bouts of insecurity with him and their new love. But, that moment, the way he was looking at her, the way he was literally loving her with his eyes, and that he was doing it in front of others made it all worth the wait.

She knew without a doubt that they were destined to be together. There were too many links, too many ties that bound them together, for it to be any other way. While she was musing over their destined fate, Bull leaned in and kissed her lips so sweetly.

"Stop over thinking it, Chaise. I love you, baby. I'm not going anywhere. Ever," he promised.

"I believe you. Because you keep your promises," she replied. "I love you, too. More than anything."

Chaise went inside to help Brianna clean their dinner dishes while the men stayed outside to clean up around the grill. She sincerely enjoyed spending time with Brianna, getting to know her, and finding out new things about her brother. And about Colton.

Brianna told Chaise about their time in the Middle East and how she got to know Bull, Rebel, Shadow and, of course, Reaper. Chaise wasn't surprised to hear about how Bull acted when Brianna showed up after being dead for three years. She imagined Bull felt very betrayed and abandoned all over again. The fact that he forgave Brianna and still called her his sister was a miracle in itself.

"He's crazy about you, ya know?" Brianna said to Chaise. "That man loves you so much. I've never seen him like this in all the years I've known him."

"I am crazy about him, too. Maybe it seems too fast? But it just feels right. I know there's no one else for me," Chaise explained.

"It was fast for Noah and me, too. I spent time with him in the desert and things progressed rapidly, even when I thought there was no future for us. But after he was discharged, he showed up here in Miami, at a bar where I was celebrating my birthday with some friends, and we've been together ever since. Well, with the exception of the three years when I was dead, but he was still my only one then, too. When you know, you know."

A little while later, Bull and Chaise left the Steele's Miami mansion and headed home. That word had seemed so foreign to Bull at first. But now that the case was closed, and his dad was retired and back with his mother, *home* sounded better and better. The best part was that Chaise considered his house as her home. As *their* home.

When they got home, Bull let Chaise walk in the house first. She immediately thought it was strange because he always insisted on making sure the house was secure before he let her go in. But it was late, and they were both tired so she didn't ask about it.

When she stepped inside, she gasped loudly, and her hands flew to her face. She looked around, wide-eyed, and her jaw hung open. Her heart was pounding, and her pulse was racing. She couldn't believe what she saw in front of her.

There must have been one hundred lit candles scattered throughout the house, their flames flickering and casting shadows on the walls. There were red rose petals lining a path from the garage door, through the kitchen to the den. The den held dozens of flowers in various sizes and arrangements. Soft, romantic music filled the air and set the mood.

In the center of the den sat a table with a large, white box wrapped with a huge, red velvet bow. Chaise turned to find Bull standing just behind her, watching her every move, and gauging her reaction.

"When? How?" she stammered.

Bull smiled. "I would never reveal my methods, babe."

Chaise admired the different flowers, taking time to smell them and appreciate their beauty. Her eyes kept straying to the box that waited for her. Bull smiled, knowing it was killing her to wait. She eventually made her way to it and looked at him for permission.

"For me?"

"For you, baby," Bull answered sweetly.

Chaise was busy carefully untying the bow and opening the box. When she removed all the internal stuffing, she found a small, black velvet box. She held her breath as she opened it to find a sparkling, diamond ring. She turned quickly to Bull, her eyes questioning the ring's intention, but he wasn't standing beside her.

He was kneeling on one knee. His eyes wordlessly implored her to accept his promise of forever. He took her hand in his and then stole her heart all over again.

"Sierra Chaise Steele, I think I've known since I met you that you would change my life. There was something about you—even that first night—that drew me to you. Now that you've shown me what real love is, I can't live without you. Will you marry me, Chaise?"

"Yes—oh my God, yes, Colton!"

Chaise fell to her knees in front of him and wrapped her arms around his neck. Bull kissed her, slowly and sweetly at first, and the desire and urgency increased along with their tempo. Bull gently led her to lie down, and he made love to her for the rest of the night. On the floor. On the couch. In the shower and eventually in their bed.

"Now that we've christened the house, maybe we should get some sleep," Chaise joked.

"I guess I can let you sleep for a little while to recharge your batteries. Then you're mine again," Bull said before sleep overtook him.

The next morning, Bull woke to hearing Chaise on the phone, telling Brianna about how he proposed. She was so excited and animated, it made him want to do it all over again, just to please her and make her feel loved.

He realized they were so much alike in that they didn't feel loved by their father when they were younger. They were both abandoned —but in different ways. His protective instincts went into overdrive when he thought about how Chaise and Noah's father must have treated her. He knew it had to be severe for her to refuse to return home when her life was in danger.

He vowed she would never have that problem again. She would always have a safe place to call home—physically and emotionally. He found he loved the responsibility of being "the man of the house," and Chaise enjoyed letting him take the reins. It made her feel safe and kept her anxiety at bay.

She didn't know that Bull had asked for Noah's permission to propose to her until Brianna explained it. The two men had a long talk about what it would mean to their families, their friendship, and their working relationship. Noah knew that no matter what, once Bull made a commitment, he would honor it to his death.

There was no doubting the love between Chaise and Bull. Noah assured Bull that he would be honored to have him as his brother-in-law. Noah's talk with his sister had only cemented his decision even more. They would be Aunt Chaise and Uncle Bull to Noah and Brianna's baby. They would be one big, happy family.

Bull slipped out of bed and eased up behind Chaise. He wrapped his arms around her, startling her, but she didn't miss a beat in her description of his proposal. "Tell her all the neighbors know my name is 'Oh God, Colton' now," he murmured in her ear.

Her face turned beet red, and she playfully swatted him away. He laughed when she answered Brianna's question. "Oh, Colton said to tell you 'good morning,' that's all."

Chaise ended the call and took a seat in Bull's lap. "I'm so happy. Thank you for everything you did last night. It was perfect!"

"Anything for you, my love," he replied sincerely.

"Things are happening so fast. Your parents are moving down here soon," Chaise said.

"That's right. They're selling the house in Alabama and moving here to be closer to us," Bull replied with a smile.

"Brianna said her dad wants to offer me a job with his hotels. I'll be the Human Resources Manager for all his hotels, but I'll mainly work out of the new one they're building here. It's exciting, isn't it?

Starting a new life together?" Chaise asked, carefully watching his reaction.

"It's better than I ever thought it could be," Bull answered as he repositioned Chaise so that she straddled him.

Chaise leaned in and kissed him in response. "Thank you for not giving up on me when you had every reason to just walk away."

Bull shook his head from side to side. "If I had to pick one thing that I would rather die than live without, it would be you. I really never thought I'd say this, but I can't wait to make you my wife."

"Well, Mr. Lanier, why don't you give me a preview of the honeymoon?" she asked seductively.

"Mmm, I'd be glad to, future Mrs. Lanier. Your first preview will be a lesson in *Bull riding*," he wiggled his eyebrows suggestively at her. "But first, I need a date."

Chaise's eyes crinkled at the corners and her lips twisted to the side as the thought about her wedding date. Bull smiled at how cute the gestures looked on her. "I think a late April wedding. Noah and Brianna's baby will have already been born and then our whole family can be there with us."

"April it is. Now, it's time to try on your spurs," he said as he jumped up and ran down the hall with Chaise wrapped around him, laughing hysterically.

"Couldn't ask for a better start to a new life," Chaise said dreamily.

EPILOGUE

The hissing of oxygen flowing through tubes, the dinging of patient call lights, and the sterile smell of the hospital brought back memories of Brianna's hospitalization—a memory Noah would much rather forget. This visit to the hospital was under different circumstances, but no more desirable.

Chaise had received an urgent phone call from Sara Steele, their mother. Steve was in the hospital and the news was not good. He was rushed by ambulance to the emergency room during the night and was taken straight into surgery. Sara was frantic to reach all her children. Steve was in pain but awake and asking to see them.

When Noah first heard the news, he was hesitant to agree to see him. He didn't think the hospital, post-surgery, was the best place for a family reunion after so many years apart. Sara insisted, however, and between Brianna and Chaise, Noah really didn't stand a chance.

Noah, Brianna, Bull, and Chaise all walked silently down the corridor to Steve's room in the ICU step-down unit. His condition was being carefully guarded but he wasn't in such dire straits as to need the constant monitoring of the ICU nurses.

Chaise held on to Colton's hand tightly as they walked. The

impending visit weighed heavily on her mind. The anxiety level began building in her chest and she knew the only thing that kept her attack under control was the fact that Colton was with there with her. She felt him squeeze and tug on her hand lightly, asking her to look at him.

"I'm here, baby. Whatever you need, I'm here for you," he said warmly.

She nodded and squeezed his hand as she leaned into his side. "I can't imagine doing this without you here."

The beeping of the heart monitor and the ticking of the IV machine were the only sounds in the room. Sara was asleep sitting up in her chair and Steve was resting in the hospital bed with his eyes closed.

Brianna spoke up. "Maybe Bull and I should wait outside the room to give you and Chaise time to talk to your mother alone."

Noah shook his head. "No. *This* is my family now—you, our baby, Chaise, and Bull. We go in together."

Noah walked into the darkened room first and Sara sleepily opened her eyes. When she saw Noah, her eyes grew wide, and she jumped up from her chair. As she rushed to him, with her arms widespread and tears in her eyes, Noah felt the regret wash over him. It had been too many years since he'd seen his mother.

He wrapped his arms around her and whispered his greeting in her ear. "Hi, Mom. How are you holding up?"

She pulled back and looked from him to Brianna, who stood proudly beside Noah. Sara's eyes dropped to Brianna's small bump and her hands flew to cover her mouth. "Noah?"

"Mom, this is my wife, Brianna. Brianna, this is my mom, Sara," he replied in hushed tones.

Sara looked at Brianna and suddenly threw her arms around her neck. Sara hugged her tightly as she cried softly. Brianna patted her on the back and whispered soothing words to her.

Sara opened her eyes and saw a large, formidable figure behind Brianna. Once her eyes adjusted, she saw his arm was wrapped around her daughter, Chaise. Turning Brianna with one hand, Sara used her other arm to grab Chaise and pull her in for a group hug.

When Sara let go of them, Chaise made her introductions. "Mom, this is Colton, my fiancé. Colton, this is Sara, my mom."

"Fiancé?" Sara asked and both Bull and Chaise nodded. "I'm so glad I didn't miss the wedding! Or my grandbaby's arrival!"

"You aren't having a family reunion without me, are you?" a weak voice called out.

All heads snapped to the direction of the voice. Steve's automatic pain medicine dispenser gave him another dose of pain medicine as Noah and Chaise moved to his bedside.

"Hi, Dad," Chaise replied. "How are you feeling?"

"Better now that the two of you are here," he answered. "I have something I need to say to you both."

Noah took a deep breath and readied himself to leave and take his family with him if Steve decided to start his usual rant. "Go ahead," Noah replied.

"I'm sorry, kids. I'm so sorry. I love you both and I want you back in my life. Not just because of this but finding out you have Stage Three colon cancer is definitely a wake-up call for how you've lived your life. I look back and I'm not proud of the type of father I was to you two. I want a chance to make it up to you. I want to walk my baby down the aisle. I want to be a good grandfather," Steve choked up on his last words.

The room was silent. Both Chaise and Noah were stunned speechless at his admission and his request. Noah looked around at his family and they each nodded their approval.

"Apology accepted, Dad," Noah replied quietly. "Let's be a family again."

The pain medicine took effect and Steve soon slipped back into a deep sleep. Despite the prognosis, Chaise knew that her family would be whole again. Somehow everything would work out as it was intended to be.

They stood, gathered around their sick father, chatting and

making introductions as Steve went in and out of sleep. Their future was ahead of them and no matter what it brought, Chaise, Colton, Brianna, and Noah would face it together.

There is strength in numbers and in family ties.

doorframe with their weapons drawn, the guards were disarmed with minimal effort.

The team moved fully into the room, completed their full sweep, and untied the hostages. "US Army," Reaper introduced himself. "Is anyone injured?"

"Not bad. I can walk," one man answered. The others replied that they weren't injured.

Reaper pointed to the man who was obviously stronger than the others. "You stay with him—" he pointed to the slightly wounded man "—right behind me. We move at the speed of the weakest person." He finished giving the instructions on how each hostage would follow them out so that a member of the team covered each man.

"Big Eye, Reaper," he said into the radio. "Recovered. Exiting with five."

"Copy that, Reaper," came the reply. "Eyes on you."

Reaper transferred the connection from the handset to the speaker in his helmet so the recon plane could easily communicate with him. The group of men formed a line and began their withdrawal from the compound. The echo of heavy footfalls and voices became louder from the direction in which they were headed.

The voice in his helmet alerted him. "Reaper, Big Eye. Multiple hostiles are blocking your current route. Turn left at the next intersection. Proceed to the window. Extraction team being relocated."

"Copy," Reaper replied and proceeded on the updated route. Slinging his gun over his shoulder by the strap, he picked up a chair and busted a pane of the glass of the small panel window. Once the shards were cleared, he placed the chair in front of the window and motioned for Bull to go first. "Cover."

Bull nodded and deftly moved through the open window to take his place outside. "Men approaching," he said quietly into his comm.

"Big Eye, Reaper. Confirm extraction team location."

"Reaper, the team is less than half a klick from your current location."

"Copy," he replied.

He relayed the information to Bull as he helped the first hostage through the window. Rebel and Shadow remained in position with their rifles at the ready as Reaper fed the remaining men through the small opening.

"Your turn, ladies," Reaper said to Rebel and Shadow.

"Age before beauty." Shadow smirked at Rebel and jerked his head toward the exit.

"I'll be waiting on the other side of that wall to kick your ass," Rebel chuckled as he climbed out nimbly.

"You're up, big guy," Reaper said.

Shadow shouldered his weapon and followed Rebel. "Let's go, Reaper. Playtime is over," Shadow said from outside the window.

"Reaper, Big Eye. Multiple hostiles approaching your location. Take cover."

As Reaper started to turn toward the window, the first of the combatants turned the corner and spotted him. The hostile raised his rifle and took his aim at Reaper. A shot rang out and the man crumpled to the floor before he could squeeze the trigger. Reaper stepped on the chair and dove through the window, landed on his hands, and rolled in a somersault to lessen the force of his landing. Rebel simultaneously moved to cover the team, his rifle trained on the small opening.

As more men entered the hallway, Rebel squeezed the trigger of his automatic rifle. One by one, one insurgent after another fell to the floor.

"Let's go," Reaper yelled to the hostages.

They began their trek across the compound grounds toward the back wall. Armed men began pouring out of multiple doorways behind them. The men yelled curses in Arabic as they ran toward the fleeing hostages. Rebel turned and began to fire his weapon, hitting his mark repeatedly as he covered the team and hostages. One man fell from Rebel's covering fire, but he was still determined to kill the American infidels who had defiled his residence. While lying on his stomach, he raised his rifle with his bloody hands and tried to steady his shaking arms.

He fired his gun and the bullet whizzed by Rebel's head, way too close for comfort. The close proximity of the bullet to his head only fueled Rebel's anger. He turned his gun back to the wounded man and returned fire. The bullet struck the man in the head and left a gruesome, gaping wound in its wake.

A portable tactical ladder suddenly appeared over the wall, and Reaper directed the hostages to it while he and the other men provided covering fire. Several members of the extraction team climbed over the wall and moved into position in the yard, helping deter more armed opponents from approaching them. Once everyone was safely over the wall, they ran to the waiting helicopters and were safely lifted out.

Tears of joy and gratitude flowed down the faces of the rescued men. Rounds of sincere "thanks" and "thank you so much" were repeated over and over as the weight of reality set in. They were so very grateful to be going home to their families. Happy, healthy, and largely uninjured, thoughts of what could have been played through their thoughts and sent shivers down their spines.

In the courtyard of the terrorist compound, two young boys left the safety of the darkness and approached the corpse of the man who had kept shooting even after he'd been injured. The eldest of the two dropped to his knees beside the body, then dropped his pistol as his knees struck the dirt. Tears formed tracks over his cheeks through the dust that had collected on his face.

"I'm sorry, Father," he said to the lifeless man. "I failed you. I'm your firstborn, and I failed to do my duty."

The younger brother placed his hand on the older one's shoulder. He was young, but he inherently understood the despair his brother felt. Family honor had been instilled in them since birth. Following orders, making their father proud, and taking a stand for their country weren't just ideals they talked about around the dinner table. The two boys had lived it every day of their young lives.

"Orphaned at barely thirteen," the older one said aloud. "It's all my fault."

2

CHAPTER TWO

SEPTEMBER

Current Day

The end of summer was marred by a different kind of ending. The rounds of chemotherapy and radiation therapy had begun to take their toll on the elder Steele man. The cancer that had weakened his body progressed rapidly, and the toxic treatments had a hard time keeping up with the new cell growth. The chances of improvement had begun to dwindle, and the doctors were forced to consider Steve's other options.

"Mr. Steele, it doesn't appear the treatment is working as well as we hoped we it would," Dr. Patel began. "It may be time for you and your wife to start discussing your final wishes, what lengths you're willing to go to for treatment, and at what point you want to stop treatment altogether."

Sara's soft whimpers were the only sound in the room. Steve stared at the wall straight ahead of him as he processed the bad news. Noah and Brianna sat beside Sara, both unable to string a few words together into a coherent response. Colton and Chaise sat on the other side of the bed, with Chaise holding Steve's hand while tears streamed down her face unchecked.

"Thank you, Dr. Patel. Sara and I will discuss it," Steve finally spoke.

Dr. Patel nodded and, before leaving the room, said, "Let me know if there's anything I can do to help. I'm sorry to be the bearer of such bad news. We will keep hoping for a significant change soon."

Steve and Sara both nodded at Dr. Patel in appreciation before Sara leaned over and laid her head on Steve's shoulder. Her tears dripped onto the sleeve of his hospital gown until it was soaked all the way through to his skin. She slowly started moving her head from side to side and muttering, "No. No. No."

"*No!*" she screamed before the sobs racked her body and her cries became long, guttural moans.

Steve maneuvered until his arm wrapped around her body, and he gently pulled her closer to him. Crawling up on the bed, Sara laid down beside Steve, wrapped her arm around him, and they simply held each other in their shared pain. Through all the ups and downs in their marriage and their family, one thing had remained constant: at the end of it all, their love was still as strong as steel.

"Dad," Chaise choked out, "we'll get a second opinion. Dr. Patel is great, but he could be wrong."

Steve shook his head. "He's the best, baby girl. He's not wrong. I had to stop my treatment a few days ago because of the severe reactions. They put me on IV rehydration for a while. If my body can't tolerate the treatment, there's nothing to keep the cancer in check.

"I plan on sticking around for a few more months anyway, so I can die a happy man. I'm going to hold my first grand baby." He looked at Noah and Brianna. Then he looked at Chaise and Bull, "And I'm going to walk my baby girl down the aisle to give her away to an honorable man who loves her. Most of all, I'll die a happy man knowing my family is whole again, and you'll all be at my side when I go.

"Sara." He paused as she raised her head from his chest. "I'm ready to get out of this hospital and go home now."

"Dad," Noah spoke then cleared his throat. "Are you sure that's really a good idea?"

"We've already talked about my options for home health care, son. I'll have around-the-clock nurses so your mom can still just spend time with me," Steve explained. "It's hard on her being at the hospital all the time."

"It's not just that, Dad. There has to be something else we can do." Noah's exasperation filled his voice.

Steve smiled at Noah. "I appreciate your concern more than you'll ever know, son. But, I'd rather spend my remaining days with my family, at home and comfortable. I'll still go for chemotherapy and radiation as long as I can, with home health care to help us out with the extra care at home."

Sara left the room to find Dr. Patel and arrange for her husband's discharge home. The weight on her heart was heavy as she walked the hospital corridor. Thinking that this could be their last trip home together threatened to knock her to her knees. She drew her strength from deep inside as her legs carried her forward until she found Dr. Patel. She approached him with a lump in her throat, inhaled deeply, and exhaled slowly.

"Dr. Patel, my husband has decided he'd like to go home. Can you arrange for his discharge and home health care as soon as possible, please?" Sara asked, rushing her words before she lost the courage to speak them.

Dr. Patel's kind eyes softened as the meaning behind her words took hold. "Yes, Mrs. Steele, I'll be glad to do it right away." Calling a nurse over, Dr. Patel gave her instructions on Steve's discharge and had her call social services to begin the paperwork for his home health care. Turning back to Sara, Dr. Patel tried to reassure her. "This is very difficult, but you'll have a lot of help and support through it. I'm very sorry I didn't have better news to deliver."

Unable to stop the tears flowing from her eyes, Sara quickly whisked each one away, only to have it replaced by another. "It's not your fault, Dr. Patel. We both know you've done everything you can

WICKED NIGHTS INTRO

1

CHAPTER ONE

Ten Years Earlier

"Eyes on target," Reaper whispered into his comm.

The rest of the Delta Force team remained in place with their muscles tensed and ready to move when the command was issued.

"Big Eye, Reaper. Can you confirm friendlies are still in the southwest corner of the compound?" Reaper asked into the handheld radio to the reconnaissance plane that flew overhead.

"Roger that, Reaper. Thermals show five stationary warm bodies, one in motion inside the room, and one stationary outside the door."

"Copy that. Going dark. Reaper out."

He pressed the microphone button on his neck to talk to his team on the ground. "Positions."

One word was all it took for Bull, Rebel, and Shadow to move quickly into their places. They moved silently across the grounds to surround the area where the hostages were held. The houses inside the compound were all connected by doorways or covered breezeways, obviously built over time as the need to expand arose. They were constructed of a mixture of sunbaked mud and clay brick, with flat roofs and very few windows. As they covered the major entryways of the house, each man alerted their leader when he was in place and ready to take control of the situation.

When the news first broke that hostile insurgents had taken five American contractors hostage, Reaper knew his team would soon be called to intercede. The terrorists were demanding the release of one of their leaders in exchange for the five American men they currently held. For every day the government waited to make the exchange, the extremists vowed they'd behead one of the hostages. Reaper's team specialized in getting in and out of secure places, safely extracting the hostages, and effectively disabling the resistance.

When everyone was in place, Reaper gave the one-word command. "Go."

With his weapon drawn, each man crept silently through the dark in his assigned hallway until the four met in the back corner of the house. As they reached the last turn, they prepared to meet the resistance waiting for them. Rebel took his position, crouching low to the ground, ready to cover Reaper when he bolted to the opposite wall. Shadow and Bull prepared to move into similar positions immediately after the initial foe was incapacitated.

Like the well-oiled machine they'd trained to be, they executed their plan flawlessly. When the guard saw Reaper step into the hallway, his brain barely had time to register the shock before Rebel's double-tap took him out. Shadow and Bull moved into the lead positions as they continued to the door. Shouting in Arabic, followed by painful yelps, alerted the team that their enemies inside the hostage room were aware of their presence. Three men took their places on either side of the door, and then Shadow hit the door with a well-placed kick. He quickly jumped to the right side of the door, out of the way before the men inside the room opened fire.

The location of the bullet spray in the mud bricks across the hall gave the men a good indication of the enemies' locations inside the room. Rebel and Bull faced each other before one took the high position and the other took the lower one. As the guys swung around the

WICKED NIGHTS BLURB

First comes love. Then comes marriage. Then comes a shiny new baby carriage.

But is life ever really that simple?

An unknown danger lurked in the distance, and a family's hope began to fade into despair. Just when everything in life appeared to be perfect, will the family of Steele Security be prepared for the approaching wicked nights?

do. We'll just have to keep trying and pray for a miracle. Thank you for your help."

Turning to walk back to Steve's room, Sara thought the corridor had never seemed so long before. Each step was harder for her to take than the last. Each breath became harder to breathe as she felt she might hyperventilate at any moment. The makings of a full-blown panic attack were threatening to take over and put her in a fetal position, crying and rocking in the corner.

One thought kept swirling through Sara's mind as she moved slowly down the hall.

"How can I do this?"

Hours later, the family had moved Steve from the hospital back to his home just south of Miami. The beachfront estate had every amenity a first-class businessman could hope to surround himself with. Steve Steele had made his name and fortune as the CEO of a major insurance company.

His shrewdness in running large, complex organizations had turned him into a highly sought-after commodity. Since his official retirement, he'd realized the important things he'd missed out on in life. Instead of focusing so much on making a name for himself in the marketplace, he realized he should've focused on making a better impression with his children. He'd decided the most important project he could work on was repairing his family bonds.

Then one night he landed in the hospital with unusual stomach pains and a stomach so upset he couldn't bear another second of it, and everything changed. That was the night of his emergency surgery. The night the surgeon broke the news that he had cancer and it was already advanced. He watched his plans evaporate before his eyes. No way to reconcile with his children. No time to repair what he'd so thoroughly destroyed.

Then Noah and Chaise appeared in his hospital room. At first, he thought it was a reaction to his pain medications. A hallucination conjured by his mind there to taunt him. But then he realized his visions were real as he watched Sara hug them through her tears. His children had returned—two of them anyway. There was still one son unaccounted for, but he at least felt he had a chance now.

As he lay in his own bed, Steve reflected solemnly on Dr. Patel's words. "I've worked all my life, only to retire and learn I have cancer. Terminal cancer, for all intents and purposes," he whispered to himself. "How did this happen?"

Hearing voices approach, he cut his eyes to the door and waited for Sara and the home health nurse to appear.

"Is there anything I can get you, honey?" Sara asked sweetly as she walked in.

"Just you." He smiled.

"You have me. You've always had me," she assured him as she took her spot on the bed beside him.

"I'm a lucky man," he said as he kissed her head.

"Hello, Mr. Steele. I'm Hope, and I'll be one of your nurses." The nurse extended her hand and smiled.

"Hope," Steve said thoughtfully. "I need hope, too."

She nodded, understanding his meaning. "I need to get your vitals and do your initial medical assessment. It won't take long."

"I don't seem to have any other plans right now." Steve smiled. "Let's get it done."

NOAH PACED BACK and forth in the great room of the house he'd grown up in. "There has to be something else we can do."

"We'll figure something out, babe. We're not giving up yet," Brianna assured him.

Sara walked into the room and all eyes snapped to her. "Hope is going over his medical information and getting his vitals. I thought I'd come check on you while they're busy."

"Mom, we're fine," Noah assured her. "You need to rest. This is taking a lot out of you."

"I'm just trying to stay busy," she admitted. "It's easier than sitting and thinking about everything."

"What can we do to help?" Brianna asked Sara. "Just say the word and we'll do it."

"We're all doing everything we can right now," Sara replied, taking Brianna's hand. "Don't feel obligated to stay here. He's not dying today. It just wasn't the news we had hoped to hear."

Noah, Brianna, Chaise, and Bull stayed with Sara as Hope worked with Steve. A couple hours later, Hope joined the family in the great room. "Mrs. Steele, I've finished with my assessment. Mr. Steele is sleeping now. That's completely normal, so don't worry. All the moving, transferring, and people poking at him just made him more tired than usual."

"Thank you, Hope. Please call us Steve and Sara," she replied with a tired smile.

"I'll be back tomorrow with more help and we'll set up our schedules. Here's my contact information," she said, handing Sara her card. "If you need anything, call me at any time."

After Sara walked Hope out, she returned to her family. "It's so good to see you all here. You're welcome to stay, but you really don't have to. He'll sleep the rest of the night, and we'll start chemotherapy and radiation again tomorrow."

"We'll go and let you get some rest then, Mom," Noah replied as he kissed her cheek. "Call if you need anything."

Chaise stood and hugged Sara. "I love you, Mom. Do you want me to stay with you?"

"No, baby," she replied. "Go home with Colton and rest. I love you all. More than you'll ever know."

After they said their goodbyes, Sara climbed into bed with Steve and snuggled up next to him. Her hot tears slid slowly out of her eyes as she drifted off to sleep.

THE MOOD in the Steele Security office was still somber a week after Steve's home health care started. His treatments had resumed and, with the help of medications and hydration treatment, he began to tolerate the side effects better than before. Concern for his health and future weighed heavily on the entire extended family.

"You know," Brianna began. "Your mom reminds me so much of my neighbor in Colorado. I didn't realize how much I'd depended on her to keep me sane while I was away from you. I miss her."

"I'd like to meet her," Noah replied earnestly. "With everything that's happened in the last few months, we've barely had time to slow down. We should take a week or two and go see her. You can show me around and tell me all about your life in Boulder."

"Really?" Brianna perked up. "Do you think your parents would be okay with us leaving?"

"Yeah, I talked to Mom this morning and she said we need to stop acting like Dad is dying tomorrow," Noah chuckled. "She's right, though. Everyone has called at least once a day to ask how he is feeling. If we need to come back early, we'll have the jet so we can leave at any time."

"Let's go," Brianna agreed. "I want to surprise Mrs. Stanton, and I guess I have a lot of explaining to do to her, too."

"We're going, too," Bull chimed in.

Noah's eyebrows rose in question.

"Don't look at me like that, Reaper. Brianna is my little sister, and I missed three years with her, too. If you two are going on a stroll down memory lane, I'm strolling with you," Bull demanded as he crossed his arms over his chest.

"Using that logic, Shadow and I are going, too," Rebel spoke up.

"Hell, yeah," Shadow added. "We're not sitting this one out."

"I'm with the guys on this one, Noah," Chaise added and winked at Brianna.

"Looks like you're outnumbered, big guy." Brianna smiled. "We're taking the whole family to Colorado."

Noah glanced around the room at the family that had been at his side for nearly every major event in his life. "Fair enough. I'll have them get the jet ready to leave first thing in the morning. We'll have to brief Roman tonight and let him know he's in charge while we're away. This should be an interesting trip."

"Of course it will be. Look who's going with you," Shadow quipped.

Noah groaned and the room erupted in laughter. "I'm taking my woman home now. Meet us at the airstrip at eight tomorrow morning."

"I'll call Roman on my way home and give him the rundown, Reap," Rebel offered as he walked to the door. "See you bright and early in the morning."

"I'm right behind you, man," Shadow replied. "Have a good night, everyone."

"Let's go, Chaise. You have womanly duties to perform," Bull commanded.

"Bull. Seriously." Noah gave him a disgusted look.

"What?"

"She's my sister," Noah complained emphatically.

"Yeah, I know," Bull spoke slowly. "It's her turn to make dinner tonight, and I need her to help me pack my suitcase. What did you think I meant?"

"Nothing. I don't want to think about it," Noah amended quickly.

"Oh, wait. You thought I meant..." Bull smiled broadly. "Good idea. She definitely has those womanly duties to perform tonight."

"Get out," Noah ordered. "Get out of here right now."

"Come on, Colton," Chaise laughed. "You have some manly duties to perform for me, too."

"I can't hear you," Noah replied as his hands covered his ears. "Can't hear a word. Get out."

Chaise and Bull walked out the door laughing together and left Noah and Brianna alone. Brianna walked over to Noah, straddled his lap as she faced him, and kissed his lips. When he opened his eyes, she pulled his hands down from his ears. "They're gone now. You're safe."

"Thank God. I'll never get used to hearing that," Noah admitted.

"She's grown and he loves her, Noah. You have to accept that." Brianna smiled. "Where is your brother? Have you heard anything yet?"

"Not a word. He's deep undercover and hasn't checked in with his handler in a while now. Shadow said that's completely normal, especially if he's gathering a lot of intel and can't risk blowing his cover," Noah sighed. "I just hope that's the case, and it's not because something bad has happened to him."

"You've had a long enough day," Brianna decided. "It's time for you to take me home and perform some husbandly duties for me."

"It sounds so much better when you say it, wife." Noah's eyes darkened. "It's all my pleasure to perform my husbandly duties for you."

"Not *all* your pleasure," Brianna quipped. "I happen to get a lot of pleasure from it, too."

"Time to go," Noah replied as he shut his laptop. "Now I can't wait to get you home."

He stood, taking Brianna with him as she wrapped her legs around his waist. Her baby bump at sixteen weeks was just big enough to be noticeable but not enough to get in the way. Noah held her close to him, and she took the opportunity to kiss and lick his neck as he carried her out to the car.

"You're killing me, woman," he growled.

"Maybe I'll give you a special treat while you're driving," she purred in his ear.

"You want me to wreck," he chuckled. "Not that I'll try to stop you or anything."

"It's a good thing our SUV is nice and roomy," she replied. "I have better access to you."

"That does it. We're not going anywhere until I'm done with you. We'll just have to be like horny teenagers in the backseat."

"If you insist," she agreed.

"Damn, I love your pregnancy hormones," Noah said as he opened the back door of the SUV. After he carefully placed Brianna inside, his take-charge personality emerged again. "Strip. We're taking advantage of these new black-out windows."

"All yours, big guy. Show me what you got for me."

Noah climbed in, started the car to blast the air conditioner, and joined Brianna in the backseat. Without a thought of who could see them and not caring who might hear them, Noah took his time in exploring every inch of Brianna's body, further sealing their love and bond to each other.

"Whoa, that was hot." Brianna sat up to adjust her clothes. "We need to do this more often."

"Only if you insist." Noah smiled smugly and leaned over to kiss her softly.

"I love you, Noah," she said as she stroked his face.

"I love you, Brianna. More than life itself."

BOOKS BY A.D. JUSTICE

Steele Security Series

Wicked Games (Book 1)

Wicked Ties (Book 2)

Wicked Nights (Book 3)

Wicked Intentions (Book 4)

Wicked Shadows (Book 5)

Crossing Lines Series

Fine Line

Blurred Line

Hard Line

The Vault Series

Precarious: Warning, Part One

Insidious: Warning, Part Two

Treacherous: Warning, Part Three

A HOMETOWN NOVEL

Intent

All I Want

All I Need

Entice (coming soon!)

The Crazy Series

Crazy Maybe (Book 1)

Crazy Baby (Book 2)

Crazy Love (Book 3, Free Short Story)

Dominic Powers Series

Her Dom (Book 1)

Her Dom's Lesson (Book 2)

Covis Realm, Easthaven Crest Series

Cloaked

Deceived

Unveiled

Stand—alone Books

Saving Grace

Completely Captivated

Immortal Envy

Mistletoe Not Required

Just One Summer

ABOUT THE AUTHOR

A.D. Justice is the award-winning, *USA Today* bestselling author of several series and stand-alone romance novels in various romance genres, including romantic suspense, contemporary, and paranormal.

When she's not writing, she loves spending time with her alpha male husband in the Northwest Georgia mountains. They're living out their own HEA, frequently on horseback with a dog in tow.

She is also an avid reader of romance novels, a master of procrastination, a chocolate sommelier, a twister of words, and speaks fluent sarcasm. An avid animal lover, she has two horses, two cats, and two very spoiled dogs.

She loves chatting with her readers. You're welcome to stalk her across all social media!

Connect with her online!

Newsletter
Facebook Reader Group
Website

facebook.com/adjusticeauthor

instagram.com/authoradjustice

bookbub.com/authors/a-d-justice

amazon.com/author/adjustice

pinterest.com/adjusticeauthor

ACKNOWLEDGMENTS

First and foremost, I want to thank my Lord and Savior for His continued forgiveness of a sinner.

To my husband: I love you! Thank you for putting up with the late nights, long weekends and the less than stellar kept house. Writing the book didn't help much with any of that, either. :)

To my Street Team: Y'all are the best! Thank you for being my beta readers, my sounding boards, my biggest supporters and the best all-around people in the world! Love all of you!

To my readers: Thank you for taking a chance on a new indie author! I love hearing from everyone so stop by my page and say hello!

To my assistant: Tabitha Charisse, thank you for all your help and support. You are very much appreciated.

To my BFFs: I don't know how I managed to do anything correct before I met the best friends anyone could ever ask for. T.K. Leigh and Michelle Dare, I love both of you!

To the bloggers: None of this would be possible without your help, support and tireless pimping! I love everyone in this great group of people! I can't name one without naming everyone because you've all been so helpful and wonderful friends.